He held u s against his. "Tess sa

"Yes. That's the plan." Hopefully, her voice didn't reflect the pinch of uncertainty that had crept into her thoughts.

His gaze dropped to her lips. "I probably shouldn't kiss you again if you're leaving."

He was right, yet her heartbeat picked up.

"Well, in another month you won't have the opportunity. Really, this could be your last chance." What was she saying right now?

"You know what they say," she continued, "you should make the most of every opportunity." The rush of energy he generated inside of her had taken over.

She *wanted* him to kiss her. Right now she wanted him.

PRAISE FOR SARA RICHARDSON

"With wit and warmth, Sara Richardson creates heartfelt stories you can't put down."

—Lori Foster, *New York Times* bestselling author

"Sara Richardson writes unputdownable, unforgettable stories from the heart."

—Jill Shalvis, *New York Times* bestselling author

"Sara [Richardson] brings real feelings to every scene she writes."

—Carolyn Brown, *New York Times* bestselling author

The Summer Sisters

"This is sure to win readers' hearts."

—*Publishers Weekly*

One Night with a Cowboy

"Richardson has a gift for creating empathetic characters and charming small-town settings, and her taut plotting and sparkling prose keep the pages turning. This appealing love story is sure to please." —*Publishers Weekly*

Home for the Holidays

"Fill your favorite mug with hot chocolate and whipped cream as you savor this wonderful holiday story of family reunited and dreams finally fulfilled. I loved it!"

—Sherryl Woods, #1 *New York Times* bestselling author

"You'll want to stay home for the holidays with this satisfying Christmas read."

—Sheila Roberts, *USA Today* bestselling author

First Kiss with a Cowboy

"The pace is fast, the setting's charming, and the love scenes are delicious. Fans of cowboy romance are sure to be captivated." —*Publishers Weekly*, Starred Review

A Cowboy for Christmas

"Tight plotting and a sweet surprise ending make for a delightful Christmas treat. Readers will be sad to see the series end." —*Publishers Weekly*

Colorado Cowboy

"Readers who love tear-jerking small-town romances with minimal sex scenes and maximum emotional intimacy will quickly devour this charming installment."

—*Publishers Weekly*

Renegade Cowboy

"Top Pick! An amazing story about finding a second chance to be with the one that you love."

—Harlequin Junkie

"A beautifully honest and heartwarming tale about forgiveness and growing up that will win the hearts of fans and newcomers alike." —*RT Book Reviews*

Hometown Cowboy

"Filled with humor, heart, and love, this page-turner is one wild ride."

—Jennifer Ryan, *New York Times* bestselling author

No Better Man

"Charming, witty, and fun. There's no better read. I enjoyed every word!" —Debbie Macomber, #1 *New York Times* bestselling author

WISHING *on a* CHRISTMAS COWBOY

Also by Sara Richardson

Heart of the Rockies series

No Better Man
Something Like Love
One Christmas Wish (novella)
More Than a Feeling
Rocky Mountain Wedding (novella)

Rocky Mountain Riders series

Hometown Cowboy
Comeback Cowboy
Renegade Cowboy
Rocky Mountain Cowboy (novella)
True-Blue Cowboy
Rocky Mountain Cowboy Christmas (novella)
Colorado Cowboy
A Cowboy for Christmas

Silverado Lake series

First Kiss with a Cowboy
One Night with a Cowboy
Last Dance with a Cowboy

Juniper Springs series

Home for the Holidays
The Summer Sisters

WISHING *on a* CHRISTMAS COWBOY

SARA RICHARDSON

A STAR VALLEY NOVEL

FOREVER
New York Boston

This book is a work of fiction. Names, characters, places, and incidents are the product of the author's imagination or are used fictitiously. Any resemblance to actual events, locales, or persons, living or dead, is coincidental.

Forever
Hachette Book Group
1290 Avenue of the Americas, New York, NY 10104
read-forever.com
twitter.com/readforeverpub

First Edition: October 2022

Forever is an imprint of Grand Central Publishing. The Forever name and logo are trademarks of Hachette Book Group, Inc.

The publisher is not responsible for websites (or their content) that are not owned by the publisher.

The Hachette Speakers Bureau provides a wide range of authors for speaking events. To find out more, go to www.hachettespeakersbureau.com or call (866) 376-6591.

ISBNs: 978-1-5387-2588-7 (mass market), 978-1-5387-2589-4 (ebook)

Printed in the United States of America

OPM

10 9 8 7 6 5 4 3 2 1

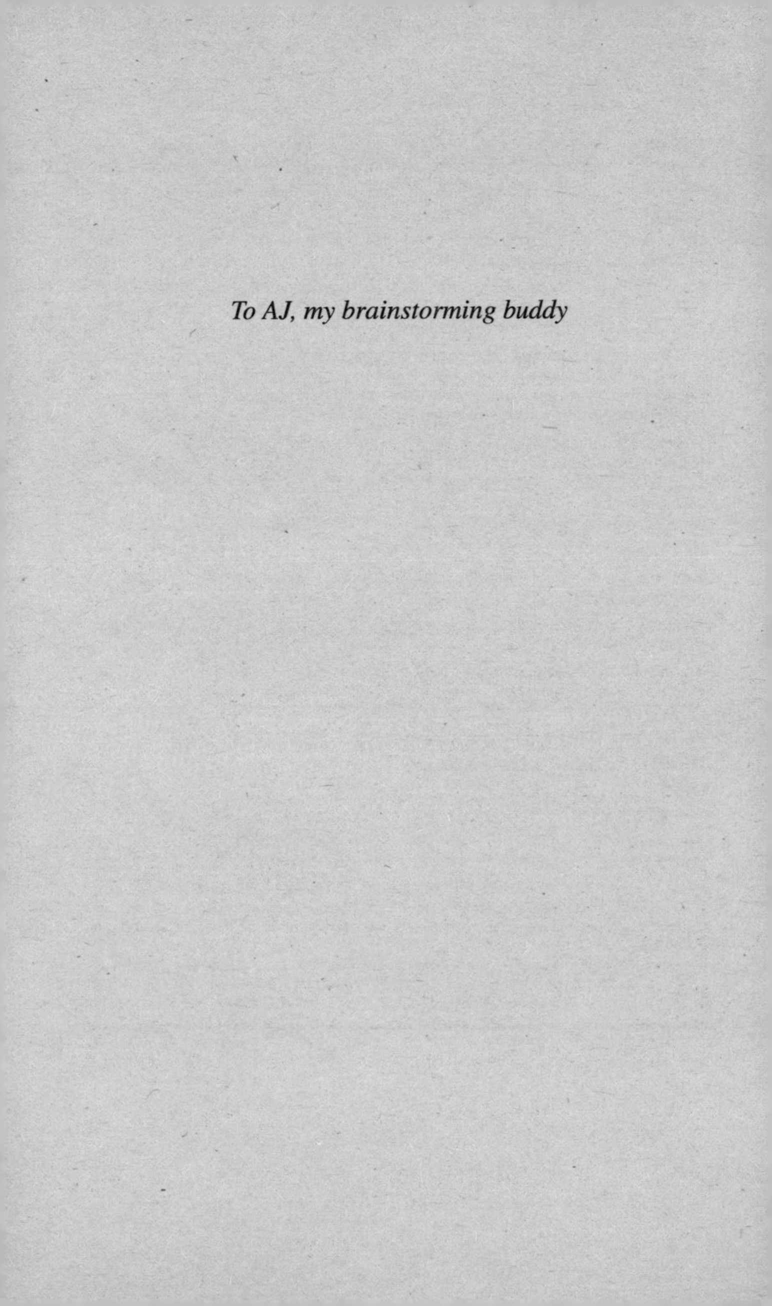

To AJ, my brainstorming buddy

WISHING *on a* CHRISTMAS COWBOY

CHAPTER ONE

"This is it. This is how my life will end."

Kyra Fowler eased her compact SUV up yet another narrow switchback somewhere in the godforsaken wilderness of Wyoming, the pine branches scraping both sides of the car like a fork screeching against a porcelain plate. She was going to die out here.

Fifteen miles ago, her faithful GPS man with the hot British accent had decided to abandon her not three miles after she exited the lonely two-lane highway that had led her somewhere into the vicinity of Star Valley Springs, Wyoming. Apparently the town happened to be a literal hidden gem. Since she'd lost service on her phone, she'd been driving on these sorry excuses for backroads for an hour and still saw no signs of civilization. She had, however, watched a bear dart into the woods a few miles back, so there would be no getting out of the car under any circumstances.

She eyed her fuel meter, which had dipped dangerously

low. Most likely she'd eventually run out of gas and, after a few nights surviving in the frigid overnight Wyoming fall temperatures, she'd succumb to hypothermia. She'd watched enough evening news to know that was how these scenarios always ended.

Stepping on the brake, Kyra took a second to massage her temples, warding off a headache. This whole situation had to be some sort of really bad joke. When the Law Offices of Edmundson and Podgurski had called to inform her that her estranged father had passed away, Kyra had reluctantly agreed to travel all the way from Fort Myers to Jackson, Wyoming. She'd arrived for the reading of his will only to find out that the illustrious Kenneth Fowler hadn't left her—his only blood child—a typical inheritance. Nope. In order to make up for his abandonment eighteen years ago, her father had left her a *town* in the middle of nowhere. Star Valley Springs, population three hundred twenty eight at the last census count.

A town! As if she had any use for an entire town.

But that wasn't the worst part. A humorless laugh slipped out. Oh, no. The worst part was that this *gift* came with certain stipulations on what she could do with her new town. Such as, she couldn't sell any of the very expensive land, businesses, or homes she now owned until the improvements specified in his will were made.

"Thanks, Dad."

Kyra eased her foot back onto the gas, the SUV crawling forward so she wouldn't dent the undercarriage on the rocks and tree branches littering the road. "I don't understand." She hadn't wanted anything from Kenneth—hadn't *needed* anything from him since the day he'd walked out on her and her mom to build a new family with Kyra's best friend's mother.

Why couldn't he have left the town to Lyric, his stepdaughter? Thoughts of her childhood friend never failed to stir up an aching nostalgia. She and Lyric had been inseparable once. Until her father ran off with Lyric's mother and moved the poor girl to this frozen place. Kyra had never blamed Lyric—her friend had been just as shocked as she'd been when they learned that their parents had been having an affair.

Kyra slowed the car to navigate a hairpin turn, nerves pulsing in her stomach. What would it be like to see Lyric now? After all this time? When she'd learned about her father's death, she'd thought about getting in touch with her old friend, but she didn't know what to say. They'd secretly emailed a few times after Lyric had moved away, but Kyra's mother found out and forbade her from ever talking to her friend again.

Ugh. She stepped on the brakes once more and let her head fall back. Why had her father wanted to complicate her life now? He should've left Star Valley Springs to Lyric. Then Kyra wouldn't have had to take a three-month leave of absence from her nursing job to deal with this mess. The mountains of Wyoming were the last place she wanted to be from now until Christmas, but her father hadn't exactly given her a choice. At first, she'd thought about refusing the inheritance, but then Mr. Podgurski had informed her the town was valued at well over one million dollars and developers had already been sniffing around.

She couldn't pass up one million dollars.

Urging the car on, Kyra followed yet another bend in the rutted blacktop, coming to a stop at a fork in the road. The path to the right appeared to have fared slightly better than the left, so she turned the wheel and continued driving beneath the thick canopy of trees. If she hadn't been lost she might've called the view outside her windshield beautiful, with the golden aspen leaves interspersed among the deep green pine branches all backlit in the setting sun, but her tensed shoulders and persisting headache stole the landscape's shining glory.

She was never going to get out of here. She would have to ration out the lone chocolate bar she had left in her purse and spend the entire night—

Wait a minute. A car! Parked up ahead near a small pond. Kyra picked up speed. It was a truck, actually. It looked like something straight out of the seventies, an old rust-colored Ford lifted onto big monster tires, but who cared what the truck looked like? Someone else was out here. And they probably weren't lost.

Kyra pulled off the road and parked next to the truck. No one sat inside, which meant she had to go on a scouting expedition. After slipping her pepper spray into her pocket, she climbed out of the car and approached the pond. "Hello?" Maybe if she spoke loud enough she'd scare all the bears away.

Ripples formed in the middle of the pond, and someone surfaced. A man. He let out a whoop before wiping his face with his hands, and then he proceeded to swim across to the far side. He must not have noticed her.

"Excuse me," Kyra called, walking to the shoreline.

The man jerked his head as though she'd startled him.

"Hi there." She waved, hoping she didn't have to use the pepper spray in her pocket. "Um, I seem to be a little lost and I was wondering if you might be able to help."

Without responding, the man started to swim toward her—his powerful arms making his freestyle stroke Olympics-worthy. He made it about halfway across the pond but then stopped and seemed to tread water while he sized her up.

She sized him up too. He wasn't scary looking, per se, but he did have a bit of a wild look about him. His dark shoulder-length hair was slicked back, and stubble shadowed his jaw. He could be a mountain man. Or a serial killer. It was hard to tell.

She thought about informing him she was armed with pepper spray, but then he finally said, "You must be looking for Jackson Hole."

"No." Any moron could find the biggest tourist town this side of the Rockies. "Actually, I'm looking for Star Valley Springs. My GPS quit on me, and I've been driving around for the last hour." Or decade.

"Sure. I can help." The man went into the freestyle stroke again, and now that he'd gotten closer she caught a glimpse of various tattoos covering his biceps.

"You might want to turn around," the man said as he approached the shoreline.

Turn around? She noticed a heap of clothes on a rock nearby. "Oh." Because he was naked. "Right. Sure. I'll definitely turn around." Maybe she should run too. What kind of man swam naked in public? Was this public? Maybe she'd ventured onto private property...

"All right. I'm good," he said behind her.

She turned back around but lost her train of thought when she caught sight of his bare, glistening chest. Another tattoo covered his left pec—the Navy SEAL trident emblem. Her gaze drifted down to his worn jeans, which sat low on his hips, showcasing chiseled muscle along with more than a few jagged scars.

"You wanted directions?"

Kyra blinked the rest of the world back into focus. How long had she been staring at him? "Um, yes. Directions." She straightened, forcing her gaze to stay above his neck. "Like I said, I'm lost and I really need to get to Star Valley Springs."

The man seemed to take his time pulling on a heathered green T-shirt that brought out the hazel hues in his eyes. "The town is a good half-hour drive from here. About ten miles, but the roads aren't the greatest."

"I've noticed." Next time she would have to rent a Jeep to get around this area. What was she thinking? There wouldn't be a next time. After Christmas she was going to sell Star Valley Springs to the highest bidder and use the money to finally build a new life for herself in London. That money would literally make her dream come true.

"It'd probably be easier if you follow me." The man sidestepped her and headed for the truck. "Less chance you'll get lost. There are a lot of turns and old logging roads out here. I can lead you out."

"That would be great." Kyra got back into her car and started it up only to see the low fuel light blinking at her. Would she even be able to drive for a half hour without running out of gas?

Next to her, the truck's engine revved.

"Wait!" She scrambled to get out of the car. Thankfully the truck's window was down. "I'm about to run out of gas." Humiliation pinched at her cheeks. She'd never had to be rescued. Her mother had drilled into her that she couldn't rely on anyone else in life, and she hadn't.

Now she was both lost and out of gas...and completely dependent on this man she didn't even know.

Her incompetence didn't seem to faze the man. His left shoulder lifted in a lazy shrug. "Hop in, then. We can pick up some gas and I'll bring you back to get the car later."

He made the solution sound easy. Hop in. With a complete stranger.

You can't trust anyone. Though Kyra's mother passed away two years ago, her voice still constantly echoed in Kyra's head. What choice did she have? Her mom would probably tell her to hike out of the woods on her own before getting into a car with a tattooed mountain man, but daylight would fade fast, and she didn't want to stay out here alone. "Let me grab my luggage."

She popped the hatch on her SUV, but the man met her back there. Without a word he lifted her carry-on bag out of her car and put it in the bed of his truck. "Anything else?"

And there she went ogling him again. It was hard not to, what with his broad shoulders and chest. A man didn't develop that body type without some serious dedication. "Nope. Huh-uh. No more luggage. Only my purse but I'll get that." She darted to the front seat and retrieved her purse before locking the doors. After patting the pepper spray in her pocket once more, she opened the passenger's door and climbed up onto the step so she could catapult herself into the truck.

"Quite the leap up here," she commented, going for levity. But there was a tremor of fear in her voice. This might very well turn out to be the worst decision she had ever made. No one knew she was out here. He could kidnap her and take her back to his mountain hovel and no one would ever know where to find her…

"Gotta have some good clearance on these roads." The man clicked in his seatbelt and waited for her to do the same.

Right. She had to stop the trembling in her hands so she could summon some coordination. At least the inside of his truck didn't indicate he enjoyed kidnapping damsels in distress. It was tidy and faintly smelled like the inside of a coffee shop. "I really appreciate this," she said as the man steered the truck onto the road. "I'm not usually so needy and irresponsible. My name is Kyra, by the way. Kyra Fowler."

"Ah." The man's head tipped back in a gesture of understanding. "You're Kenny's daughter, then."

"Technically, I guess." Not that she wanted to talk about their very complicated relationship. "And you are—?"

"Aiden. Aiden Steele." The man made a quick left onto another rutted road, the bulky tires bouncing her all over the place.

Kyra crossed her arms over her chest. Sheesh. She should've worn a sports bra. "How did you know Kenneth?"

"Everyone in Star Valley Springs knew Kenny." The man kept his eyes trained on the road, but something told Kyra he didn't have to. His body seemed to adjust for every bump and curve before they hit. "Most people make it a point to get to know the man who holds their fate in his hands." He shot her a sideways glance, his jaw tensing. "Or woman, as the case may now be."

A series of bumps rattled Kyra, and she was glad she wasn't the one driving. "Well, I won't be holding anyone's fate in my hands, thank you very much." She clutched the handle above the door to steady herself. "My father mandated that I have to oversee some work on the town and then I'll sell as soon as possible."

"That so?" Aiden swerved around a large boulder that had rolled onto the shoulder of the road.

"Yes." She couldn't read his expression. The curve of his lips hinted at amusement, but his eyes had narrowed slightly. "I had to take a leave of absence from my job to come up here." And within a few months, hopefully she'd have a new job—a whole new life—at the hospital she'd applied to in London. That's what she'd been working toward for the entire last two years. She'd gone back to school to become a nurse practitioner so she could finally move on. Not that Aiden Steele needed to hear her life story or her plans for the future. "So do you swim out here a lot?" she asked, hoping the change in subject wasn't too obvious.

"Couple times a week." There was that shrug again, casual and carefree. "It's one of the many hot springs around here. Temperature stays at around a hundred all year long. The minerals are good for the body."

Yes, they'd obviously been very good for his body. Kyra focused her gaze out the windshield. The trees had started to thin some, and the road was dipping lower into a valley.

"I was sorry to hear about your dad." Aiden studied her, but she wasn't sure what he was looking for. Emotion? "He was a helluva guy. Saved this town from becoming another Jackson Hole tourist trap when he bought up all the land. Everyone around here really respected him."

A long-standing resentment heated her veins. "I didn't

know my father." She might as well get that out of the way now. She understood how these small towns worked. Everyone knew everyone else's business. So they might as well hear this from her up front—she wasn't here to reminisce or sing Kenneth Fowler's praises or even learn about what kind of man he'd been. It was too late to know him.

Eighteen years ago he'd left her behind, plain and simple, so she'd left him behind too.

CHAPTER TWO

What the hell had Kenny been thinking when he left Star Valley Springs to this woman?

Aiden snuck another look Kyra. When he'd first seen her standing on the bank of the spring, he'd been sure he was dreaming. It wasn't so much her wavy blond hair—he usually preferred dark—or her curves that had commanded his attention, though they didn't have him complaining. What had really stunned him was her face—all perfect contours and softness. And her blue eyes…soulful and bright. Now, though, everything about her seemed…rigid. From the way she sat so tall and straight to the way she'd fashioned her hair into a tight, neat ponytail to the way her mouth had pulled into a thin, straight line when he'd mentioned her father, whom she clearly didn't want to talk about.

Funny, because that was all he wanted to talk about right now. Aiden had never once questioned the man's judgment. Kenny had moved to Star Valley Springs fifteen years ago, purchasing the ranch adjacent to the one Aiden's brother-in-law's family owned. Times were hard then. Rising taxes, drought, supply cost increases. You name it, all the ranchers and businesses were taking hits left and right. But Kenny had made it big as a consultant in the oil business and started buying up all the land in town to preserve those spaces—to protect them. The second a developer bought in anywhere near Star Valley Springs, land prices would shoot up, taxes would rise again, and big chains and box stores would push out all the hardworking local businesspeople. Like his sister. Aiden couldn't let that happen.

"So, have you been to Star Valley Springs before?" he asked in a sorry attempt to make conversation. What a lame question. She'd already told him she hadn't known her father. Why, though? He hadn't known the man long, but Kenny treated people in town like family. He'd looked out for everyone. How did the man not know his own daughter?

Aiden shot Kyra a sideways glance. Asking her dumb questions wouldn't get him more information. What could he say? He was out of practice. It'd been a while since he'd had the luxury of speaking with a beautiful woman. He'd had a few other things on his plate, namely keeping his sister's ranch afloat while he tried to run a construction business to help pay his own bills. Life in Star Valley Springs kept him too busy to think much. He'd moved here with his SEAL team buddies two years ago. They'd lost Jace—his brother-in-law—on their last mission, and when they'd joined up, the four of them had made a pact. If anything ever happened to one of them, the other three would take care of the family he'd left behind, whether it be parents, siblings, or, in Jace's case, a wife and two young daughters.

His brother-in-law had used his dying breath to remind Aiden of the pact, and he'd sworn to Jace that Tess and the girls would never have anything to worry about. Especially losing their home. And he'd kept that promise. He wasn't about to let this woman come in now and ruin everything.

"No. I've never been here before." Kyra seemed inclined to stare out the window while they crossed the bridge over the river. "It's pretty." She delivered the words somewhat begrudgingly, as if they were hard to admit.

Pretty? "It's one of the most beautiful places on earth," he corrected gruffly. Aiden stared out ahead of them at the town that looked so small tucked in between two awe-inspiring peaks. Gold and green dotted the mountainsides, with most of the leaves still barely hanging on. "Star Valley is pristine and untouched." Unlike the large city to their south. Jackson had become an abomination with its overpriced amenities and celebrity vacation homes. "It's real Wyoming."

Kyra uttered a noncommittal grunt, and he almost laughed. She was trying to deny the beauty of the place even though it was spread out right in front of her. That could only mean one thing. She was a stubborn one. "Where are you from?" he asked, pausing longer than he needed to at the stop sign on the outskirts of town.

She still wouldn't look at him. "Fort Myers."

So maybe she preferred the beach to the mountains. "It's pretty there." But not breathtaking like the Tetons.

"It's okay." Her eyes seemed fixated on the mountains.

"But I'm hoping to move to London after the first of the year. I applied for a job there."

"London?"

This time she stared directly at him. Must've been his horrified tone.

"What's wrong with London?" Kyra demanded.

Why did he find it so easy to look into her blue eyes? "Nothing." He'd been to London more than once. In his previous line of work he'd traveled the world on missions. And sure, London was a cool city to visit, but he wouldn't want to live there. "It's crowded is all. Too confining." Maybe at one time in his life he would've been fine there, but these days he needed space, room to wander in the opposite direction of his ghosts.

Kyra looked away first. "Well, I love it there. The history, the sights, the people."

Aiden stepped on the gas again, heading down Main Street en route to Kenny's place on the west side of town. Driving through, he couldn't deny that the actual town of Star Valley Springs wasn't much to look at. There were only a few establishments on the main drag—the Meadowlark Hotel and Café, a souvenir shop, the ancient town hall, a small market, and Star Valley Feed and Supplies, the store his sister owned to keep her ranch land afloat. But as an old mining-era town with square brick buildings and plank walkways lining the streets, the place did have a certain charm.

"We passed the gas station," Kyra informed him, craning her neck to peer down a side street.

"We're heading to your dad's house." He increased his speed as the neat rows of small bungalows thinned to larger acreages. "His ranch is out here on the west side. Not too much farther."

"I thought we were going to get gas so we could pick up my rental." A high-pitched ring gave the words a panicked tone.

"It'll be too dark to get back there tonight." Aiden turned onto Kenny's driveway. For being so wealthy, the man had built a simple log structure to call home. That had been Kenneth Fowler, though—never showy, always down-to-earth and easygoing. He glanced at Kyra. Evidently the apple sometimes did fall way far away from the tree. "I thought you'd want to stay at his house tonight. Isn't that why you grabbed your luggage?" He'd assumed she didn't want to try to navigate her way to town in the dark.

"I grabbed my luggage because I don't need someone breaking into my car to steal the only clothes I have with me." Instead of looking at him, she seemed to be studying her father's house out the passenger's window.

"Yeah, I've heard bears really like Samsonite suitcases." Aiden couldn't help but tease her. "Seriously I can't remember the last time I locked my truck in Star Valley. You don't have to worry about that kind of thing around here."

"Well, I always operate under the assumption that you never can be too careful," Kyra said stiffly.

He'd felt the same way before moving to Star Valley. "I can pick you up first thing in the morning and take you to your car. I promise that'll be a lot easier than trying to drive through the woods in the dark." He parked the truck in front of the porch, but Kyra stayed buckled in her seat as though she was afraid to get out.

"I don't have anything to eat."

"Sure you do." Aiden killed the engine. "Your dad's freezer is stocked with casseroles. Everyone in town knew you were coming." What they didn't know was that she'd apparently come to ruin things for them all.

"Casseroles?" Kyra still stayed put and stared out at the house, but Aiden had to get things moving along here. He had an agenda to see to.

"Yep. That's what people do here. They take care of each other." He got out of the truck and pulled her suitcase from the bed, rolling it over to the passenger's door.

Kyra finally climbed out slowly, hesitating. "I don't even have a key."

"The door's never locked." He carried the suitcase up the porch steps for her. "I think the Star Valley Ladies Aid Society cleaned for you too yesterday." Those women had been tight with Kenny's wife before she moved away. They'd been chattering about Kenny's long-lost daughter for a week now.

"The what?" She still hadn't come up the steps.

"I like to think of them as the matriarchs of the town." Aiden tried not to sound impatient, but he didn't have time for this. "Each of the members have lived in Star Valley forever and they're the ones who coordinate help when people need it the most."

"Oh...kay." She made her way up the steps, warily eyeing the front door. "But I don't need anyone's help. I can handle things on my own."

Coulda fooled him. "I'd wait to say that until you try Minnie Vitten's chicken pie if I were you." Aiden nudged her suitcase closer to her and then trotted down the steps. "They all left you phone numbers on the counter in case you need anything." He slid into the driver's seat of his truck again. "I'll be back at eight o'clock tomorrow," he called through the open window before peeling out and cruising down the driveway. Instead of heading for his cabin down the street from Tess's ranch, he drove back into town and parked in front of the Meadowlark Café and Hotel.

The café was *the* place to be in Star Valley Springs on a Friday night. Technically, it was the only place open past seven o'clock, which made it a hangout for everyone.

True to form, he found Silas and Thatch sitting at the bar, along with the other regulars who didn't like cooking for themselves most nights. "We've got a problem." Aiden claimed a stool on the other side of Thatch.

"You're tellin' me we have a problem." His friend gestured to his plate, where a half-eaten burger sat. "Lean beef is all Louie had left for my burger. He's not gettin' the good stuff in until the Monday delivery."

"Quit your gripin'," the man grouched from behind the bar. Louie Vitten and his wife, Minnie, had owned the Meadowlark Hotel and Café ever since he'd inherited the relic from his grandfather. Both in their late fifties, they were staples in this town—rough around the edges like most of the people here, but their hearts were pure gold.

"Lean beef." Silas shook his head. "Crying shame. Burgers weren't meant to be lean."

"Bunch of whiners." Louie slid a frosty glass of Aiden's favorite pale ale across the bar to him. "They wouldn't have even known if I hadn't told 'em." The man's brown eyes seemed especially sharp tonight, and most of his graying hair had come out of his long ponytail. "They say the lean stuff is better for your heart. You can't even tell the difference."

"Yes I can." Thatch poked at the burger with a knife. "It's not greasy enough. And my heart is top-notch. I don't need lean be—"

"We have a *real* problem," Aiden interrupted. Though he appreciated the warning on the beef. It looked like he wouldn't be ordering a burger until Monday. "I was at the swimming hole earlier and a woman showed up."

Silas, Thatch, and Louie all froze.

"I'm gonna need another beer for this story," Silas said, signaling Louie.

"Sounds like a good one," the man agreed, filling another glass from the tap.

"It's not that great of a story. Trust me." It wasn't some sordid rendezvous with a stranger. Kyra was hot, don't get him wrong, but he wouldn't be getting tangled up with her. "It's Kyra Fowler. She's in town to settle Kenny's estate." He explained how she'd gotten lost and that he'd dropped her off at her father's house. "She wants nothing to do with Star Valley Springs," he finished. "She wants to sell to a developer. And you know what that means." What it would mean for all of them.

"Those damn millionaires she's gonna sell to will push us out of our homes and jobs." Louie slung a towel over his shoulder while murmuring curse words.

"Turns out she didn't even know Kenny." Aiden still couldn't fathom why the man would've put their town in jeopardy by leaving everything to her. He should've talked to Kenny about his plans. But no one could've known a heart attack would take the man down without any warning. One day he was having a beer with them at the café, and the next he dropped dead in his barn.

"Star Valley Springs should've gone to Lyric." Silas pushed away his plate. "She loves this town."

Lyric was Kenny's stepdaughter. Though her mother had moved to Arizona to live with her sister after Kenny's death, Lyric still lived a few blocks away and ran a yoga studio and holistic health store out of her home. "I can't imagine why he would leave this place to an outsider."

"According to Minnie, Lyric knew her stepsister before their parents got married." Louie filled himself a glass from the tap. "Sounds like it was kind of a messy situation. Like Kenny had an affair with Lyric's mom and then left his ex-wife and Kyra behind to move here."

Yikes. So maybe Kyra resented her father for leaving. She sure hadn't made it sound like she'd kept in touch with Lyric. "I can't understand why he would leave her the town, then."

"He must've had his reasons." Thatch shrugged. "Kenny was a planner, a smart businessman. He always knew what he was doing. Maybe you're misjudging Kyra."

Leave it to Thatch to play the devil's advocate. "She told me she's staying through Christmas to fix up the place like her dad outlined in his will, and then she's going to sell and move to London."

"Why would she move there?" Silas asked, wearing the exact same expression Aiden had.

"I don't know." He'd spent less than thirty minutes with the woman. "I don't know much about her. But I do know she is determined to sell this place as soon as she can." And they should all be plenty worried.

"You can't let that happen, Aiden." Louie leaned into the counter. "You have to find a way to stop her."

"Me?" Since when had he become this town's savior? "We all have to stop her. Together."

"You already have a plan." Thatch studied him. After working counterterrorism operations with him, Thatch and Silas could both read his thoughts. And he could read theirs.

"It'll be like another mission," Aiden told them, the plan taking shape as he spoke. "We'll get everyone in town in on this. Operation Save Star Valley Springs."

"I like it." Silas had his game face on—every bit as serious as he'd been when they'd found themselves in the deserts of Afghanistan.

"We have to turn her," Aiden went on. "Show her what makes this town unique and desirable. We need to make her fall in love with Star Valley Springs."

"Or with someone in Star Valley Springs," Thatch quipped. "As long as she's single. And I think you're the right man for the job. Out of all of us, you've landed the most dates."

That had been in a different time, though, a different life. Before he'd lost Jace. In those days he'd never gone home from a bar without a woman, but that last mission had changed everything. "I'm assuming she's single." He hadn't seen a ring on her finger, and she'd said *she* was moving to London. There hadn't been a *we* involved. "But I'm not talking about seducing her. I'm talking about helping her see the heart of this town."

Louie was slowly nodding along. "That's exactly what we gotta do. Give her the star treatment. Show her that she could find a family here the same way her dad did."

"Exactly." A family. Aiden couldn't be sure, but it didn't seem like Kyra had many connections.

"I'll get Minnie working on things with the Ladies Society," Louie offered. "They can befriend her and help her out with stuff. And I can start spreading the word here."

"Perfect." That meant everyone in Star Valley Springs would know the situation by Sunday. Aiden turned to Thatch and Silas. "And all of a sudden Cowboy Construction is going to be too busy to take on any projects." As they were the only contractor in town, Kyra would need to enlist their help to complete her projects.

Thatch finished off his beer. "We've got the cattle drive coming up at the ranch anyway. That's the perfect excuse to delay taking on any other projects."

The cattle drive. He'd almost forgotten that next week a group of volunteers from town would move Tess's stock from the high pasture to the low meadow for winter. They usually made a weekend out of it, enjoying camping along the way and cowboy cuisine throughout the trek. Aiden laughed. "I wonder if Ms. Fowler has ever been on a cattle drive. This might be her chance to have a new experience."

The more they could involve her in the events around town, the more she would see the value in being part of their community.

CHAPTER THREE

The distinct aroma of coffee made Kyra bolt upright in bed. How could it possibly smell like coffee when she was still in bed? Unless…

She held her breath and, sure enough, there were voices downstairs. Female voices. More than one, which shouldn't have been possible considering she'd locked the door before she'd gone to bed last night.

Throwing off the covers, Kyra scooted out of bed and hastily dressed. There couldn't be any dangerous intruders down there. What kind of criminals would break into her father's house to make coffee?

Before going to find out, she made her way into the en suite bathroom of what appeared to be the guest room. After finding herself alone in her father's house last night, she'd chosen to sleep in the room that had the fewest personal touches. Mostly she'd tossed and turned in the queen-size bed that had magically been made up with crisp, clean sheets.

It was eerie being in a stranger's house that she now owned. She'd made it a point not to open one closet or cabinet door—except in the kitchen, when she'd had to search for a plate to eat a few bites of the lasagna she'd found in the freezer. She'd found a note attached to the pan.

> Welcome! We're so happy you're in Star Valley Springs. This lasagna was made with love especially for you! Heat it up at 350 degrees for an hour and enjoy! —The Star Valley Springs Ladies Aid Society

Weird. This was all so weird.

Leaning over the sink, Kyra splashed water on her face and then rose to pull her hair into a ponytail. A shower would have to wait until after she investigated who might have invited themselves into her father's kitchen at seven o'clock in the morning.

The whole house seemed to creak as she made her way down the wooden staircase, and the voices in the kitchen hushed.

"Do you think she's up?" someone whispered loudly.

"Should we go check?" another woman asked.

"I'm up," she announced, turning the corner.

Three women wearing aprons stood near the stove and the sink, their hands busy with various tasks. The shortest one dropped a spatula she'd been holding on to the counter and rushed forward. "Kyra, welcome to Star Valley Springs!" She ushered her fully into the kitchen. "I'm Minnie. And this is Doris." She pointed to the woman who had long black hair threaded with silver. "And that over there is Nelly." She gestured in the direction of the woman who'd paused from doing dishes.

"Such a treat to meet you!" Nelly sang. Judging from her fleecy white hair, she might've been the oldest in the group.

"Um, nice to meet you too?" Or at least it might've been if they hadn't broken into the house. "I'm sorry. How exactly did you get in here?"

"Oh, your dad always left a key underneath the welcome mat." Minnie withdrew a key from the pocket of her paisley apron. "He always said, 'the door's open for anyone to walk through.'" Dimples accented her smile. "That was one of his favorite phrases."

"Okay." She wouldn't know any of his favorite phrases because she hadn't talked to the man in eighteen years. Kyra did her best to maintain a polite, albeit tight, smile. "But what are you doing here?"

"We're making you breakfast." Doris opened the oven and presented a pan of blueberry muffins, each bigger than Kyra's fist.

"Why are you making me breakfast, exactly?" She wasn't trying to be rude, but couldn't they tell they were overstepping? Seriously. Who broke into a house to take over the kitchen?

"Kenny was like family to everyone in this town, which means you are now too." Nelly filled a coffee mug and brought it to a place setting that had been laid out on the kitchen island. "Now sit, sit. We have quiche and muffins. Oh! And bacon. We can't forget the bacon."

"Oh, I don't eat many carbs." But she would drink the coffee. She was going to need a lot of coffee to get through the next three months.

Kyra sat on the stool while the three women served her more food than she would ever be able to eat this early in the morning. Back home, she ate exactly two hard-boiled eggs before leaving the house for her twelve-hour shifts.

"We want you to know we're here to help whenever you need us." Doris added a couple of slices to bacon to her plate.

"With whatever you need," Minnie added, refreshing her coffee even though she'd only had a few sips. "That's the thing you need to know about Star Valley Springs. We take care of each other around here."

"I can see that." Kyra clutched her coffee mug, unsure of how to tell them she didn't need anyone to take care of her. Thanks to her father, she'd learned how to take care of herself a long time ago. "I appreciate all of this." She pushed her plate away. "But you should know that my father and I didn't have any kind of relationship." She had no idea what stories he'd told his friends about his former life—or even if he'd mentioned he had a family that he'd up and left for something better. "I'm only here to deal with his estate and do what he required me to do in his will." And she didn't want them to get any ideas about her staying.

"Of course, sweet pea." Minnie patted her hand. "We know you have quite the career back in Fort Myers. Your daddy was so proud of you becoming a pediatric nurse practitioner. It was all he could talk about."

"What?" Kyra yanked her hand away, bitterness boiling over. "We weren't in contact. I'm not sure how he would've even known what I did for a living."

"Oh." Minnie shared nervous looks with Doris and

Nelly. "Well, I know he made many mistakes—he was always the first to admit that—but he followed your accomplishments and always bragged about how well you were doing."

"That's enough talk about all that." Nelly seemed to sense Kyra's urge to run out of there. "We know you have a lot to do, and the Ladies Aid Society is here to help. We can help with yard sales, cleaning out the house, donations. You name it."

Kyra couldn't name it. She couldn't even think. How could her father have pretended he had any right to be proud of her? "You know what?" She pushed off the stool. "You can help. You can organize donations for everything in this house. I don't want to go through his things. Just give it all away." She quickly left the room before any tears could fall.

This was all so wrong. A month ago she'd had no feelings about Kenneth Fowler. For the first eight years after he left, she'd hoped he would come back. Or that he would at least come and see her, be a part of her life. But by her senior year in high school, she'd finally given up. So when he'd sent her a few letters through college, she returned them unopened. He hadn't wanted anything to do with her when she was a child, so he didn't get to be part of her life as an adult.

Kyra crept up the stairs, disregarding the framed pictures hanging on the walls—images of the mountains and wildlife and various angles of the ranch house. Had her father taken them? She didn't even want to wonder. She didn't want any of this—the confusion, the mystery about why Kenneth had left all of this for her when he had a family she wasn't a part of.

After walking into the guest room, she shut the door—shut everything out—and sat on the bed, staring at the wall. Maybe coming here wasn't worth the money after all. Maybe she should call up the lawyer and tell him to forget her inheritance. She picked up her phone from the nightstand, but a knock stopped her from dialing.

"Kyra?" a soft voice called. "It's Lyric. Can I come in?"

Her heart lurched. The last time Kyra had seen her, Lyric had been sobbing. They'd met secretly at a park right after Kyra's father had told her mother he was in love with someone else. One week later, he'd moved away with his new family, and she'd had to mourn the loss of her best friend and her dad at once.

All of that was supposed to be ancient history. She should be over the past. But the tears burning in her eyes proved that coming here only served to remind her of all she'd lost—her father and her best friend and a family. She was being forced to grieve all over again.

Kyra blinked back the tears and rose from the bed, determined to straighten her backbone against the emotion. She shouldn't feel anything anymore. When she'd gotten the call from the lawyer, she figured she would have to see Lyric eventually, and she'd told herself it wouldn't be hard. But the quaking in her knees begged to differ. Still, she had no choice but to open the door and let the woman in.

"Oh, my God." Her former friend simply stared at her. "You look amazing. I can't believe you're here."

"Trust me. I can't believe it either." The monotone couldn't be helped. She was doing everything she could to keep her emotions in check. Lyric had changed. The woman in front of her had the same large, dark, expressive eyes and winsome dimples, but everything else was different. Her sleek jet-black hair had streaks of dark purple and she wore flowy bohemian pants and a peasant top.

"I'm sorry to just show up like this, but I figured the Ladies would be here and thought you might need backup." Lyric didn't walk into the room, but instead shifted nervously outside the door. "I can only imagine how much you resent me. I'm so sorry, Kyra. For everything that happened between our families."

Honestly, she had resented Lyric for a while. How could she not? Her friend had gotten the family Kyra had lost. But in the last email her friend had sent—the one Kyra's mother had found—Lyric told Kyra that her father was going to bring her out to Wyoming to visit. He'd promised. But the visit had never happened. She hadn't even heard from her father. Ironic he'd decided to bring her out here to visit now.

"What happened in the past wasn't your fault," she finally managed to say. Neither one of them had had any say in their parents' decisions back then. "I didn't blame you." She ushered Lyric into the guest room, sure that Doris, Nelly, and Minnie were eavesdropping at the bottom of the stairs. Ever since she'd arrived in Star Valley Springs, Kyra had felt exposed somehow—like these people she'd met knew more about her life than even she did. And she couldn't stand the vulnerability.

"I don't understand any of this," she told Lyric. God, it hurt to look into the woman's eyes. For years they'd shared everything. Lyric had been the sister she'd never had. But that had been a long time ago. Kyra steeled herself against the flood of memories. This was too hard. Too much. She didn't want to be here. "You should have all of Kenneth's assets. You were more of a daughter to him than I was."

"I wasn't his daughter." A sad smile dimmed the light in Lyric's eyes. She settled herself into the chair in the corner of the room. "I never called him dad and he never called me his daughter. He was good to me, but he wasn't my father. We both understood that."

But she'd lived with him in this house. Growing up here, she had to know every nook and cranny in this place. It had been her home. Kyra lowered herself to the edge of the bed. "I don't want any part of his life." Not his house or his things or his connections in town. "I'm not sure I can stay here. It's too hard." Even now, emotion tightened her throat. She wouldn't be able to hold it off forever.

For ten years, her dad had been her hero. Her mother loved her, she'd never doubted that, but she'd rarely smiled. She always told Kyra to act more mature. Her dad had always been the one she'd laughed with and played with and had been silly with. And then one day her father had left, taking that animated, light-hearted part of her with him.

"Why did he do this?" she asked Lyric, a few tears slipping past her defenses. "Why didn't he leave everything to you and your mother?"

Lyric seemed to hesitate, her gaze darting to the window. "With all of Kenny's investments, my mom got plenty. More than she'll ever need." She rose from the chair and sat next to Kyra on the bed. "And he left me an inheritance too. But he was adamant that you would get the town and the house. I know you probably have a lot of questions." She stared down at her hands. "I wish I could give you some answers. But it's not my place.

I suspect if you stay for a while, you'll understand his reason in time."

"I'm not sure I want to understand." She'd worked so hard over the years to shut the man out. It might be impossible to let him back in now.

"I get it, but selfishly I'd love for you to stay for a while." Lyric's smile still crinkled her nose the same way it had when she was five years old. "I know we might never be friends after everything that's happened, but it's good to see you."

"It's good to see you too." Lyric's warmth melted away some of Kyra's loneliness. "I could probably use a few friends right now." She had no idea how she was going to get through the next few months on her own. "Speaking of friends... I guess we should get downstairs, huh?"

Lyric laughed. "Unless you want them to ambush you up here, probably."

Kyra found herself smiling. "Those ladies sure are persistent."

"That they are." Her friend followed her out of the room. "In fact, I'm going to sneak out the front door. I have to teach a yoga class, and if Nelly sees me she'll force me to stay for breakfast."

Kyra paused before going down the steps. "Thank you for coming by." Somehow seeing an old friend made her feel less... lost.

"Anytime." She led the way downstairs. "I left my number on the counter in case you ever want to talk. Or if you have any questions. I know this is pretty overwhelming. I'll do everything I can to help you, but I also don't want to intrude."

"I appreciate that." Kyra promised they would talk

later and told her goodbye. As soon as the screen door shut, her three fairy godmothers closed in.

"Oh, good!" Nelly made it to her first. "You came back down. Your breakfast is getting cold."

"Not to worry. We can warm it right up." Doris linked her arm through Kyra's and urged her in the direction of the kitchen.

"I'm afraid breakfast will have to wait," Aiden called through the screen door. "Kyra and I have a date to go pick up her car. I've already filled the gas cans. They're in the back of my truck."

Minnie gasped. "A date?"

"It's not a date." Kyra separated herself from the women, wishing she had taken the time for a shower after all, especially when Aiden stepped fully into the house looking like he'd put some effort into his appearance. He wore a button-down plaid shirt with his cowboy jeans, and his beard appeared trimmed. Was that product in his hair too? Kyra self-consciously ran her hand over her hair, pushing stray strands back toward her ponytail.

"Ready?" Aiden held the screen door open for her.

Not really. She hadn't been ready for any of this. "Of course." She passed by him with her jaw set and her eyes focused straight in front of her, but she couldn't ignore the man's alluring woodsy scent.

"Wait!" Minnie chased them down and handed Aiden a basket. "Kyra didn't get to eat her breakfast, so I wrapped up the muffins for you two."

"You know how much I love your muffins." Aiden's smile could've charmed the pants off a nun.

"Have fun, you two!" The woman stood back and gave them a happy wave while Kyra settled herself into the passenger's seat of his monster truck. Using the old-school crank, she rolled down the window. "It's not a date," she reminded Minnie.

"Of course not." Minnie's head bobbed in an exaggerated nod. "We'll clean up here. Don't you worry about anything."

"Thanks." Those women were so efficient, maybe they'd have the whole house emptied by the time she got back. Wouldn't that be nice?

"I see you got a visit from the Ladies this morning." Aiden started the truck and they rolled down the driveway.

"Yeah. It freaked me out a little." Why did she find it so hard to look at him? Kyra shook her head. This was ridiculous. Yes, Aiden was gorgeous. And ripped. And he had this thoughtful way of speaking. But she had never been timid around a man. She was confident and independent, and not even this sexy cowboy/former Navy guy (she assumed based on his tattoos) could change that. So there. She looked directly at him. "I wondered who could possibly be in the house when I locked the door last night."

He laughed in a low, gravelly tone. "No use in locking doors around here. Almost everyone has a key out somewhere."

"I'll have to remember to bring mine in tonight." Before he thought she was ungrateful, she added, "At least until I'm showered and dressed."

Aiden's wide grin stirred something in her. "They can be nosy, but they're also good people," he said. "Minnie owns the Meadowlark Hotel and Café with her husband, Louie. Those two pretty much run the town. They're important people to know."

"I'm sure they are." But she wouldn't be getting to know them. Whatever her father's motivation for putting her in this situation, she'd come for one purpose only. "I won't have much time to get to know anyone. I have a lot of work to do in a short amount of time. Speaking of...do you know anything about Cowboy Construction?"

"Sure. I know they're the best in town." Aiden seemed focused on driving. They'd already left the town behind and were starting up the mountainside.

"That's good, because from what I can tell, they're the only contractor in town." Within a hundred-mile radius, actually. "And I'll need a contractor." She'd gone over the list of stipulated improvements again last night: Put a new roof on the town hall—the number one priority given the fact that snow would be flying soon; repair and paint the gazebo in the town's park; and re-drywall the inside of the antique and souvenir shop. There was no way she could do any of that by herself.

"So I saw Lyric leaving when I got to the house," Aiden mentioned casually.

What was with the abrupt change of subject? Kyra gave him a side-eyed glance. The Ladies weren't the only nosy ones in town. "Yes, I spoke to her." Once again, Kyra was reminded that everyone in Star Valley Springs had an open window into her life, and she desperately wanted to shut them out. No one around here knew her, but the whole town likely already loved Lyric.

What wasn't to love? The woman seemed every bit as genuine and open and giving as she had been when they were young. In contrast, Kyra probably came across as cold. But what did they expect? She was an outsider.

She didn't know them. She hadn't even known her own father...

"Was it tough to see her?"

The question came as a surprise. Or maybe not so much the question as the way Aiden delivered it—quietly concerned for her.

Once again, he obviously knew more about her than he should, but his empathetic tone of voice immediately disarmed her. "It was a little tough," she admitted. "But good too."

Kyra looked out the window, blindly watching the trees pass. After her father had taken off she'd been left to wonder why he'd wanted to be Lyric's father and not hers. Around the holidays she'd always wondered if Lyric and her father were making Christmas cookies together like he and Kyra used to. Had they gone out for ice cream sundaes after a tough day at school the way she and her dad used to? Had her father taken Lyric to a nice dinner to celebrate all of the A's she'd gotten on her report card?

"Hey, how about we take a muffin stop?" Aiden swerved the truck onto a dirt pull-off at the side of the road. "This is a great view of the valley."

"A muffin stop?" Even with the heaviness in her heart she had to laugh. "What if I told you I don't eat muffins?"

"Then I'd say you've never tried Minnie's muffins or you'd eat them all the time." He snatched the basket off the seat between them and got out of the truck.

By the time Kyra had climbed out, Aiden already had the tailgate down and a blanket spread over the bed.

"Fancy," she commented, trying to decide how she was going to climb up there.

"I'll give you a boost." He held his hands together, and she stepped into them so he could prop her up.

Once she'd gotten settled, Aiden hopped up and sat next to her. "What d'you think?" He spread out his arms in front of him in grand presentation. "Star Valley Springs isn't so bad, is it?"

"I never said Star Valley Springs was bad." From their perch high on the mountainside the valley looked like a painting, with all of the orange and red and yellow leaves blurring together and the shimmering river lazily bending and curving with the landscape. "It's a beautiful place," she acknowledged.

But it wasn't the place for her.

CHAPTER FOUR

"You're right. These muffins are amazing." Kyra popped the last bite of Minnie's blueberry muffin into her mouth and dusted the crumbs off her hands.

Aiden tried not to watch as her mouth moved, but she had perfect lips and a rare smile that gave his heart a jolt. He smiled too. The woman had gone from saying she'd take a few bites to finishing off the whole thing while they'd talked about her job as a pediatric nurse practitioner. He had to say... Kyra Fowler impressed him.

"What's Minnie's muffin secret?" She neatly folded up the muffin wrapper and stashed it in the basket. "I never could bake."

Man, she looked so relaxed—completely different from the woman he'd first met yesterday. "Don't know what her secret is." He finished off his own muffin and stuffed the wrapper back into the basket. "She won't tell a soul. Not even Louie knows."

"Well, whatever her secret is, those carbs are worth

every bite." Kyra scooted forward and hopped from the truck's tailgate to the ground. "I guess we should get going. I've got so much to do today if I want to stay on schedule with all of my projects."

"Right." He had a lot to do too. Namely get back to the ranch so he could brief Silas and Thatch on the state of the mission. The first step in operation Save Star Valley had been to befriend Kyra, which was proving a little too easy. But they would have to move into phase two as soon as possible—delay her construction projects so she'd have to spend more time in Star Valley Springs.

Aiden locked up the tailgate and got into the truck.

Kyra already had her seatbelt on. "You never told me what you do in Star Valley."

No, he'd been purposely avoiding that conversation. Once she found out he owned Cowboy Construction, she'd only want to talk about business. And he wanted to know more about her. For the sake of the mission, of course. "I help out on my sister's cattle ranch a lot." Not a lie. The ranch work did take up at least half of his time.

"Your sister owns a cattle ranch?" She raised her eyebrows as though impressed. "That's hard work."

Yeah, she was telling him. Aiden started the engine and steered the truck back onto the road. He might as well tell her the truth. If she was going to be spending a minimum of three months in Star Valley, she'd find out anyway. "Jace, my brother-in-law, passed away. He and I served together." Jace would've retired from the Navy if Aiden hadn't talked him into staying, and then he still would've been here. His throat locked up. "I moved here after we lost him, along with Silas and Thatch—two other members of the team—to help out Tess and my two nieces on the ranch."

Kyra angled her body to face him, and her mouth dropped open. "That's horrible. My God, I'm so sorry. How long ago?"

"Two years." But it might as well have been last week. Damn, his chest ached. He should've gone with talking about the construction.

"I'm sure having you here means everything to your sister." Kyra cleared her throat as if she was holding back emotion too. "And your nieces. How old are they?"

"Morgan is ten and Willow is six." And they had both suffered far too much loss already. He slowed the truck to navigate a switchback. It was past time to change the subject. "Silas and Thatch and I also started Cowboy Construction since we wouldn't take any income from the ranch." There was barely enough coming in to support Tess and the girls.

"Oh. Wow. Good to know. We'll have to talk about my projects, then." She smiled, but her expression was more subdued than it had been five minutes ago. He shouldn't have spilled his guts to her. Now she likely felt sorry for him.

"So your nieces... are they doing okay?"

Aiden peeked at her. If he wasn't mistaken, her eyes were full of tears. "They have their hard days and their good days." Just like him. "They're amazing, though. Resilient and smart. Morgan is hilarious." Like her dad was. He couldn't bring himself to say that. "And Willow is so creative. Always making up stories." Which had been another of Jace's best qualities.

Kyra nodded, still wearing that sad smile as she stared

out the front windshield. "I bet they miss him." She glanced at him sideways. "I bet you miss him too."

His grip tightened on the wheel. "Every day." The admission came out gruffer than he'd intended. "He was my best friend. We grew up together." And then he'd let Jace down when his friend had needed him the most. A searing pain cut through him. He couldn't talk about this. Not with her. Not with anyone. "So these projects you have to get done...what scale are we talking?" No one knew what had been outlined in Kenny's will.

"I'm not exactly sure." She studied him for a few seconds, but he didn't know what she was looking for. "I need the experts to take a look and let me know the scale and scope. Kenneth left plenty of money for the work."

Yes, knowing Kenny, the man had done his research on exactly how much would be needed. Aiden turned onto the road that led to the swimming hole. "Why don't you follow me to the ranch? That's where the Cowboy Construction headquarters are. We can start to talk through what you need done." And then he could start throwing out excuses for why they couldn't work fast. He parked next to her rental and got out to fill up her gas tank.

"Thanks for doing all of this." Kyra stood by watching. "How much do I owe you for the gas?"

"Don't worry about it." He screwed the lid back on. "This is only about half a tank, so you'll have to fill up again soon."

"I'll hit the gas station later today," she promised. Though she kept aiming that polite smile at him, something in her demeanor had shifted. "And I'll follow you to the ranch, so don't drive too fast."

"Got it." He climbed back into his truck and led the

way out of the woods and down the mountainside at a crawling pace, only speeding up when he finally turned onto Tess's driveway. He parked the truck in front of the barn they'd converted for the business and hoofed it inside to warn his friends. "Kyra's here. She's parking her car outside."

"Great." Thatch stood at the coffee counter with Silas, the pot brewing and hissing in front of him. "We'll make sure to look extra busy, then."

"It took you two a while to go pick up her car." Silas cocked an eyebrow. "You get lost or something?"

Aiden sat behind his desk and fired up his laptop. "We took a muffin stop. Minnie packed some up for us to take on the road."

"A muffin stop." Thatch elbowed Silas. "Is that what kids are calling it these days?"

They both snickered.

"Dude, I know I told you to seduce her, but I didn't think you'd actually do it." Silas crossed the room and sat on the edge of Aiden's desk.

"I'm not seducing her." *Don't make eye contact.* He wasn't seducing her, but there were distinct urges happening. Urges he would deny. "I'm befriending her. We all have to befriend her if we want this operation to be a success."

His friends shared a look. "Befriending can be even more dangerous than seducing a woman," Thatch said wisely.

As if Thatch had ever had any experience befriending a woman. "Whatever. We want her to feel welcome here, so you two be nice to her." After seeing their smirks he added, "And no hitting on her."

"Copy that." Thatch saluted him.

Aiden glanced out the window and saw Kyra standing just outside. She was talking on her phone. "It's time to move into phase two of the operation—evasive maneuvers on the construction front."

"Our specialty." Silas went to sit at his desk and leaned back in his chair, kicking up his feet.

"You're supposed to look busy, dumbass." Thatch knocked Silas's boots off the desk on the way to his station. "Get out your computer or something."

"You don't look bus—"

The door opened and shut Silas up.

Kyra hurried inside, tucking her phone back into her purse. "Sorry. I had to take that call."

"No worries." Aiden got up to pull another chair to his desk so she could sit across from him.

"We were just prioritizing our projects." Silas stared at his computer screen with a serious expression, but he was probably just strategizing his next Battleship move with Thatch. Those two were obsessed.

"Yeah. Work is busy right now." Thatch frowned at his screen. "Son of a—" He stopped just in time as though remembering they had company. "We're literally sinking underwater," he muttered, glaring at Silas.

"But we'd like to hear about the projects you need done." Aiden drew Kyra's attention back to him. Those two yahoos were not helping.

"Right." Her head shook like she was trying to get her thoughts together. "Well, Kenneth had outlined three very specific upgrades I have to make." She rifled through her purse and pulled out a list. "Evidently, he was going to do them but didn't get around to it before…" The sentence trailed off. "Anyway. Um, I'm hoping to get started on the projects as soon as possible. Today would be good."

"Today?" Aiden leaned over to get a look at the list. "New roof on the town hall." That would suck. Roofing jobs were always messy and more complicated than they appeared to be. "Paint and repair gazebo in the park." That could easily be done in a few days. "Re-drywall the antique and souvenir shop." He grimaced. "Gotta admit, that's more than I was picturing."

"Yeah," Silas agreed. "That's going to take a while."

"Especially with the cattle drive delaying all of our projects," Thatch added. "There's no way we can get started today."

"Oh." Kyra sat up taller. "I didn't realize you were so busy."

"We've got a lot on our plate." Aiden made sure to sigh. It wasn't a lie. They did have some room renovations going on at the Meadowlark Hotel, though Minnie wasn't in too much of a hurry to get them done. The few tourists they had tended to come around mostly in the summer. "The biggest delay right now will be the cattle drive starting next Sunday. We have to spend all week preparing."

"Cattle drive?" Kyra asked impatiently. "How long will that be?"

"It can take up to three days," Silas said gravely.

"But it does go faster with more people." Thatch had always been the lead BS-er of the group. "You're welcome to join us. The more help we have driving the cattle, the quicker we can move them down to the lower meadow."

Aiden held back a laugh. They already had plenty of

help. Having some city slicker join them wasn't going to make things move any faster.

"Me?" Kyra laughed. "You want me to go on a cattle drive? There's no way—"

"Uncle Aiden!" Morgan nearly knocked down the door as she bounded into the office at Mach speed. "Guess what?" his niece asked, her deep brown eyes wide. She didn't wait for him to guess. "I got some new cowgirl boots!" She hiked her foot up onto his desk to show off the glittery blue leather.

He inspected them closely and let out a low whistle. "Those are sharp. Think they have any in my size?"

She giggled. "No way. You said glitter makes you sneeze."

He grinned. Morgan never forgot anything he said. "I have an allergy," he explained to Kyra.

"Well, you're not supposed to inhale the stuff." His adorable niece had recently perfected the art of eyerolling. She turned to Kyra. "You shoulda seen him. We were doing this really cool crafting project..."

"Oh, I love crafting projects." Kyra leaned closer to the girl, giving Morgan her full attention.

"Me too!" Morgan looked so much like Jace when she got all jazzed about something. Her eyes lit and her mouth curved into the same smile her father had worn. "Anyway, Uncle Aiden dumped way too much glitter on his glue and then he got his face real close to it and shook the paper so all the glitter went up his nose and made him sneeze."

Kyra laughed with Morgan. "Rookie mistake."

"Totally," he acknowledged.

"I'm still working with him," his niece said with an air

of importance. "He has a lot to learn about crafting, but he's getting better."

Spending time with his nieces had made him a better man all around, he wouldn't deny that. "Glad you came to see me, kid." Morgan's interruption couldn't have come at a more perfect time. Kyra obviously liked kids, given her job and the way she connected with his niece. "We were trying to convince Ms. Fowler to come and help us on the cattle drive."

"Yes!" Morgan clapped. "Ohmygosh! The cattle drive is so fun! You'll love it! We get to camp and ride horses. And we eat yummy food at the campfire. It's the best!"

"It is the best," Aiden agreed, nodding emphatically with a grin directed at Kyra. Give her three days in the backcountry and she would fall in love with this place the same way he had. Beauty didn't began to describe these mountains. "You would have the time of your life if you came with us." They would all make sure.

"Is that so?" The woman's mesmerizing blue eyes narrowed at him, calling bullshit on his promise. "And going on this cattle drive would allow you to take on my projects sooner?" Kyra asked as though she already knew the answer.

"Oh, yeah," Silas chimed in from across the room.

"Definitely," Thatch confirmed.

Aiden shrugged. Morgan had made his job easy.

"Then I'm in." The woman focused on his niece. "If you say it's that fun, I'll come and help out."

"Yay!" The girl hugged her and then pulled away, looking embarrassed. "I'm Morgan, by the way. Are you a friend of Uncle Aiden's?"

"I'm Kyra," she said, not answering the question.

Yesterday he'd been real tempted to call her his adversary, but today...well...she kept surprising him.

"It's nice to meet you." Morgan skipped to the door. "Since you're coming on the cattle drive with us, do you want to meet my horse? His name is Bravo."

"I would love to meet your horse." Kyra stood and slung her purse on her shoulder. Before following Morgan out the door, she paused and turned back to Aiden. "Since I've agreed to the cattle drive, I'm assuming that means you'll get me estimates and timelines for the work I need done?"

"We'll get started on that today." Aiden walked her and Morgan out the door, already thinking of what excuses he could come up with to delay the bids. "I'll be in touch."

"Uncle Aiden, do you want to come to the barn with us?" Morgan tugged on his hand. "Bravo loves you."

"Oh...I have a lot to do." They'd just finished telling Kyra how busy they were in here. Although judging from the way Silas and Thatch were staring at their screens and then sending one another death glares over their Battleship battle, Kyra had likely figured out they weren't as slammed as they'd said.

"We can hold down the fort." Silas waved him out the door. "You go enjoy a muffin or two."

If Aiden had been closer he would've decked him. "I'll be back in a few," he muttered in response to Silas and Thatch's ribbing grins.

"Why'd they tell you to go have a muffin?" Morgan led the way out the door and across the driveway to the horse stables.

"I have no idea." Evading was better than telling her that the three of them were constantly giving each other shit. After their years in the service together, they were more like brothers than friends. Unfortunately those two could see right through him. They likely detected the way he couldn't seem to keep his eyes off Kyra. "Anyway, welcome to the Dry Creek Ranch," he said belatedly to Kyra.

"My daddy built that house with his grandparents." Morgan pointed to the main house, where Tess had lived for the last twelve years. The land had been in Jace's family since his great grandfather had settled in the valley with his family as a boy, and it had always been Jace's dream to raise his family here. Aiden braced for the inevitable shot of pain that never missed its mark whenever he thought about everything his brother-in-law was missing.

"It looks like a pretty incredible house." Kyra paused to admire the simple structure. "I bet that's your room right there." She pointed to the side window with blue curtains the same color as his niece's new boots.

"Yep! How'd you know?" Morgan looked up at Kyra in awe.

"I can tell blue is your favorite color. It's my favorite color too." The two carried on an entire conversation about the color blue while they entered the stable.

Aiden watched them interact, stunned at how easily Kyra connected with his niece. Morgan had come a long way in two years, but it had taken months for him to build a rapport with her after Jace's death. Now she hardly even noticed he was tagging along. He might as well have stayed back in the office for all he was contributing to the conversation.

"This is Bravo." Morgan stopped at the third stall and

swung open the door to show off her quarter horse. "My daddy named him."

"Bravo is a great name." Kyra walked into the stall and ran her hand along the horse's muzzle.

Bravo nudged her shoulder with his nose. "He wants treats," Morgan informed her. "I'll be right back." She skipped out of the stall and disappeared.

Aiden joined Kyra next to the horse. "She loves this guy." Morgan and her father had spent a lot of time training him together before Jace passed. "You're really good with her," he said to Kyra.

She continued to pet the horse, not looking at him. "I was ten when my dad left." Her gaze lifted to his. "Not that it's the same exactly, but..."

"You know what it's like." To grow up without a father. He had no clue what Morgan had had to go through, but Kyra understood better than anyone.

"I know how it feels to try and live with a piece of your heart missing." Kyra turned her face to his. "But you do too."

Yes. He lived with a gaping hole in the very center of his heart. Aiden met her eyes, holding her gaze, and for a fleeting second the empathy he found there soothed the pain. "I thought it would get easier over time." But it hadn't. Watching his nieces grow as the weeks and months passed only reminded him their father wasn't here to see each milestone.

Kyra smoothed her hand over the horse's mane again, but she didn't take her eyes off of his. "It doesn't get easier. But you get stronger."

He opened his mouth to tell her that most days he didn't feel stronger, but his niece traipsed back into the stall and handed Kyra a carrot. "Here's the treats. This is his favorite."

"I've never fed a horse before." The woman awkwardly held out the carrot.

"It's easy. Just lay it flat on your palm." His niece demonstrated.

"Okay." Kyra did as instructed, and Bravo gobbled the carrot off her hand. "Oh, wow. He has whiskers."

The sound of her laugh loosened the bonds that bitterness and grief had coiled around Aiden's heart over the last two years. Thatch was right.

Befriending this woman might prove to be the most dangerous thing he'd ever done.

CHAPTER FIVE

For the life of her Kyra didn't know how she'd survived almost thirty years—and a whole week in Star Valley—without experiencing breakfast at the Meadowlark Café.

She sipped her coffee, which somehow tasted better than any cup she'd ever had back in Fort Myers, and tried to decide between the pineapple upside-down pancakes and the bourbon praline French toast. Seeing as how she was gearing up to be on a cattle drive for at least two days, she might as well go big.

A cattle drive. She was really going on a cattle drive? Kyra almost laughed out loud. Before coming to Star Valley Springs, her idea of an outdoorsy experience was to take her reclining lounge chair to the beach for an afternoon, and now she was about to trek across rugged mountain terrain on the back of a horse. "What was I thinking?" she muttered. Thankfully, the café was so busy no one else seemed to hear her mumbling to herself.

Truthfully, Morgan happened to be too adorable to refuse. She hadn't wanted to disappoint the girl when she'd seemed so hopeful Kyra would join them. And Kyra had no idea what kind of game Aiden was playing, but if going on this little excursion would make him work faster on her projects, she would happily become a cowgirl. Not to mention that when he'd brought up the possibility of her going, she'd seen the challenge in his eyes. And she never backed down from a challenge.

"How's your coffee?" Minnie appeared next to her, holding the carafe.

"Absolutely delicious." Kyra set down the menu and checked her watch. The contractor she was supposed to meet happened to be ten minutes late.

"It's our own special blend using beans from fair trade and organic farms," the woman said proudly. "I always add a splash of oat milk before I bring it out. That really melds the flavors."

"It's like magic in a cup." She didn't care what was in the coffee. It tasted good and she needed the caffeine. "I might need a few more cups." She'd been in town for a week and had yet to sleep through the night. There was too much to think about in that house. Too many unanswered questions. As of yet she hadn't been able to bring herself to open the closets, but that had to change today.

"You can have as many free coffee refills as you want." The woman topped off her mug. "Are you still waiting for someone else?" she asked, eyeing the empty seat across from Kyra.

"Yeah. It seems he's running a little late." And the contractor she'd called in Jackson likely didn't have cell service around here. Hopefully, he wasn't going to stand her up. She hadn't heard a peep from Cowboy Construction since she'd been at the ranch, so she needed another option.

"Oh, you're meeting a *he*?" Minnie glanced around and then leaned closer. "You and Aiden must be having a second date then," she half whispered.

"Nope. We didn't even have a first date." And she hadn't seen him since she'd left his sister's ranch, which was more than fine with her. She hadn't found her thoughts drifting to him at all. She hadn't been thinking about how his grin had made her feel all warm and skittish. Or how sweet he'd been with his niece when they were in the stable. Or how something passed between them when Aiden had held her gaze in the barn.

Nope. She hadn't been thinking about him at all

"I'm meeting someone else," Kyra told Minnie. So far Aiden didn't seem all that reliable. Besides, it might be best for her to work with someone who didn't make her heart flutter.

"Would you like to order while you wait for your…*friend*?" Minnie pressed. She was clearly dying to ask who this unnamed man was, but Kyra smiled mysteriously.

"No, that's okay. I'll wait until he gets here." She hadn't decided between the pancakes and the French toast yet anyway.

"All right, sweet pea. I'll come back around soon." The woman scurried away, leaving Kyra to check her phone.

No texts, no missed calls. Either the man was as lost as she had gotten driving in here, or he wasn't coming. She lifted her coffee mug again. He had to come, that's all there was to it. Other than Cowboy Construction, this contractor from Jackson was her only option. Every other company she'd called had said they were too busy or they wouldn't travel that far to do the work she needed done.

"Miss Kyra!" Morgan waved at her from the door.

"Hey!" She waved back, genuinely happy to see the girl. She was such a sweetheart. Kyra almost got up to meet her, but then Aiden walked into the café behind Morgan holding a younger girl's hand.

On second thought, she'd stay put at her table.

"Hey." Aiden followed Morgan to her table at a distance, urging the younger girl along with him.

Instead of responding to the man, Kyra focused on his other niece. "You must be Willow." The girl was a miniature version of her older sister.

The girl nodded in response, almost hiding behind her uncle.

"Willow, this is Kyra." Aiden gently prodded her forward.

"She's Uncle Aiden's friend," Morgan chimed in.

Were they friends? Kyra couldn't be sure. She liked Aiden's smile. She thought he was sweet with his nieces. And she'd caught a couple of glimpses of a kind heart underneath that strong, steady cowboy exterior, but could she trust him? She didn't know how to trust anyone.

"It's very nice to meet you, Willow." Luckily, with the girls here Kyra didn't have to look at Aiden. It was his grayish green eyes. They seemed to pull her in and make her talk about things she would rather forget.

"Nice to meet you too," Willow whispered. She seemed much shier than her sister.

Kyra's eyes lifted, and she found her gaze locked onto

Aiden's. Her heart responded with a swift drop. "Um, I'd ask you to join me, but I'm actually meeting someone this morning."

"That's okay." Aiden seemed to have no problem staring directly into her eyes. "These girls like to sit by the windows anyway."

"Uncle Aiden takes us out to breakfast every Saturday morning and we have a regular table over there." Morgan pointed to the opposite corner of the room.

Of course he took his nieces to breakfast every week. The man was such an anomaly. Loyal, devoted, tender with children. All within a tough ex–Navy SEAL, tattooed exterior.

"Why don't you girls sit down and I'll be over in a minute?" He let go of Willow's hand, and Morgan guided her sister away.

"Good to see you, Miss Kyra!" the girl called. "I can't wait for the cattle drive!"

"Me too," she lied. Who cared that she'd only been camping once—in her own backyard? She wouldn't let Aiden see her sweat.

"I've been working on your bids," Aiden said when the girls had walked away.

The guilt in his expression amused her. "Have you now?" She had to tease him a little. "And to think, I was ready to give up on you."

"Yeah, things have been a little chaotic." He finally looked away and kept his eyes on the girls. "But I'm almost done with putting together the estimates. I'll have them ready after the cattle drive."

"Okay, sure." She casually sipped her coffee. "I should tell you, though, I'm meeting with another contractor.

Now actually. So I might not need the estimates." Working with someone else would be less complicated anyway. Aiden would likely be a lot more tempting than this Ralph guy she'd called, and she did not want to get distracted. She couldn't treat this stint in Star Valley Springs like a vacation.

"You found another contractor to work with?"

His shocked tone tempted her to laugh. "We haven't signed anything yet, but I am talking to someone else. Since you're all so busy." Her gaze drifted to the door, where an older gentleman had stepped in and was looking around. "There he is, in fact." She stood and sidestepped Aiden. "Please excuse me."

The older gentleman looked relieved when she approached. "Are you Ralph?" she asked just to make sure.

"Yes, ma'am." His full mustache muffled the words. "Sorry I'm late. I took a wrong turn in them woods and had to find my way out."

"Don't worry about it. I've been there." She waved him to follow her. "I have a table all ready for us."

The man sat down across from her and slipped off his cowboy hat. "This town is tough to find. I didn't even know it was here, to tell you the truth. I've fished the river, but I've never made it this far down."

"I should've warned you." Kyra signaled for Minnie as she sat down.

"I see your *friend's* here." Amusement played on the woman's red-slicked lips as she placed Ralph's menu down on the table. "Can I get you some coffee, sir?"

"I'd love coffee." The man took a quick glance at the items listed. "And the logger's breakfast with over-easy eggs and bacon."

"I'll do the pineapple upside-down pancakes," Kyra added.

"You got it." Minnie jotted down their orders and disappeared.

"Thanks for coming." Kyra focused on Ralph, even though she could feel Aiden watching them. "I appreciate you taking the time to meet with me."

"Yeah, I was headed up this way for a fishing trip anyway." The man sat back, his shoulders sagging. He looked to be approaching sixty with the gray streaking through his sandy hair and the weathered lines around his eyes and mouth. "This town is a lot farther away than I thought, though."

Uh oh. That didn't sound good. "I'm willing to put you and your crew up at the Meadowlark Hotel during the work so you wouldn't have to travel back and forth." Her father had left plenty of money in the budget for paying a couple of contractors to stay close by. "Meals would be included too." And whatever else she had to entice him with to take the job. "With overtime pay for the weekends."

"It sounds like something to consider." The man turned his head to glance out the window. "This seems like a real nice town. I wouldn't mind spending a few weeks in the area. Especially since the fishing is so close by."

"Right." Maybe motivating him to take the job wouldn't be as difficult as she'd thought. "The fishing is amazing. At least that's what I've heard. I haven't exactly tried myself." But she'd heard Louie talking about fly fishing earlier...

"You got rainbows out there in that section of the river?" Ralph asked, smoothing his napkin on his lap.

Rainbows? As in the colors that came down from the clouds? "Um…"

A server delivered their food and Ralph's coffee. Perfect timing. If Kyra couldn't convince the man to stay here for the fishing, Minnie and Louie's cooking would surely lure him in.

"What do you need done, exactly?" Ralph asked as they dug in.

As quickly and efficiently as possible, Kyra went over the project list with him.

"A roof?" He shook his head. "That's bigger scale than I was thinking."

Oh, no. She was losing him. Kyra took a few bites before answering so she didn't come across as desperate. At least he seemed to be enjoying his food too. "I'm paying cash up front. And I'd be happy to compensate even more for the rush on my timeline too." She'd hoped to save some of the money from the project budget her father had designated so she could use it for her move, but now was not the time to be frugal.

"What's your timeline?" the man asked, finishing off his bacon.

Kyra braced herself. "I need the work completed before Christmas."

Ralph laughed. He actually laughed!

"I can tell ya right now that ain't happening." He buttered his toast while he spoke. "I've got openings in February but not before."

"February?" But that was four months away. "I can't wait that long. I need to get started right away." With any luck, she'd already be living and working in London by February.

"Sorry." He munched on his toast. "I'm booked out until February. I woulda told you that on the phone, but you didn't say this would be a rush job."

"It's not your fault." Kyra gave up on her pancakes. "I should've explained the situation. I apologize that you had to come all the way out here." But at least he'd gotten a free breakfast out of the deal.

"No problem." Ralph waved off her apology. "I'll try my luck on the river before I head home."

Evidently this meeting wasn't a total waste for him like it had been for her. He finished eating, and then Kyra stood to bid him farewell. "It was nice to meet you."

"You too." Ralph tipped his hat to her. "Thanks for the breakfast."

"I'm glad you enjoyed it." She, on the other hand, would be taking her pancakes home with her. After he left, Kyra sat back down to wait for the bill, defeat weighting her shoulders. So much for finding another option. Her gaze moved across the room and stopped on Aiden with his nieces. The three of them were laughing hysterically about something, their heads bent together over the table.

Geez, talk about a picture-perfect moment.

Right then, Aiden lifted his head, and his eyes met hers from all the way across the room. He held her gaze for a few seconds before looking around as though searching for Ralph. After saying something to the girls, the three of them got up and walked to her table.

"How'd the meeting go?" The man was too decent to gloat, but he had to know how it went since Ralph had already left.

Did she have to answer him? Kyra held back a gusty

sigh. "It's not going to work out, so I'll need those estimates after all."

His smile was too genuine to rub her nose in the failure. "They'll be ready for you the day we get back from the cattle drive. I promise."

"Miss Kyra!" Morgan slipped between them. "Do you want to come shopping with us? We're going to find a present for our mom. Her birthday is coming up next month."

If only she could pretend she was here for fun and shopping rather than focusing on what she needed to do. Kyra stood and decided to leave the pancakes and throw a few twenties on the table. Minnie could keep the change. "I would love to go shopping, but I need to get home. I have a lot of cleaning to get done." What good would it do her to start the construction projects if she didn't actually clean out the house? Minnie had already told her the ladies would help, but they wanted her to take the lead on sorting through her father's things. Everything else might currently be out of her control, but she could go back to Kenneth's place and finally start opening those closets.

"Do you need help?" Morgan asked. "We're really good at cleaning. Aren't we, Willow?"

The younger girl nodded emphatically.

"Oh, that's okay." Kyra put her arm around Morgan as they made their way to the door. "I don't want to ruin your shopping trip. Cleaning isn't nearly as fun." Especially cleaning out the house of a complete stranger.

"We don't mind." Morgan stopped and peered at Aiden over her shoulder. "Do we, Uncle Aiden? You shouldn't have to do it all by yourself. That's no fun either. Willow and I always help each other clean our rooms. It goes much faster."

"I don't mind." Aiden held the door open and gestured for them to go through first. "If that's what you girls want to do with your day."

Willow tugged on Aiden's sleeve, and he lowered his head. She whispered something to make the man grin. "Willow says she's very good at dusting."

"We call her the dust buster," Morgan confirmed.

Her little sister nodded proudly.

Kyra looked at Aiden, her heart stirring in that strange, foreign way. She didn't know what to make of the way he grinned at her or how he could disarm her with the right tone. She didn't know exactly how to act with him. But Morgan and Willow were both staring at her with wide, pleading eyes. How could she refuse their sweet offers of help? "If you're sure you really don't mind?"

"Not at all!" Morgan grabbed Willow's hand, and they walked into the parking lot with Kyra and Aiden a step behind.

"Are you sure it's not an imposition?" he asked quietly. "They can be pretty...persistent, but if you'd rather not have company, they'll be okay."

"It's no trouble for me." Well, cleaning was no trouble for her. Aiden, on the other hand? He had the potential to bring plenty of trouble into her life. "It's sweet of them to offer. They're pretty amazing."

"Yeah, they are." He watched his nieces with such a fondness in his eyes Kyra's heart ached. They might have lost their father, but they had Aiden to love them and to take them out to breakfast. They were lucky. He clearly made them a priority in his life, and that would give them back some of the security they'd lost...some of the security she'd never gotten back after her father had left.

"We'll meet you at Kenny's house, then," he said, following his nieces in the direction of his truck.

"Sounds good." Kyra climbed into her SUV and silently commanded her heart to settle. She couldn't name the emotion that had her all muddled inside. Fear, maybe. Anticipation. Uncertainty. But also...gratitude. She had no idea what kinds of things she would find in her father's closets, but at least now she wouldn't have to face them alone.

As she drove into the ranch house's driveway, she tried to imagine what it would've been like to grow up here. Among the mountains, in this small town where everyone seemed to care for one another, where people showed up when someone needed help. She'd never had anyone to call for help. After her father left, Kyra's mother refused to rely on anyone else for anything. *It's you and me against the world*, she'd always said. Kyra had had friends but, looking back, she'd always managed to keep at least a little distance in every relationship. None of the friendships she'd made over the years had stood the test of time. And she had plenty of acquaintances at work, but not one of them had called to check on her since she'd been gone.

The sound of Aiden's truck prompted her to get out of her car. He parked behind her, and the girls filed out, talking excitedly about their memories of this house.

"Remember the Christmas party last year?" Morgan asked Willow. "Santa came and everything!"

"Every year, Kenny had a Christmas party and invited the whole town," Aiden explained.

"It was the best!" Morgan led the charge up the porch steps.

"There was tons and tons of candy," Willow added shyly.

"That sounds like fun." Kyra hid her face as she focused on unlocking the door. Her dad had always dressed up like Santa Claus for her too. When he'd left, he'd taken the magic of Christmas away with him.

"Did you change the locks?" They stepped inside, and Aiden aimed a full, teasing grin at her.

Kyra recovered, pushing the memories out of her thoughts. "No, but I can't get my head around not locking the door." And she had removed the key hidden under the mat. "I'm a city girl. One week in the backwoods of Wyoming hasn't changed that." She tossed her purse onto the credenza in the entryway.

"Maybe a cattle drive will," Aiden suggested a little too innocently.

Don't bet on it. "All right, girls..." she said, eager to change the topic. "I thought we might start upstairs in the guest room." There likely wasn't much in those closets, so they could knock that room out pretty quickly.

"Okey dokey." Morgan tromped up the staircase with Willow right on her heels.

Aiden gestured for Kyra to go next. "So how much have you gotten done around here?"

"Honestly? I haven't even started working on the house yet," she said, all too aware of the man behind her. "It's weird." She stopped outside of the guest room. "I mean, for ten years he was my father, there all the time, a huge part of my life, and then one day he wasn't. There was only a big empty space..." There she went again, opening the vein of her past and letting everything spill out.

"I can't imagine what that must've been like for you." In any other tone, those words might've made her roll her eyes, but he said them with such sincerity that she had to step back. Kyra fought against her heart's easy response to him. *Stop*. He was not her friend. He couldn't be her friend.

"Let's start by cleaning out the closet." Sidestepping Aiden, Kyra moved quickly into the room and opened the door to the walk-in closet. "This isn't too bad." There were a lot of boxes, but they'd all been well organized on the shelves. She pulled one off to pry it open. "I'm thinking we take everything out and make one pile for donations and one pile for trash."

"You're not keeping anything?" Morgan lowered to her knees and started to dig around in the box. "Holy cow. Look at this!" She removed a large stuffed-animal dolphin that still had the tags on it. "You can't get rid of this, Miss Kyra! It's so pretty. And it's brand new!"

Willow seemed to agree, snatching it out of her sister's hands and hugging the animal tightly against her chest. "This is the softest stuffed animal ever."

"And look at this!" Morgan pulled out a bagged comforter that was covered in hearts and dolphins. Again, the tags were still on.

The girl held it out, and Kyra took the twin-size comforter out of the packaging. "It's brand new. Never been used."

"How beautiful." Morgan ran her hand over the soft material. "It even has lots of blue on it. Our favorite color."

"You're right." Kyra set aside the comforter, her pulse picking up. And dolphins had always been her favorite animal. After her parents had taken her swimming with the dolphins at an aquarium for her birthday the year she'd turned nine, she'd been obsessed…

"Ohmygoodness!" Willow rifled through the box too, pulling out posters and curtains, and little dolphin trinkets—all with the tags still on.

"Why is all this stuff in here?" Morgan asked, holding up a glittery dolphin statue.

"I don't know." Kyra couldn't manage more than a whisper. Her throat was on fire. She pulled down another box, nearly toppling over in the process, before Aiden helped steady her. He took the box from her hands and set it on the floor.

She couldn't bring herself to open it, but Morgan didn't wait. "Look at all of these clothes." She started holding up outdated sweaters and leggings and a puffy blue parka with the price tags still on.

"There's a whole wardrobe in there," Kyra murmured, backing out of the closet. Had her father gotten all these things for her? She shuffled to the bed and eased herself down to the mattress, bracing her palms against her thighs. "I don't understand." Why did her father have a whole closet full of brand-new items perfect for a ten-year-old girl?

While Morgan and Willow continued to *ohh* and *ahh* over the clothes in the closet, Aiden sat on the bed next to her.

"Those were all my favorite things." She paused to swallow tears. "My father and I both loved animals, but my mom was allergic to everything. So instead of having pets, he took me to the zoo. The dolphins were always our favorite. We even swam with them at the aquarium once." That had been their last outing together. "I never heard from him." She searched Aiden's face for any clues about why her father would've purchased all of these things and then left them boxed away in a closet for eighteen years. "Never. He left and I didn't hear from him once." Her eyes were swimming in tears now.

With the same tenderness he showed to his nieces, Aiden wrapped his hand around hers, holding her up in the sea of confusion. "I can't say that I understand either. What about your mom? Did she ever talk about your dad after he left?"

"Not much." Kyra exhaled slowly, trying to rein in her emotions. "But I remember wanting to call him, wanting to talk to him or go visit. And she told me he didn't want to see me. She said he had a new family, and he didn't want us anymore." But that couldn't have been true. There was a whole closet full of evidence telling her that her mom had lied. "Right after I graduated from college, Mom was diagnosed with breast cancer, and the past didn't seem important. We never talked about it." She'd never pushed for information. She'd never questioned the narrative her mother had fed her.

"I can't speak too much to the past," Aiden said quietly. "But I was in rough shape when I moved here. Jace had just passed away and I had no clue what I was doing on the ranch." He stared down at their hands, which were still entwined.

Maybe she should've pulled away from him, but she craved the warmth his simple gesture brought.

"Your dad took me under his wing," Aiden said. "We

didn't talk a whole lot. I usually wasn't in the mood to talk, but he taught me everything he knew about working with the cattle so I could help Tess. That's the kind of man he was. He gave a lot and didn't expect anything in return. I can't imagine he didn't want to know you." The man hesitated but then continued. "You remind me of him, actually. I mean, I know we just met, but the way you are with my nieces…so compassionate and warm? That was Kenny too."

Warm and compassionate. That had been the father she'd known for ten years. And she'd never understood how the man could've changed overnight. "Why would she lie to me?" The tears finally slipped down her cheeks, and she let them go. "Why wouldn't she let me see him?"

Aiden held her hand tighter, shaking his head as though he was at a loss. "Maybe Lyric would know."

Yes. She needed to talk to Lyric. She had to know more about their past than she was letting on.

CHAPTER SIX

Uncle Aiden? Hello?" Morgan tapped his shoulder repeatedly from the back seat of his truck. "Did you hear me? I asked if you could turn this song up."

"Oh. Sure." He hadn't heard a word his nieces were saying as they chattered excitedly about all of the new treasures Kyra had given them to take home. He turned up the radio dial, and the girls belted out some Carrie Underwood song like they were standing on a stage with her.

They'd left Kyra's place ten minutes ago, but his mind was still back there in that guest room with her. He never should've touched her. Never should've taken her hand. The contact had burned him up inside.

He was only supposed to be convincing her to keep the land. He wasn't supposed to be feeling things for her. His heart wasn't supposed to respond to her the way it had when he'd seen the sadness in her eyes.

"Uncle Aiden, why did Kyra seem sad when we left?" Willow asked over the music.

"Oh…" He took his time formulating an answer. "I think she misses her dad."

"We miss our daddy too," his sweet niece murmured.

"We sure do." And that tightening in his chest, the anger and grief still pumping through him at the thought of what had happened to Jace, only proved how messed up he still was.

"All right, you monkeys. We're home." He parked the truck in front of his sister's house, and they all piled out.

Aiden carted the fours boxes Kyra had given the girls from the back of his pickup to the porch while the girls bolted inside squealing about trying on their new clothes. His sister met him as he brought the last box up the steps.

"What's all this?" Tess eyed the boxes warily. "I thought we agreed you were going to start telling them no instead of spoiling them rotten all the time." She smiled as she said the words. She knew him too well.

Aiden shrugged helplessly. "You know they have me wrapped around their fingers." He wanted to give them everything. Everything their father could no longer provide. "But this stuff didn't cost me anything. It's from Kyra."

"Really?" Tess held the door open for him with an intrigued expression. "As in the woman whose plans you're trying to sabotage?"

"I'm not trying to sabotage *all* of her plans." Just the plan that involved her selling this town. Aiden set the boxes on the floor.

"Mmmmkay." His sister led him across the great room and into the kitchen that he and Jace had refinished four years ago. He swore memories of his brother-in-law hid in every corner of this place.

"Mama!" Willow skipped into the kitchen holding the stuffed dolphin. "Look at what Miss Kyra gave me!"

"How fun." Tess inspected the huge fluffy toy. "It's really pretty."

"It sure is," her daughter agreed before bounding out of the room.

"Why would Kyra give her an obviously expensive stuffed animal?" His sister poured a glass of iced tea from a pitcher on the counter and handed it to him. "I must be missing something. Where did you run into Kyra?"

"At the café." And he'd known it was a bad idea to go to Kenny's house with her, but the girls had been so excited. Yet again he hadn't been able to tell them no. "She mentioned she had to start cleaning out the house, and the girls insisted on helping her."

"So the *girls* really wanted to spend some time with Kyra?" Her raised eyebrows made it clear that Tess knew he was full of shit.

"You know how persistent they can be." Though he hadn't put up too much of a fight. "Anyway…we were cleaning out the closet in the guest room and we found all of these boxes full of the things Kyra loved when she was young. Everything still had the price tags on. It was like Kenny had planned to bring her out here and give her a room in his house, but he never did."

Aiden wasn't a father, yet he couldn't imagine abandoning Morgan and Willow. Just walking away and never seeing them again would tear him apart.

"That must've been hard for her to find." Tess dumped some sugar into her iced tea and stirred.

"Yeah. She got a little emotional." He avoided his sister's sharp gaze by taking a big gulp of tea.

"And you were there for her," Tess said with a satisfied smirk. "I knew you liked her."

"I feel bad for her," he corrected. "This huge burden was dumped into her lap out of nowhere and she's dealing with a lot by herself."

"I hear she's coming on the cattle drive." Tess pulled out the stool next to him and sat down. "Silas said the three of you are trying to stall on the work Kenny wanted her to do."

"For a good reason." He faced his sister. "You know what'll happen if one of those developers gets their hands on this place."

That dimmed Tess's smile. "Yes. I know. But maybe there's no stopping the changes, Aiden." She stared into her glass and swirled the ice around. "Ever since we lost Jace, you've made your whole life about the girls and me, about this ranch, but that's not really fair to you."

Not this conversation again. He thunked his glass down hard on the counter, his blood heating. "You know what's not fair? That Jace isn't here." And yet Aiden was. How did that make any sense? He didn't have a family, a wife, two kids to take care of. "I told him you and the girls would never have to worry about anything."

And he would do whatever it took to keep his promise.

Kyra had been standing outside Lyric's front door for a good five minutes and she still couldn't bring herself to knock. Torn between wanting to finally know the truth and wanting to close that door on the discovery and forget they were ever there, she stood paralyzed, taking in the many details of Lyric's wide front porch.

The outside of the house was a reflection of the woman herself—vibrant and inviting. The bright turquoise siding and the pure white trim gave the bungalow neat but cheerful lines. Various flowerpots housed plants of all varieties, crowding the porch along with various garden gnome statues. Two colorful hammock chairs hung from the porch's rafters, swaying slightly in the gentle breeze.

She and Lyric had been texting back and forth over the last few days, and her friend had sent her address and told Kyra to stop by anytime. But now she didn't know what to say. There'd been a time she and Lyric had been as close as sisters. Maybe they would've stayed close if her mother hadn't put a stop to the emails.

Pain radiated through her chest. God, what would it have been like to have a sister? Kyra's mother had kept their life small, just the two of them, blocking out everyone else who might have made their lives richer. But what if Kyra could've had a family? What if she could've had her mom but also her father and a stepmom and Lyric?

That was the real hesitation—the reason she couldn't make herself knock. Her mother had taken away the possibility for Kyra to have another family. And she didn't know what to do with the truth now. Yes, she could get angry. She could hate her mother. But what purpose would that serve?

A whining sound on the other side of the door startled her. A dog? Kyra took a step back, ready to make a fast escape, but the dog barked.

Before she could hide, the door opened. "Kyra." Lyric's smile brightened her eyes as though she was genuinely happy to see her. "Come on in." She stepped aside while a large, beautiful black-and-white husky greeted Kyra with a sniff.

"All right, Amos," the woman chided, gently nudging the dog away. "Give the poor woman some room."

"He's a beautiful dog." Kyra stepped inside the house and reached out her hand for Amos to lick.

"Thanks. He's my best guy." Lyric's laugh sounded exactly like it had when they were ten. "He's my only guy, if you want to know the truth."

Kyra knelt down and petted the dog's soft fur. She always wished she had more time to devote to a pet of her own. "Seems to me dogs are much more loyal than people."

"Exactly." Her former friend gave the dog some love too and then turned her attention back to Kyra. "Would you like something to drink? Maybe some herbal tea or kombucha?"

"Oh. No." Her stomach was too unsettled, though the scent that was wafting through Lyric's home was calming. Maybe it was jasmine? "I'm sorry to show up like this, but I really need to talk to you." Why was she so nervous? Geez, her legs were shaky.

"I'm glad you came." Lyric gestured to the sagging velvet couch behind them. "Have a seat. Let me know if you change your mind on the drink. I make my own herbal tea blends."

"I'll keep that in mind." But right now she had to get through this. Kyra lowered herself to the very edge of the couch, sitting there stiffly.

"How's everything going?" Lyric settled comfortably into an overstuffed chair across from the couch as though it was natural for them to sit and chat.

"Things have been interesting." Kyra couldn't bring herself to make small talk. "I found some boxes in the guest room closet." She watched her former friend's face closely. "They were full of clothes and décor for a girl's bedroom. Everything was brand-new. With the price tags still on."

Lyric nodded, inhaling deeply. "Yes. I left those at Kenny's request. He told my mother once that he wanted to keep those boxes for you. He never gave up hope he'd be able to give them to you someday."

"But why?" The entire foundation of her life was shaking. Somewhere inside she already knew the truth. Ever since she'd sat on the edge of the bed with Aiden holding her hand, she'd gone back over everything her mother had said about her father abandoning both of them, how she'd cut off all of Kyra's communication with Lyric. How could her mother purposely have kept her away from them both?

"Those things were all supposed to be yours." Lyric's voice gentled. "Kenny and my mom wanted to create a space for you at the house. After we moved here, they spent months shopping for exactly the right pieces to make you welcome and comfortable. I helped them."

"This makes no sense to me." Kyra had to stand up. She had to move. "You didn't say anything. When you came by the house that day—"

"I wasn't trying to keep anything from you." Her former friend—stepsister?—peered up at her, eyes full of tears. "I could tell you were shell-shocked, that's all. And you should have the power to navigate this journey at your own pace. As you're ready. I didn't want to force anything on you."

Kyra turned to look out the window, but all she saw were images of her and Lyric as two young girls. Best friends who'd done everything together. According to her mother, Kenneth and Naya started to talk and flirt when he would pick up Kyra from Lyric's house. From there the relationship apparently evolved into an affair.

"I never heard from my father after he married your mom." She didn't admit that she had been sure her father had abandoned her because Naya hadn't wanted anything to do with Kyra. "He didn't call. He didn't write. He didn't ever try to contact me until I was in college." And by then she'd decided it was too late.

Lyric stood and approached her, some of the tears spilling over. "I know it seemed like he didn't want anything to do with you, but that wasn't true," she finally said. "Kenny and my mom didn't tell me anything at the time. Other than you wouldn't be coming to stay sometimes like they'd hoped. Like *I'd* hoped." She walked to a shelf next to the fireplace, where she selected a photo album. "I had this idea that we would be real sisters. And even though your parents' divorce was painful and it was hard moving away from everything I'd known all my life, that hope was what got me through. I thought the move and the changes would've been all worth it if you were really my sister." Lyric handed the album to Kyra.

"You kept all these pictures..." She sat back on the couch and flipped through the memories of the two of them at the beach, at birthday parties, at the park, with her own tears blurring the images.

"You were my best friend." Lyric sat next to her, glancing down at the photographs with a sad smile. "When they told me you wouldn't be coming to see us at all, I was so angry. I gave them hell for years—did all the rebelling I could. For a while there I hated them for leaving you behind. It wasn't until I confronted my mother years later that I learned the truth."

The truth. Did Kyra want to hear the truth? Would it do her any good after all this time? She braced herself.

"Your mom was angry about the affair." Lyric hesitated, her fingers nervously knotting together in her lap. "I don't know all the details, but they told me your mom threatened your father. She told him that if he tried to get any custodial rights after moving away she would tell all kinds of lies about how he treated you both. She said she was going to make sure he never got to take you away from her."

Kyra slumped back against the couch and held her breath until the searing pain in her chest subsided. Knowing the truth still hadn't prepared her to hear those words. "I should've realized what she was doing." But her mother had been all she thought she had left. And then in the last several years, when her mom's health started failing, she'd been too focused on managing her care to think about the past.

"I'm so sorry." Lyric gave her hand a gentle squeeze. "I think your mom was scared that you would leave too. That you would choose to live here instead of staying in Florida with her. Your dad didn't want to put you through that kind of pain. He didn't want you to get caught in the middle of a war."

"It would've hurt me either way." She hadn't meant to snap at Lyric, but this was all too much. Too hard. "If he would've fought for me at least I would've had a father to show for the pain." She knew she shouldn't be lashing out at Lyric. But everyone else was gone, and she was left to pick up the pieces. She wanted to be mad at both of her parents. Her father had left her, and her mother had lied to her, and now she had to deal with the mess they'd made.

"I know this doesn't help much, but he regretted his choices." Lyric's voice was filled with regret too. "That's why he tried to get in touch with you when you were in college. He knew your mom couldn't stop him anymore."

"I sent all of his letters back without opening them." Her heart sat like a dead weight in her chest. Seeing his return address on those envelopes had made her so angry.

"He understood," her friend murmured. "He knew he didn't necessarily deserve a place in your life after disappearing." She squeezed Kyra's hand. "But I think that's why he left you the house and the town. He wanted you to know that he loved you. Even if he didn't get a chance to tell you himself."

"I don't know what to do with all of this." She was so tired. Her parents were both gone. None of them could go back to right any wrongs. She couldn't go back and open the letters she received in college. God, if only she would've opened them, she might've gotten to know her father.

Amos ambled over and rested his head on her knee with a whine. Kyra ran her hand over his soft fur with a fresh round of tears falling.

"I'm happy to help you clean out the house when you're ready," Lyric offered. "I don't want to impose or take over, but that's not something you should have to do by yourself. We can do it slowly, over time. And meanwhile, since you're stuck here anyway, maybe you could take the time to enjoy Star Valley a little bit—get to know the people and place your father loved so much."

"That would be good." She'd never been one to slow down and enjoy each moment as it passed. But now she wouldn't have a choice. She was here, and being in Star Valley Springs gave her a chance to know more of her father. Kyra let her head fall back to the cushion. The initial anger had started to subside, leaving behind a cold numbness. "I can't even start cleaning out the house until I get back from the cattle drive anyway."

Her friend's eyes widened. "You're going on the cattle drive?"

"It would appear so." Though Lyric's obvious shock brought on plenty of second thoughts. "How bad is it?"

"It's actually really fun." The woman quickly went from frowning to smiling. "I love going, but this year I couldn't get out of some commitments I'd already made." Her head tilted as she stared at Kyra. "Aiden invited you go?"

"More like challenged me to go." Even though the man wasn't there to see her, she straightened her spine. "It was almost like he thought I wouldn't be able to hack it out there." Maybe she wouldn't survive the trek. She caught Lyric's gaze. "Should I be worried?"

"Nah." The woman waved her off casually. "You'll be fine. I actually think you'll have a great time. It's beautiful country, and you'll get to know everyone. The cattle drive is a perfect way to enjoy some of your time here." Lyric's dimples reappeared. "And I have a feeling Aiden will be keeping a close eye on you."

The comment brought a steady flow of heat through her body. Not two hours ago she'd sat with him on the bed crying while he'd held her hand. She'd never cried in front of anyone besides her mother. "What's that supposed to mean?"

"I've heard things, that's all." The woman's eyebrows peaked. "Minnie said you two went on a date."

"A date?" It felt good to laugh after all the crying. "Seriously? She packed up some muffins for us to take along while he drove me to pick up my car in the middle of the woods. I would hardly call that a date." But it had been the first time she'd glimpsed the man's depth and kindness. She didn't say so, though.

Lyric raised her arms in front of her. "All I'm saying is I have a feeling about you two. I get feelings a lot. Intuition, my mom called it. And I think Aiden likes you."

Her heart seemed to accelerate at the news, but she tamped down the response with a shake of her head. "He knows I'm planning to move to London. This is all temporary." A short detour on her life's map. That was all this stay in Star Valley Springs could be. "I think I'm ready for that drink now. Do you happen to have anything that will take the edge off a headache?" All the tears and emotions and thoughts and memories had started to make her temples pound.

"Kombucha has many healing and restorative properties." Lyric popped up to her feet. "Especially my homemade recipe." She offered Kyra a hand to help her stand. "Oh, and after the drink, we could always do some meditative yoga in my studio. I'm a certified instructor. I teach at the resorts in Jackson on the weekends, but I take private clients in my home too."

"Sure. Why not?" Between the kombucha and the yoga and Lyric's friendship, maybe she would be able to sort through the anger and the sadness and the helplessness she felt right now so she could move forward.

CHAPTER SEVEN

Why don't you just call her already?" Silas secured a duffel bag to the straps attached to his horse's saddle.

"I have no idea what you're talking about." Playing dumb, Aiden tightened the ropes holding his sleeping bag onto the bundle of gear he'd situated on Recon's back. His horse shifted from side to side, impatient to hit the trail. Aiden felt the same way. All morning a nervous energy had plagued him. He hadn't heard from Kyra since he'd sat with her in the guest room at her father's ranch yesterday, but that hadn't stopped him from thinking about her.

"We're talking about Kyra." Silas shoved an elbow into his ribs. "Come on. You've been looking at the driveway every other second for the last ten minutes. Call her already and see if she changed her mind about coming."

"I hope she didn't change her mind. That would ruin everything." This was supposed to be an integral part of their mission to encourage her to hold on to the town.

"We'd better all hope she didn't change her mind. Getting her out into those mountains is the best way to get her to fall in love with this place." Yet again he craned his neck so he could see out the stable doors. The other volunteers were milling around outside the house, but Kyra still hadn't come.

His friend stopped fidgeting with the saddle straps. "Do you think it's possible she'd love it enough to stay? Even if she does like all of us and the town, you think she'd want to build a life here?"

"No." Kyra had already made her plans clear. She had her heart set on London. "But I'm hoping at the very least she can see this place as a second home. A place to visit when she can. That's why we need her to build connections here." The more she got to know everyone, the more she would see how selling would negatively impact them all. Maybe that would be enough to motivate her to at least turn the land and her holdings on Main Street into some kind of trust they could help her manage. Kenny had mentioned a trust not three months before he'd died.

"You sure that's the only reason you're so eager to see her?" Silas teased. "Because from what I saw when she visited Cowboy Construction, there's plenty of chemistry simmering between you two."

"There're also plenty of reasons I can't go there with her." And he had to remind himself of those reasons every time he got close to her. "She's not planning to build a life here." And his life would always be where his sister and nieces were.

"No one said you had to marry her or anything. But it wouldn't kill you to have a little fun." His friend crossed his arms and stared him down. "How long's it been since you've spent time with a woman anyway?"

Too long. Silas and Thatch made the trek to Jackson for some nightlife a few times a month, but he never went with them. "I have other priorities."

"Well, you're a better man than I am." His friend whacked him on the shoulder. "Because if I had a woman like Kyra looking at me the way she looks at you, I'd be all over that." He started to lead his horse out of the stable.

Aiden took hold of the lead rope attached to Recon's halter and hurried to catch up with Silas. "What d'you mean, how she looks at me?"

"Oh, come on." His friend paused just outside the stables. "You may have sworn a vow of celibacy since we've moved here, but you're not clueless. She blushes when she looks at you. Her cheeks get pink. And she looks at you a hell of a lot. I could tell that even from the few minutes in the office last week."

Aiden's blood started to pump faster, but it wasn't because of what his friend had said. A car had turned onto the driveway...

"Looks like you had nothing to worry about." Silas led his horse to the fence and tied him up.

"Uncle Aiden!" Morgan waved from the front porch. "Kyra's here! She really came!"

Yes, she had. And damn if his whole body hadn't warmed up at the prospect of seeing her.

After securing Recon's lead rope to the fence, Aiden went to meet her as she got out of the car. He tried not to spend an awkward amount of time admiring her, but he couldn't seem to look away either. She'd traded in her usual dark jeans for a lighter pair—tattered around the edges. And instead of a sensible gray or black sweater like she usually wore, she'd put on a blue-and-white-checkered flannel. And that wasn't all. "Are those cowboy boots?" He openly gawked at her footwear.

"Cowgirl boots." Her smirk was full of sass. "I didn't exactly pack any cattle drive–appropriate clothes to wear, so Lyric lent me some of her things."

"You look good." Wait, that wasn't supposed to come out of his mouth. "I mean the clothes. They look good on you." Aw hell, what was he doing? *Shut up.* Maybe he did need to hit the nightlife scene with Silas and Thatch before he completely forgot how to talk to a woman.

"Thanks." Kyra's smile brushed off his awkwardness. She opened the back door and pulled out a duffel. "Where should I put my bag?"

"I'll take care of that." Then he would have something to focus on so he didn't have to talk to her. Evidently, talking to a woman wasn't at all like riding a bike. Aiden took the bag from her and brought it to the horse he'd rigged up especially for Kyra while Morgan led the woman around introducing her to all of the horses.

"This is Blondie," Morgan said, approaching the horse Aiden was working on.

"I've only ridden a horse when someone else was leading it." Kyra seemed to keep a healthy distance from the animal. "In a straight line on the beach."

Whoa. He'd figured she wasn't exactly an experienced rider, but she'd only ridden one time? He'd have to keep an eye on her. "Blondie is as gentle as they come," Aiden assured her. "She knows the route, and she's always calm." That horse had been around the longest, and he totally trusted her. After all, Kyra had to enjoy herself this weekend or his whole plan would backfire.

"All right, Blondie." The woman eased a step closer. "You'll have to go easy on me."

The horse stood straight and still while Aiden finished strapping on the bag. When he looked up, he noticed Kyra watching him.

"I probably should've asked how you want me to help on this cattle drive," she said nervously.

"We watch the cows to make sure they don't wander off." Morgan took the lead on explaining. "It's really fun. We get to be outside riding all day long, and then we camp up at the high meadow tents and have a fire and roast marshmallows."

"Yes, the marshmallows are the most important part." Aiden loved teasing his niece. "We actually only do the cattle drive for the s'mores."

"Oh, Uncle Aiden." Morgan sure resembled her mother when she rolled her eyes at him.

Everyone else who'd volunteered to help with the ride—Louie and Thatch and Silas and James from the bait store and Tess and Willow—started to crowd in on them, waiting for their marching orders. In Jace's absence, Aiden had become the unofficial trip leader.

"Kyra, it's nice to finally meet you." Tess stepped forward to greet the woman with a welcoming smile. "My brother has told me a lot about you."

Aiden sent his sister a warning glare. Now was not the time to make any insinuations about the two of them.

"It's nice to meet you too." Kyra shook his sister's hand. "I've enjoyed spending time with your daughters."

"They've loved hanging out with you too."

Aiden was relieved Tess didn't add, "And so has my brother" to the end of that sentence.

"We'd best get going." The faster he moved this along, the less opportunity Tess would have to embarrass him. "Why don't we all mount up and meet in the meadow?"

Everyone else started to scatter, but Kyra studied the saddle on her horse. "Mount up?"

Right. He had to remember this was all new to her. "I can help you." Aiden ignored his sister watching them as she helped Willow onto the horse they were going to share.

"Here. I'll give you a boost." He held his hands together so Kyra could step into them and then lifted her high enough that she could swing her leg over and pull herself into the saddle.

"Whoa." She gripped the saddle horn. "Blondie is much taller than she looks."

Aiden untied the lead rope and put the reins into Kyra's hands. "She knows what to do. You only have to give her little hints. Gently tug the reins right to turn right, left to turn left, and pull back to stop her." Blondie was already so in tune with the route she wouldn't need much guidance. The horse was usually happy to follow Recon around.

"Okay." Kyra pulled the reins to the right and the horse responded, turning. "Got it. That's not so hard."

"See? You've got this." He untied Recon and then pulled himself up onto the saddle, guiding the horse next to Kyra's.

"Yeehaw!" Morgan trotted ahead of them into the meadow.

"This is actually fun." Kyra swayed with the horse's movements, but she looked relaxed.

"You're doing great." His niece had stopped to wait for them to catch up. "You look like a real cowgirl, Miss Kyra."

Aiden found himself admiring the woman again. That was the biggest smile he'd seen on her face since he'd met her.

"Yo, A-dog," Thatch called.

He turned to see his two friends smirking at him. They'd caught him checking her out for sure.

"Are we going to get this party started or what?" Silas demanded.

"Yeah." He had to get his focus back on track before this whole trip went south. "Thatch and Silas, you take the lead. Tess and Willow, James and Louie, you run the flanks, and Morgan, Kyra, and I will run tail." He had to stay with Kyra to make sure she got the hang of riding.

That was his story and he was sticking to it.

"Come on, Bravo!" Morgan rode her horse in a few circles while the group started off.

Wearing a determined look, Kyra steered Blondie next to Recon. "So where are the cattle?" she asked, glancing around them.

"We'll find them near the high meadow and round them up." He kept a slow, methodical pace, making them lag behind everyone else. "Shouldn't take us too long to get up there."

"Uncle Aiden, do I have to stay in the back?" He could tell Morgan was trying not to whine. "Can I ride a little faster just for now?"

"Go for it." Morgan was most likely itching to feel the wind in her hair, and that would give him the chance to talk to Kyra alone for a while. He waited until Morgan had left them in her dust and then started in. "So you obviously went over to talk to Lyric." He glanced at her boots. "How'd it go?" He'd been wondering what she'd found out, how she was feeling, what she was thinking ever since he'd sat on that bed with her. He couldn't seem to stop wondering about her.

Kyra fixed her eyes on the mountains in front of them. "Lyric told me that my mom threatened my father with a nasty custody battle and then made sure I had no contact with him." Her voice quieted. "That's what I was expecting to hear, but somehow being prepared didn't make the conversation any easier."

"I'm sure it didn't." If they hadn't been sitting on horses he would've reached for her again. What a horrible feeling it must be to learn the truth now. When there was nothing she could do about it. "How do you feel?"

She took her time responding, and Aiden let the sound of their clomping horses fill the silence.

"My feelings seem to change on an hourly basis," she finally said. "Sometimes I'm really angry at both of them. And then in other moments I'm just sad."

"Makes sense." He knew from personal experience that anger was easier to manage than the sadness.

"My mom took a lot away from me." Kyra's jaw had set as though she was fighting back emotion. "But my father is the one who left. And I know she was hurting and scared."

"Yeah. Fear does strange things to people." He knew that from experience too.

The woman peered at his face, searching his eyes. "Were you ever afraid? On your missions?"

"All the time." He'd never admitted as much to anyone

else. "But I was never afraid for myself." He hadn't been out there fighting for himself. "I was afraid for Silas and Thatch. And for Jace." And then his worst fear was realized when the enemy struck down his brother-in-law and he couldn't save him. He caught Morgan in his gaze up ahead of them. "Now I'm afraid for the girls. I'm afraid their hearts will never fully recover from the loss." He was terrified they would hate him someday when they learned more details about their father's death.

"I can understand that." Kyra tugged on the reins, pulling her horse to a stop. She waited for him to stop too. "But in thinking about why my mother did what she did, I've realized that fear is a form of control. And it doesn't leave a lot of room for joy in your life."

Aiden looked into the woman's eyes, finding them full of a hope that had eluded him.

"There's still so much joy in your nieces, Aiden." Her expression stirred something in him. How'd she find it so easy to smile after losing her mother and her father? After everything she'd learned about her past? "And you get to be part of their lives. You get to be part of their joy."

"Thank God for that," he said as he watched Morgan trot around humming to herself.

Kyra jiggled the reins and started Blondie moving again. "This place really is incredible." Her head panned, looking from one peak to the next. "It doesn't even look real. It's like staring at a painting. I'm not sure I've ever seen a sky that blue."

Aiden raised his eyes to the mountains stretching in front of them. He'd seen this view so many times that it was easy to take it for granted. But witnessing the vista with Kyra made him see the grandeur through a different lens. "It'll keep getting better as we ride higher," he promised, suddenly eager to show her everything—the trickling waterfall at the west edge of the high meadow, the grove of golden aspens near the camp, the backside view of Red Mountain.

"Think you can ride a little faster?" Her smile beckoned his. "We have a lot of ground to cover." And he couldn't wait to see the wonder through her eyes.

CHAPTER EIGHT

"Say cheese." Aiden snapped another picture while Kyra struck her best pose in front of the waterfall.

"How about one more?" the man asked, raising her phone again. "Smile."

He didn't have to tell her twice. Kyra likely hadn't stopped smiling once all day. Aiden had been right about the scenery on this little trek. This was the third waterfall they'd stopped at, and each one seemed to get prettier. Kyra turned away from the camera to admire how the brook cascaded down over the moss-carpeted boulders behind her.

She'd always thought that the turquoise waters of the gulf offered some of the world's most stunning scenery, but that was before she'd spent time in the mountains. The other volunteers milled around the stream, letting the horses drink while they chatted like they didn't see the magic in this space quite the way she did. They were probably used to waterfalls.

"Hopefully, I got some good pictures." Aiden handed her phone back to her. "Of course, with you in the spotlight it would be hard to take a bad picture."

What a line. Kyra could feel her smile growing. She'd never been one for flirting—because she was usually so terrible at it. But Aiden made flirting fun. "You're just saying that so I quit stopping at every little waterfall we see." Admittedly she'd been a little ridiculous when it had come to taking pictures of the scenery. "There's so much to take in."

"I'm happy to stop and take pictures whenever you want." Aiden grinned. "Even if it takes us two extra days to get the cattle to the lower meadow."

"Well, in that case..." Kyra knelt to capture a few more shots of the waterfall from a closer angle.

Aiden crouched next to her, glancing over her shoulder as though trying to see what she saw. "So you're glad you came on the cattle drive, then?"

Goose bumps rose on her neck at the closeness of his voice. "Yes." She stood upright, her knees wobbling. "I still haven't figured out exactly why you wanted me to come, but I'm glad I'm here." She wouldn't have wanted to miss these views.

Aiden rose to his full height, standing close enough that she could see flecks of sliver in his eyes. "I thought you should see the whole area. Since you own the town and all."

Kyra narrowed her eyes at him. "That's the only reason?" Because it had kind of seemed to her that he was trying to distract her from her projects for some reason. And his plan was obviously working. As much as she hated to admit it, the scenery wasn't the only distraction.

"Of course that's not the only reason." His grin teased her again. "If you hadn't come, I would never hear the end of it from Morgan."

Laughing felt easier somehow out in the mountains. "Well, truthfully, Morgan is the only reason I came in the first place. I couldn't disappoint her."

"Morgan was the only one you wanted to spend time with?" Aiden's gaze pressed into hers, and there was no hiding the truth. She'd had more fun with him over the last few hours than she'd had in a long time.

"You two sure seem to be enjoying yourselves." Tess could not have timed her interruption better. The woman turned to her brother. "I haven't seen you smile this much in a long time."

Kyra couldn't seem to dim her happy expression, but Aiden's face suddenly turned to stone. "Kyra wanted more pictures," he muttered. "But I need to ride around and make sure the cattle haven't spread too far." Without another word or a glance at her, he stomped away.

Whoa. The mood between them had sure changed fast. "We were having fun. I thought..." She shouldn't have said that out loud, but Aiden's sudden withdrawal had given her vertigo.

"I should've kept my mouth shut." Tess sighed. "I was just happy to see him smiling again. Truthfully, I think he's forgotten how to enjoy life. Or maybe he doesn't think he's allowed to enjoy life."

Kyra detected the note of concern in his sister's tone. "It seems like losing Jace was hard on him." She'd noticed that something happened to the man when he spoke about his brother-in-law. His voice got lower and rough, and tension gripped his jaw.

"Aiden takes too much on himself," his sister said. "He always has."

"All right, everyone, let's mount up," Aiden barked from the meadow before Kyra could respond. "I'll ride lead this time with Morgan. Silas and Thatch, you bring up the rear. Everyone else can fall in. We're close to the camp, so no more stops until we get there."

Kyra studied him from a distance. Was this the same man who had flirted with her five minutes ago?

"You want to ride together?" Tess asked as they walked in the direction of their horses.

"Sure." Since it appeared Aiden wouldn't be assisting her anymore.

"Come on, baby girl." Tess boosted Willow up and helped her get settled in the saddle before mounting the horse.

Feigning confidence, Kyra stuck her leg in the stirrup of Blondie's saddle and swung her leg over, not so gracefully grunting and inching her way to a seated position. Every time they'd stopped earlier, Aiden had assisted her with the mounting-a-horse thing. But look at her. She'd done it all by herself. She didn't need him at all.

Still, disappointment squeezed at her heart as they started off.

The cowboys took care of pushing the cattle into a herd, with Morgan hooting and hollering alongside them.

Kyra and Tess and Willow rode along the right side, keeping a nice, slow pace. Mountain peaks surrounded them on all sides, and about half of the colorful leaves still clung stubbornly to the tree branches, with the golds and reds contrasted against a clear royal-blue sky. Beautiful, but she didn't dare try to pull out her phone to take another picture.

"Please tell me I'm not the only one with a seriously sore rear end." Tess laughed. "I'm out of riding shape."

"You're not the only one," Kyra confirmed. In fact, she might have to sit on the horse all evening. Who knew if she'd be able to walk once she got off?

"At least we're almost there." Tess pointed up ahead of them. "You can start to see the tents."

Kyra squinted. Sure enough, a cluster of large white structures came into view on the other side of the meadow.

"So Aiden said you're planning to move to London." Tess shaded her eyes from the sun and glanced at Kyra.

"Uh, yeah." Today was probably the first day in a long time she hadn't thought about London once. "After I wrap up things in Star Valley Springs."

"Why London?" Tess asked, letting Willow take the reins.

"My mom took me there when I graduated from high school." That trip had given her some of the best moments of her life—visiting the palace and walking over London Bridge and hiking in the Lake District. Her mother had seemed so relaxed and happy. "Two years after we went, she got cancer." And the memories of London were what had gotten Kyra through. "While she was sick I started to research living there. And it became this dream I relied on to get through some hard days."

"I'm sorry your mama got sick," Willow half whispered in her sweet way.

"Thank you." Kyra shifted in the saddle.

"I totally get holding on to a dream through tough

times," Tess said. "I'm still holding on to my dreams for this place, even with Jace gone."

Kyra peeked over at the woman's face. Her smile appeared wistful. She wanted to tell Tess how sorry she was, how much she appreciated their family's sacrifice, but with Willow sitting on the same horse, she only said, "Aiden told me what an incredible person he was."

"My daddy was the best!" It was the loudest Willow had ever spoken in Kyra's presence.

Tess kissed the top of her daughter's head. "Yes, he was."

If anyone had asked her about the tears in her eyes, Kyra would've blamed the sun or the wind, but truthfully she was still trying to process what she'd learned about her own father, about his absence in her life. Hearing Willow and Morgan talk about their daddy made her own loss feel that much closer. Would she have had the same bond with her father that those girls had with Jace if she'd been given the chance?

She blinked away the tears as they rode into the outskirts of the camp, where four large white canvas tents were clustered around a rock fire ring and picnic tables. Following Tess's lead, she tugged Blondie to a stop.

Uhhhh... Kyra judged the distance to the ground. It looked like a long way down.

Before she could figure out the best way to dismount without any help, the sound of pounding hooves drew her gaze across the camp. Aiden and Recon were galloping toward them at breakneck speed.

That man was all cowboy—the dusty jeans, the wide-brimmed black hat casting a shadow over his face, the way his body moved in tune with the horse. She couldn't stop watching him.

"There's something about a cowboy," Tess murmured, a teasing ring to her voice.

"Oh. Uh." Kyra almost said she'd been watching the horse, but the woman would likely see through that excuse.

"Aiden is the best there is." His sister patted Kyra's leg with a conspiratorial wink and then slid off her horse before helping Willow down.

Kyra didn't have time to say anything before the cowboy in question pulled his horse to a stop next to her. "Need help getting down?"

"Probably." But this crush she had on him was starting to get out of hand. Even other people were starting to notice. The entire afternoon they'd been riding she'd forgotten about her purpose for being here. She'd forgotten that she was moving to London as soon as possible. He'd made her forget, and then he'd suddenly bailed on her with no explanation. The last thing she needed in her life was a man well versed in the art of walking away.

"Swing your leg over and slide down," he instructed. "I'll catch you."

Sure he would. He would catch her and hold her and make her feel all sorts of things she shouldn't be feeling for him. And then he'd likely disappear again.

"That's okay. I've got this." Kyra held on to the saddle and clumsily found her way to the ground, rolling her right ankle slightly before finding her footing. "See? No problem." She held back a grimace.

"You're a natural." Aiden went to work tying her horse to a fence post.

"Miss Kyra!" Morgan sprinted out of one of the tents. "You're bunking up with Mom, Willow, and me!" She stumbled down the steps. "I'll take your bag to your cot for you."

"Thank you." Kyra took a few steps on her ankle. It ached but there was no obvious damage done.

"You okay?" Aiden dropped his gaze to her boots as though he'd noticed something was off.

"I'm great." She detached her bag from the saddle straps and handed it to Morgan.

"I'll put you next to me!" the girl called, running in the opposite direction.

With her and Aiden left alone, Kyra took the opportunity to get her projects and purpose for being here back on track, lest she forget again. "Have you finished working on my bids yet?" She should've asked him that question first thing this morning.

"Oh. Actually, no." He removed his bag from Recon's saddle. "I'm still waiting for some materials costs from one of our suppliers. But he should have everything back to me by next week."

That would be two weeks that she'd been here and had gotten nothing done. "You're not stalling this on purpose. Are you?" She decided to come out and ask him. "Because I have a life I need to get back to." A life she had been waiting to live for a long time. "This money from my father can give me a whole new start. In the past, I haven't had a say in what's happened to me, and for the first time I get to choose the life I want." She couldn't undo her parents' mistakes, but she could make damn sure she didn't make her own.

Aiden stared at her, unmoving. A rigidity worked

itself into his jaw. "I'll get you the bids as soon as I have the numbers. I promise." He looked like he might say something more, but instead he turned and walked away.

"Sheesh, what's his problem?" Morgan had snuck up behind her.

Kyra was ready to throw up her hands. "I have no idea." The man had gone from being warm and flirty and helpful and kind to cold in the span of a few minutes.

"Huh." The girl seemed to shrug it off much more easily than Kyra could. "My mom asked me to come and get you. Willow has a rash and she was wondering if you'd look at it."

"Of course." She left Blondie tied up at the fence and followed Aiden's niece into the tent. The setup was pretty rustic, but at least there was a wooden floor platform instead of dirt, and lanterns lighting the dim space.

Tess and Willow were seated on a cot, and the girl was crying.

"Hey there, sweetie." Kyra knelt in front of her. "What's the problem?"

"I'm itchy." Willow sniffled, rubbing her hands up and down her arms.

"But you're not supposed to itch," Morgan insisted. "Right, Miss Kyra?"

"Well, sometimes scratching a rash can make things worse." She took the younger girl's hand and gently straightened her arm.

"She complained a little bit this morning," Tess told her. "But it's gotten much worse."

Nodding, Kyra inspected the red, splotchy bumps. "It looks like typical dermatitis to me." She saw it all the time in Florida. “Have you switched soaps or laundry detergents or anything?”

“Yes, this week, actually.” Tess put her arm around her daughter. “The store was out of the brand I’d been using, so I bought something else.”

“That’s probably what triggered it.” Kyra stood up and went to her bag, which Morgan had placed on a cot nearby. “Happens to me all the time.” She dug out her all-natural aloe cream and walked back to Willow. “This will clear it right up and stop the itching.” She tweaked the girl’s nose. “I have sensitive skin too.”

The girl stopped crying and smiled. “Then I’m just like you.”

While Kyra smoothed the cream on Willow’s arms, Tess sorted through the girl’s bag searching for clothing that hadn’t been washed in the most recent loads. “Here. You haven’t worn this shirt in a few weeks.” She helped her daughter pull it on.

“That should make a big difference.” Kyra stashed the cream back in her bag. “We can reapply tomorrow morning before we leave.”

“Thank you,” Willow said with another shy smile.

“Yes, thank you.” Tess sat back down on the bed, looking tired.

Once again, Kyra felt that stab of sympathy for her. She couldn’t imagine having to do everything for two children on her own.

“You saved us a trip to the doctor,” Tess said. “The closest family practice clinic is over an hour and a half away.”

“Seriously?” Kyra sat on the cot across from her. “That’s pretty inconvenient.”

"Yeah. It's not ideal." She ruffled her daughter's hair. "So any time we need a quick strep test or something, we have to make a day of it."

"But you're a doctor!" Morgan paused from smoothing out her sleeping bag on the cot next to Kyra's. "So you could move to Star Valley Springs and be our doctor!"

"Oh." She laughed a little. "I'm not a doctor, exactly." She'd known nurse practitioners who'd started their own clinics, but that wasn't her path. "I might be getting a job in London."

Morgan stopped moving. "But that's like a whole ocean away."

"It's an easy plane ride." Tess rose from the bed, a bright smile on her face. "Now let's go bug Uncle Aiden about getting the s'mores ready instead of giving Kyra a hard time."

"S'mores!" The girls both launched out of the tent at Mach speed, leaving Kyra alone with Tess.

"I know you have your heart set on London, and I think it's amazing that you're pursing your dreams." She squeezed Kyra's arm. "But just know you'll always have a place here too. If you ever want to come back and visit. If I've learned anything over these last few years it's that it takes a village to raise a family. And you're more than welcome to be a part of ours."

CHAPTER NINE

Aiden stirred the fire he'd built with a stick, watching in a sleep-deprived haze as the flames gained momentum. The first light of dawn fringed the eastern horizon with soft pink and purple hues. No one else would likely be up for another hour, but he hadn't been able to stay in bed.

Usually he slept great during a campout—there was something calming about the fresh mountain air, the peaceful quietness. But there was also something about what Kyra had said yesterday that he couldn't get out of his head.

For the first time I get to choose the life I want.

The woman had been dealt a crappy hand with her parents' divorce and her dad taking off like that. As great a man as Aiden had always thought Kenny to be, he couldn't imagine walking out on his kid.

Watching his two nieces navigate the death of their father had shown him what kind of pain a loss like that causes. The circumstances were nowhere near the same—Jace was a hero who'd made the ultimate sacrifice, and Kenny had chosen to walk away—but Kyra had still lost her father, the man she depended on. And who was Aiden to deny her the inheritance that should be rightfully hers?

Behind him, a zipper sounded, and Tess crawled out of the tent. "Whew." She stood and stretched, then zipped her fleece coat all the way up to her chin and pulled on her wool hat. "It's chilly out here." She joined Aiden by the fire and sat on one of the stumps they used for seating. "Please tell me you have the coffee going."

"Should be done in a few." He nodded toward the coffee percolator he'd filled and set on the grate over the fire. "You didn't sleep well?"

"You know I never do out here." His sister had always preferred four secure walls around her, even when their family had gone camping as kids. She didn't have to make the treks up here with Aiden overseeing the cattle drives, but he knew she did it because the girls loved camping out. "What about you? You're not usually up this early."

"I've got a lot on my mind." He used a hot pad to pull the percolator off the grate and then filled two mugs with the dark, rich coffee.

"Does this have anything to do with why you were avoiding Kyra last night?" His sister took a cup from his hand.

"I wasn't avoiding her." He didn't know why he bothered lying to Tess. She never let him off the hook.

"You didn't say a word to her all night," his sister argued. "You kept yourself so busy with dinner and cleanup and counting the cattle that you didn't even play cards with us." Her eyes narrowed. "You always play cards with us on the cattle drive."

"I'm not sure I can do it." There was the truth. "I'm not sure I can—or should—try to convince her to hold on to the town instead of selling it off." Aiden reached into the duffel bag full of kitchen supplies and found the cast-iron griddle. He might as well get breakfast started while they sat here. Everyone else would be up soon, and he wanted to get an early start on the day.

"Because you like her too much to manipulate her." Tess set down her coffee and found the box of pancake mix and the large mixing bowl they'd brought.

"She has dreams." He had to leave his feelings out of this. Yesterday had only proven he didn't know what to do with feelings. One minute he'd been wrapped up in Kyra, and then the next he'd run away from her. *You two sure seem to be enjoying yourselves.* One sentence from Tess was all it had taken to bury him in guilt. How could he enjoy himself when Jace was gone?

Aiden shut down that line of thinking. "Besides, Kyra hasn't had it easy." She should have the chance to find some joy in her life. "But if we don't convince her to keep what Kenny gave her, we'll lose everything eventually." When the developers started to build their resorts and vacation homes, the taxes would go up to pay for the infrastructure. The Meadowlark would quickly go out of business. Tess's feed store that helped keep the ranch afloat would likely be put under by the larger chain stores offering the same products at cheaper prices.

"Maybe you should be honest with her." Tess measured

out the water and eggs, adding them to the mixing bowl before stirring with their camp spoon. "Tell her the truth instead of stalling and trying to trick her into falling in love with Star Valley."

"I'm not sure what good the truth would do." He greased the griddle with a pat of butter and got ready to flip the pancakes Tess started to pour. "She wants to move to London, and she needs money to do it." If he explained to Kyra what would happen when she sold Star Valley Springs, he'd be pressuring her to make a sacrifice he had no business asking her to consider.

"Maybe she only wants to move to London because she has no one keeping her here." Tess's impish expression ribbed him. "You can't tell me you're not attracted to her."

Could she be talking any louder? "I can't start a relationship with anyone right now," he said in a low whisper. The fact was, he didn't deserve that kind of happiness when it had been taken away from his best friend and his sister.

"That doesn't make any sense," Tess said impatiently. "Why can't you start a relation—"

"Hey, kids, what's cookin'?" Silas sauntered to the fire ring and yawned loudly.

"Pancakes." Grateful for the interruption, Aiden flipped the neat rows of batter Tess had poured.

"Here." Tess handed Silas a paper plate. "First one up gets first dibs."

"Works for me." His friend held out his plate while Aiden piled on the pancakes.

"Want some homemade syrup?" Tess offered him a jar.

"You know I do." Silas drenched his pancakes and then

took a bite. "Damn, Tess. I really should've married you before Jace did."

Aiden was ready to get up and tackle the idiot over that comment, but his sister only laughed. "You wouldn't have had a chance in hell."

"I know." Silas's face sobered. "Jace was the best one out of all of us."

Truer words had never been spoken. And yet here the three of them were, still living when Jace had died. Aiden flipped another row of pancakes. Could he really call what he was doing right now living? He had a job that kept him busy so he could keep his mind off other things. He had Tess and the girls to worry over so he could keep his own guilt regarding the past at bay. But he didn't have any dreams for himself. Not like Kyra did.

If he was being honest, he didn't see much of a future for himself past tomorrow. Everyone else might eventually move on. Tess could fall in love again, get married. Someday the girls would go off to college, and his diversions would be gone. He'd be stuck and alone...

"That one's burning." Tess pointed to a pancake that was starting to char on the edges.

"Oops." He scooped the burnt pancake off the griddle and tossed it into a nearby trash can. That slip-up was a prime example of why he didn't spend too much time thinking about the past or the future. He needed to stay in the present for his own peace of mind.

As the sun rose higher, the rest of the group started to emerge from their tents, joining them by the fire.

Kyra was last to arrive.

Aiden bent his head over the griddle to keep the

endless supply of pancakes going, but his gaze continued wandering to her. He'd never seen the woman's face so unguarded, a contented smile on her lips, the glow of happiness in her eyes.

"I can't believe how good I slept," she said to Tess and Morgan.

"You were out cold," his niece confirmed.

"I've never slept all night in a tent." Kyra took a plate from the pile. "But I have to say, I think that's the best night of sleep I've gotten since I left Florida." She sat on the stump next to him, and Aiden put a few pancakes on her plate.

"I didn't know you cooked."

How did she smile so easily at him when he felt torn and conflicted every time he looked at her?

"Our boy here makes one helluva pancake." Thatch held out his plate for thirds.

"I'll have to keep that in mind." Kyra was likely joking, but suddenly he imagined himself bringing her breakfast in bed, kissing the syrup off her lips.

Aaand it was time to go back to avoiding her.

Aiden flipped the last batch of pancakes and then directed the clean-up and packing efforts so they could head out for the lower pastures before the sun got any higher.

"All right, everyone," he said when they'd loaded the gear and were circled up. "Same formation as yesterday morning." Yes, that would put him at the back of the pack with Kyra again, but Tess was right. He couldn't ignore the woman. He'd been the one to invite her out here in the first place. And they'd have Morgan with them as a buffer.

"Can I be the leader again?" Morgan begged. "I want to go fast!"

"Oh. Sure. I guess." So no buffer after all. Luckily, though, he had to pay close attention to the cattle on the way down so none of them strayed. He could distract himself with cattle.

"All right, M-dog." Silas gave Aiden's niece a high-five. "You're gonna ride with the elite team today. We'll try to keep up with you."

"Good luck!" The girl nudged her heels into her horse's girth and took off, with Thatch and Silas lagging behind. Aiden marveled again at what a skilled rider Morgan had become. She was growing up…

"We're heading out too," Tess said. She and Willow and the rest of the volunteers rode to the outsides of the herd, leaving him and Kyra to push from behind.

Once they noticed the horses riding the lines, the cattle started to move. They knew the drill. These drives usually went down without too many complications.

While Kyra rode straight ahead, Aiden spent the first few miles sweeping, steering his horse back and forth from one end of the herd to the other. It might have been overkill, but this way he didn't have to talk to Kyra and fool himself into thinking he could make her happy. When he talked to her he felt different, not so burdened. But the feeling wouldn't last. The feeling never lasted. Eventually the cycle would repeat itself, and he'd be back to despair.

Aiden turned Recon to sweep to the other side and saw Kyra struggling a few feet away.

"Whoa." She pulled her horse to a stop. "Blondie's acting weird. She's tossing her head and grunting."

He slowed his horse and looked over his shoulder. "Okay, ease up the reins a little and give her some breathing room."

"I'm hardly doing anything." Kyra let the reins go slack, and the horse started to shuffle to the right and then to the left.

"Easy, girl," Aiden said soothingly. What had her so riled up? He guided Recon closer, but Blondie swiveled her head to the right and then bolted in that direction.

"Oh, God!" Kyra slumped forward on the horse, holding on to the saddle while the reins dangled.

"Shit!" Aiden directed Recon after them, pushing him into a canter. "Yah!" He crouched low while he worked the reins. "Pull up! Get the reins and pull up," he shouted over the wind.

"I can't!" She lifted her head but wouldn't sit tall. "I'm going to fall off!"

"Come on, Recon." Aiden pushed the horse harder, but Blondie had decided to accelerate, heading for the woods.

"Damn it! Blondie! Whoa!" A helplessness Aiden had felt before washed through him as he followed them down the mountainside. "Hold on! You have to hold on!" He never should've convinced Kyra to come on this trip.

If anything happened to her, it would be on him.

CHAPTER TEN

Okay, *this* was how she was going to die.

Trees flashed by in a blur while Blondie dodged to the left and the right. Kyra held on to the saddle so tightly her knuckles ached, and she leaned forward trying to maintain her balance. "Please, Blondie." She wasn't sure if she was yelling or whispering. "Stop."

But the horse pounded on, jarring Kyra's head and shoulders. She squeezed her eyes shut, blacking everything out. This could not be happening.

"I'm right here!" Aiden's voice sounded close, but she couldn't see him.

"Hang on!" he yelled. "I won't let anything happen to you."

Something *was* happening to her. She was tearing down the mountainside on the back of an out-of-control horse. Oh, God! They were going to hit a tree…

"Whoa." Aiden grunted.

Was Blondie slowing? At first Kyra couldn't tell, but

then she lifted her head and opened her eyes. Aiden was alongside the horse pulling on the reins. "Easy, Blondie," he murmured, easing them to a stop. "That's it." The man jumped off his horse and put his hands on Kyra's waist, prodding her to slide off.

Thank. God. She fell out of the saddle in a boneless heap, but Aiden caught her, holding her up. It seemed every muscle in her body shook. From fatigue? Terror? She had no idea.

"Are you okay?" The man held his arms around her. She couldn't be sure, but it felt like he might be shaking too.

"I think so?" She was so winded one would've thought she'd done the sprinting instead of Blondie. "I... wow. I really thought that was going to end badly." She let her forehead tip forward to rest on his shoulder, only for a second, only so she could try to breathe normally.

His hands were strong against her back. Strong but also trembling. "I'm sorry," he uttered. "I never should've made you come on this trip." Aiden's chest heaved. "You could've been seriously injured..."

"I wasn't." Kyra forced herself upright, smiling against the fear in his voice. "I'm fine. Really." Her knees wobbled, but she could stand. She could walk. She hadn't died! "I was probably a little overdramatic." Maybe she should've tried harder to stop the horse; it was just that they were going so fast, everything had felt too out of control.

"It's not your fault." A dark expression crossed his face. "It's mine."

"It's not your fault either," she told him. Tess's words came back to her. *Aiden takes too much on himself. He always has.* She didn't want this situation to be one more thing that burdened him.

Aiden's arms fell to his sides, and he studied her closely. "Nothing hurts?"

"Nope." She took a few steps, moved all of her limbs. "I'd say everything is in working or—"

A strange sound in the nearby brush cut her off. Wait, was that a moo?

Aiden's eyes met hers, and he pressed a finger to his lips.

The noise came again, louder and forlorn.

"It's a calf." The man left the horses and Kyra standing there and started to search the bushes. "Here. His leg is tangled in some barbed wire."

She stumbled to where Aiden had kneeled and pushed back the branches. Sure enough, the sweetest little wide-eyed brown calf was lying on its side.

"Oh, the poor baby." She knelt beside Aiden. "Will he be okay?"

"I think so." He carefully started to unwind the barbed wire from the animal's leg.

The calf squirmed and mooed.

"You're all right." Kyra petted his head. He had the softest hair. "He's so cute." She'd never noticed the way calves' ears stuck out or how their wide, round eyes looked so innocent.

"That's good. Keep him calm for me." Aiden reached into his pocket and pulled out some kind of multitool. "I didn't even notice one had gone missing." He clipped at the wire.

"You're a good boy," Kyra told the calf.

The animal's cold nose brushed against her arm. "I've

never gotten this close to a cow before." And she kind of loved it. "He's much softer than I would've thought. What's his name?"

"Name? He doesn't have a name. He's still a baby. About six months old." Aiden made another cut to the wire. "I'm sure his mama's missing him. I think Blondie knew he'd come down this way. That's why she took off like that. She takes her job pretty seriously."

"It's a good thing she did." Kyra looked into the calf's eyes and smoothed her hand over the tufts of hair at the top of his head. "What if we would've left him out here?"

"He wouldn't have made it." Aiden cleared the last of the wire and then nudged the calf to stand up. "I should've been paying closer attention."

"I didn't see him wander away either." He could just as easily blame her for not watching. "And neither did any of the other volunteers, for that matter." Or they would've been down here looking for him. Kyra pushed to her feet.

The calf wobbled for a few steps but then marched to a patch of green grass near the riverbank and started munching.

"I'm glad we saved him." Her near-death experience had been totally worth it. "I think we should name him Brutus."

Aiden tilted his head, one corner of his mouth hiked up with amusement. "We typically don't name the live-stock."

"How come?" Kyra knelt in front of Brutus, and he licked her nose.

"Uh...well." The man hesitated, rubbing the back of

his neck. "It's not a good idea to get too attached to the animals on a cattle ranch."

"But why—oh." Because high-quality, grass-fed cattle ended up on people's dinner plates. "No. I'm sorry." She shot back up to her feet. "You can't do that to Brutus."

The calf gazed up at her with those endearing eyes while he lazily chewed on grass, and her heart cracked in half. "I'll pay you every month to make sure he gets to live a long, healthy life." They couldn't kill Brutus. They just couldn't. "He can be like the mascot of the ranch instead of...you know..." She couldn't bring herself to say, *Instead of becoming a hamburger.*

"Please, Aiden. Brutus is special. You can't let him die."

The man's lips folded. If he was trying to hide that smile, he was doing a very poor job.

"I'll take that under consideration," he finally relented. "But I can't make any promises. It's really up to Tess. She's the ranch boss."

"I'll talk to her." Kyra planted a kiss on the calf's head. "Don't worry, buddy. You'll be fine. Nobody's going ship you off to any butcher under my watch."

"Hopefully, he won't pull any more disappearing acts either." Aiden joined her next to Brutus and knelt, inspecting his leg. "Looks like mainly superficial wounds. I'll have to clean him up when we get them down to the lower pasture, but it could've been a lot worse. It's a good thing that leg isn't broken."

Kyra patted her new friend's head again. "Why? What would happen if his leg was broken?"

Aiden's silence was all the answer she needed. *Sheesh.* She would never make it living on a cattle ranch.

The man stood up and regarded the two horses who'd

also started grazing behind them. "Let's give Blondie and Recon a few minutes of rest before we head back. I'm assuming Tess realized we disappeared. They'll stop and wait for us."

"A few minutes would be good." Now that she'd stopped shaking and the poor calf was up and walking, she looked around. Stray golden leaves still dangled above them on the gnarled tree branches, but most were scattered in a carpet under their boots. The river whooshed peacefully nearby and a gentle breeze carried the scent of drying grass.

"You're sure you're okay?" Aiden approached her, and the closer he got, the harder her heart pounded. She might as well have been back on the runaway horse again.

"I'm sure," she half-whispered, getting lost in the intensity in his eyes. Awareness prickled across her skin, warm and tingling. She liked seeing him look at her like this. Open and interested. He didn't seem so burdened when she stared into his eyes.

Aiden's gaze searched hers. Whatever he was looking for, she would let him find. The pull to him seemed to strengthen every time he got close, and she was tired of fighting.

"I'm really glad you're not hurt." He stopped a foot away from her. "I was worried."

"Thanks for rescuing me." Kyra stepped into the distance between them. "Again." Somehow Aiden had seemed to always be there when she needed someone.

"Thanks for not falling off that horse." His lips twitched into a grin. "Seeing you get hurt would've killed me."

This was killing her—standing so close to him without touching him, without acting on the impulses firing through her. Screw it. She could've died. She could've been thrown from the horse and seriously injured—and if she had been, she would've regretted never doing this. Kyra brought her hands to Aiden's jaw and guided his lips to hers.

A low moan droned in his throat for a second as he started to kiss her back, and she responded by moving closer, pressing herself to him. Aiden's arms came around her, holding her the way he had after she'd fallen off the horse and into his arms. She opened her mouth to him, touching her tongue to his, drowning in the warmth, the rush, the desire he stirred in her.

Thank God she hadn't waited to do this. Lyric had been right. She had to learn to seize the moment.

Their mouths moved together, exploring, teasing, and when the man nibbled on her lower lip, Kyra had to pull back to catch her breath, to look into his eyes.

His were dilated and darker, hungry. "I shouldn't be kissing you."

"What a coincidence." She buckled her hands behind his neck in case he got any ideas about stopping. "I shouldn't be kissing you either." This was a time-out from her life—from her real life starting—a detour on her life's map. "But here we are."

"Here we are." His gaze dropped to her lips. "I don't want to be anywhere else."

"Me neither." She moved to her tippy toes to reach his lips again, to taste his mouth, to feel his strength against her body.

"Jesus, Kyra," her murmured helplessly against her lips. "What're you doing to me?"

"I'm not sure." She only knew what she was doing to

herself—finally indulging a craving she'd had since she'd seen Aiden swimming in that pond. She pressed her hips into his, feeling his desire for her, a fire starting low in her belly.

"Aiden!" Tess's voice sounded far away. "Kyra!"

His sister was calling for them.

Kyra pushed her palms into his chest, forcing herself back. "They think we're lost."

"I know I am." The man closed his eyes and sighed. "Tess has always had impeccable timing."

The misery on his face made her laugh.

"Aiden!" Tess shouted again, this time from somewhere in the vicinity.

"Damn it." The man turned away from Kyra and paced to where Brutus was drinking out of the stream.

She tried to get herself together before his sister found them too, patting down her hair, fanning the heat from her face.

"Kyra!" Tess sounded more frantic.

"We're here," she called, stepping from under the trees into a clearing.

Tess came into view on the small rise at the edge of the forest alone. She must've left Willow with everyone else. "There you are!" She rode to meet them and quickly dismounted her horse. For a few seconds she looked back and forth between the two of them, her eyes seeming to calculate the situation. "We noticed you two disappeared, but I see we had nothing to worry about," she finally said with a laugh.

"We had a runaway." Kyra couldn't seem to meet Aiden's sister's eyes. Who knew what the woman thought of her? Messing around with her brother on a cattle drive.

God, she'd never been so embarrassed. "We didn't even see the sweet little guy take off, but Blondie knew."

The explanation didn't wipe the smile off Tess's face. "I see."

Oh, yes. The woman clearly saw more than Kyra wanted her to. "I'm glad you found us, because I wanted to talk to you," she said, going for a distraction. "I would like to contribute a monthly stipend to the ranch for Brutus's care so he can live there forever."

The woman squinted at her. "I'm sorry... what?"

"Brutus? This calf?" Kyra walked to her buddy and gave him a pat. "He's not going to end up like your other cows. He's going to be the ranch's mascot."

"Mascot?" Tess aimed an inquisitive glance at Aiden and shook her head, but he raised his arms in surrender.

"Don't look at me. I told her Brutus's fate would be in your hands."

"Brutus and I bonded." Kyra leaned down and rubbed noses with him. "I couldn't live with myself knowing he ended up on someone's dinner plate. I know it sounds silly, but..."

"It's not silly." Aiden's grin hinted that the two of them now shared something secret. "It's sweet. Right, sis?"

Tess shook her head again, this time laughing. "Right. Whatever you say."

"Look, there's my house!" Morgan pointed straight ahead of them, circling her horse back to meet up with Kyra. "We're almost home."

"I can see that." She slowed Blondie's pace and gazed down the mountainside at Tess's ranch nestled into the valley. How had a few days flown by so fast?

"I don't want to go home," Willow murmured from Tess's horse a few feet away.

Kyra felt the same. When she'd agreed to go on the cattle drive, she hadn't envisioned loving her time in the mountains. But between the camping card games and the meals cooked over the fire, and the constant stunning scenery, she was sad to see it all come to an end. The girls had both been attached to her hip for the duration of the trip, which hadn't allowed for any more secret rendezvous with Aiden in the woods. Not that she was complaining. Willow and Morgan were sweet and funny—a joy to be around. Besides, the whole kissing Aiden thing probably wasn't the best idea anyway.

Her eyes followed the man as he angled down the slope on Recon's back, a telltale heat humming inside of her. It might not have been the best idea to kiss that cowboy, but she couldn't say she regretted it either.

"Do you want to have another sleepover when we get home?" Morgan asked Kyra. "I don't want you to leave. I'm going to miss you."

"Honey, I'm sure Kyra has a ton of stuff to do," Tess broke in. "And you have some chores to do too."

Seeing the disappointment on the girl's face, Kyra steered Blondie over to her. She'd gotten pretty darn good at wielding the reins. "I do have some things I need to get done. But we can get together soon."

"Pinkie promise?" The girl reached out her hand, and they sealed the deal with a pinkie shake.

"I hope Brutus will be okay." She looked back to the west, toward the lower pasture, where they'd left the cattle to graze.

"He'll be fine," Tess assured her. "His mama takes good care of him."

"We can ride up to visit him too," Morgan said. "I know the way."

"I'd love that." After this week, horseback riding might become one of her new hobbies. Not that it would be easy to do in London...

"You're welcome to come and hang out any time." Tess led the way down the switchbacks until they'd reached the stables, where the group was dismounting and starting to unpack their gear.

Aiden stood near the entrance waiting for them. "You survived your first cattle drive." He held out his arms to help her down.

Her *first* cattle drive? Kyra slid off the horse and into his arms even though she had gotten pretty skilled at dismounting herself. Who knew? This might be the last time she was in Aiden's arms. "Do you have plans to challenge me to another cattle drive?" She stepped back and cocked an eyebrow at him.

"You never know," he murmured, his gaze lowering directly to her lips.

"Girls, we really need to hurry up and brush down these horses." Tess waved them into the stables, leading the horses along with them.

"Promise you'll come see us soon!" Morgan called.

"I promise." Kyra waved at her and Willow. She'd join them for a proper goodbye as soon as she had had a moment with Aiden.

He stood gazing at her, his cowboy hat shrouding his eyes in shadows. "Do we need to talk about the kiss?"

"Hmmm. Not sure. Do we?" She didn't know what

else to say. Would talking about the kiss ruin the memory? Would he tell her what she already knew—that it shouldn't happen again?

"It was a good kiss." Aiden took off his hat and hung it on a nearby fence post.

Now she could see the desire simmering in his eyes. "Yes. It was a good kiss," she agreed, nearly breathless. "So let's leave it at that for now." She already knew why it shouldn't happen again. She didn't need to hear the reasons. Her time in Star Valley Springs was fleeting, and Aiden clearly still had a lot of issues working through his grief. Neither one of them was in a place to start something serious. "I'm trying something new while I'm here. Living more in the moment instead of overanalyzing and making plans." These might be the only few months in her entire life when she would have the luxury to live in the moment.

"I like that." The man stepped closer. "Does that mean you wouldn't be opposed to kissing me again?"

No. She would definitely not be opposed. Her insides had started to melt again, but her phone trilled from her pocket.

Heat rushed to her face as she dug it out and glanced at the screen. It was Podgurski, her father's attorney. "I need to take this." Pulse racing, she stepped away from Aiden and brought the phone to her ear. "Hello?"

"Miss Fowler? John Podgurski here. I hope this is a good time."

"Yes, hi." She swallowed hard. Aiden had her throat all knotted up. "How can I help you?"

"I wanted to check in and see how the work on the town is coming," he said briskly. "I've received calls from three developers who are interested in purchasing the land and businesses you own in Star Valley Springs."

"Oh, right." Kyra wandered farther away from the stables. "I'm afraid the work hasn't really begun yet. But we should start next week." Hopefully. Unless she got distracted again...

"That's no problem. I know you've been dealing with a lot." His tone held a requisite sympathy. "I know each of them are eager to talk to you. They're looking at other properties in the valley too, and I would hate for you to miss out on this opportunity. Would you like me to go ahead and set up some preliminary meetings with them? I'm happy to facilitate those here at the office in Jackson."

"I guess it would be good to start talking to the potential buyers." Kyra's eyes wandered up the mountainside to the peaks in the distance. "Why do they want the land? I mean, what're they going to do with it?"

"From what I can tell, they have plans to improve the area, offer more goods and services. More conveniences for the locals and tourists alike."

That was good, right? Star Valley Springs needed more conveniences. Then Tess probably wouldn't have to drive an hour and a half to take the girls to the doctor. And Louie and Minnie would get more customers into the café. "All right." She shielded the phone from the breeze. "You can set up some meetings. Just let me know when I need to be there."

"Wonderful," Podgurski said. "It'll likely take a few weeks to get everyone on the same page. I'll keep you posted."

Kyra said a quick goodbye and then turned to find Aiden standing behind her. "Everything okay?"

"Uh, yeah." Whether she wanted to acknowledge it right now or not, she had to stick to a timeline. This wasn't a vacation. "That was my father's attorney. I'm going to be meeting with some developers about selling."

Aiden nodded, his eyes never straying from hers.

"So I'll really need those bids from you as soon as possible." After that conversation with Podgurski, living in the moment no longer seemed like an attainable goal.

CHAPTER ELEVEN

Aiden snatched the estimate off the printer and went back to his desk, checking over his work to make sure the numbers added up.

"I thought we were putting off Kyra's jobs." Thatch stood on the putting green across the office, lining up a shot, while Silas watched with a critical eye.

"We were." Kind of. He wasn't about to admit how torn he'd been on that front since the cattle drive. Yes, he wanted to keep things in Star Valley Springs the way they'd always been, but he didn't want to hold Kyra back from living her dream either. "We have to get that roof done before the snow flies anyway. That's what Kenny wanted." Before the man had passed so unexpectedly, he'd mentioned wanting to get a new roof on the town hall before Christmas. "I sure as hell don't want to be standing up there freezing my ass off in another two weeks." According to the good old Farmer's Almanac they'd have an early blizzard this year.

"Good point." His friend sunk the putt and then sucker-punched Silas. "That's horse. I won. Pay up."

"Lucky shot," their friend grumbled, digging out his wallet.

"Besides, I think Kyra's starting to like Star Valley Springs." She'd seemed happy out there in the mountains, living in the moment. Hell, she'd made him live in the moment too, instead of feeling so stuck in the past. She'd seemed to relish everything—taking all those pictures, pointing out every cool tree or rock formation...and the kiss. He hadn't expected her to touch her lips to his, but when she had...well, he was a goner.

"She's starting to like Star Valley Springs?" Silas went back to his desk. "Or she's starting to like *someone* in Star Valley—"

The door opened and cut him off, allowing Aiden to plead the fifth on that line of questioning. He knew he was playing with fire when it came to Kyra, but he couldn't quite bring himself to commit to backing off either. It was that damn kiss. It had knocked something loose in his head. Or in his heart. Since the cattle drive, there'd been almost a week of radio silence between them, but that hadn't stopped him from thinking about her. He'd heard around town that she'd been busy cleaning out her father's house, and he hadn't wanted to crowd her. She'd said she wanted to take things day by day, but he was finding that hard to do.

Tess traipsed into the office wearing her typical work boots, jeans, and a flannel. "I need one of you manly men to come and check my work," his sister announced. "I installed a new garbage disposal in my kitchen, but I want to make sure I did it right before I actually turn it on."

A new garbage disposal? Aiden tossed the estimates he'd printed onto his desk. "I didn't know your garbage disposal broke. Why didn't you ask me to take care of it?"

"I don't need you to do everything for me." Tess glared at him with her hip kicked out in full sass mode. "In case you haven't noticed—which I'm pretty sure you haven't—I'm a perfectly capable woman."

"Yeah, you are." Silas leaned back in his chair and kicked his boots up onto his desk while he stared appreciatively at Aiden's sister.

"I'll come and check." Aiden stomped to Silas's desk and knocked his feet back to the floor lest he get any ideas about checking Tess out like that ever again. Tess was way too good for him. "Let me email these bids over to Kyra first."

"Ah, the bids." His sister met him at his desk and glanced at the papers. "So you're actually going to do the work for her instead of putting her off now? That's quite a change in tactics."

Aiden avoided her eyes. He'd been avoiding her eyes ever since he'd kissed Kyra so Tess wouldn't figure out he had something to hide. "We were always going to do the work. We were simply going to delay it. But now I'm not so sure there's a reason to delay."

"Because it would appear she's falling in love with Star Valley Springs," Thatch said from his desk.

"She's falling in love, all right." Tess's smirk proved she already knew too much. "Did he tell you two the ranch now has a mascot?"

Here we go. Aiden opened his laptop to send off the bids, ignoring the chatter around him. If he didn't say anything, maybe they'd move on.

"A mascot?" Silas seemed to give Tess his full attention.

"Yeah." His sister sat on Aiden's desk. "Kyra couldn't bear to think that one of the calves would eventually become beef so she convinced Aiden that we needed to keep him as a mascot instead. And he *agreed.* I believe his exact words were, 'it's sweet.'"

Damn. Tess had always been such a tattletale.

"Whoa." Thatch shook his head sadly. "Someone's got it bad. I'm afraid he's a goner."

"Whatever." Aiden closed his laptop and stood so he could bail on this conversation. "Keeping Brutus is in the interest of Operation Save Star Valley. If Kyra has an animal here, she'll want to come back and visit him. She won't want his home to be sold off out from under him." The important thing was that she had started to care. "I only agreed because her attachment to the livestock works in our favor." He was such a liar.

"You sure you only want her to come back and visit Brutus?" Thatch asked in a mocking tone. "Because rumor has it Tess interrupted something between you two out there on the cattle drive."

"Hey." Aiden gaped at his sister. *Whatever happened to the code of silence between siblings?*

"What?" Tess pushed off his desk and walked to the door. "They dragged it out of me when I rode back up to rejoin the group. I only said it had *seemed* like I'd interrupted something." Her innocent expression turned devious. "But now, thanks to your reaction, we know for sure. Don't we, boys?"

"We're not saying it's a bad thing." Silas raised his hands in front of him. "About time you got a little action. I've been worried about you, man."

"I don't need you to worry. I need you all to butt out of my business." Aiden made it to the door and held it open for Tess. "That includes you," he said, following her outside.

"Why me?" His sister whirled to face him. "I like Kyra. I'm freaking willing to give up five grand to keep a perfectly good grass-fed steer from the butcher for her. I think it's great that I interrupted you two when you were..." She widened her eyes as though waiting for him to fill in the blank.

Forget that. Aiden stomped on ahead of her into her house.

"Kissing?" Tess badgered behind him. "You two were totally kissing, weren't you? You had to be. Her face was flushed, your shirt was all askew. You kissed her."

Instead of answering, he kept going straight into the kitchen, sidestepping the tools strewn around the floor, and got himself under that sink.

"I don't see what the big deal is," Tess went on, her voice muffled. "You *should* be kissing women. And dating. And having a life."

Oh, really? He slid out from under the sink so he could see her face. "When's the last time you went out?"

"I have two kids," his sister shot back.

Exactly. And he needed to be there for her and the girls. They were his priority. Even though he wasn't half the man Jace had been, he would do his damnedest to be everything those girls needed. Aiden felt around the floor until he located the wrench outside the cabinet and then went to tighten all of the bolts in place. Except they were already pretty tight. From what he could see, Tess had done good work here. Nothing felt loose, and she'd managed to get all of the pieces into the right places.

He scooted out from under the sink. "How long did this take you?" And when the hell had Tess learned how to install a garbage disposal?

"I don't know..." His sister started to collect tools, putting them back into Jace's toolbox. "I watched a video online and then I guess it took me about two hours."

"Not bad." Aiden secured the wrench in the toolbox. "But you should've told me you needed this done. You know I'm happy to help you out around here." She had enough on her plate without having to worry about fixing things around the house. Aiden turned on the faucet and flicked the light switch to the right of the sink. A quiet grinding noise made it clear his sister knew what she was doing.

"Yes!" She danced around the kitchen. "I did it! See? I don't need you around all the time."

What was that supposed to mean? "You don't *need* me around or you don't *want* me around?" He turned off the switch.

"Don't be an ass." His sister paused her dance and shut off the faucet. "You know the girls and I love having you around. I'm just saying... if you ever did want to spread your wings and fly, the girls and I would be okay."

Not this again. "Well, I wouldn't be fine. You guys are my family." With their parents taking their retirement seriously and constantly going on all of their fancy cruises, it was mainly just the four of them. "I like doing things for you and the girls." Ever since Jace had died and Aiden had walked away from his Navy career, he had been grasping for purpose. He'd always been a protector, a soldier. Taking care of his family was all he knew.

"I know you like doing things for us," Tess said more

gently. "But I need to start doing things for myself too. I was in a bad place after we lost Jace. I realize that. And now I'm ready to move forward, to really take on this single mom thing."

There had been a change in his sister over the last several months. For the first year after Jace's funeral, she'd had little energy. She'd spent a lot of time in her room by herself. She'd managed to put on an occasional smile for the girls, but he'd seen the weariness and grief behind it. Now, though, Tess had gotten her spark back. And he was glad. He just didn't know where that left him. He couldn't stand in the way of her growing and taking on the world, even if it left him feeling lost.

"I want to start paying you and Silas and Thatch for the work you're doing on the ranch." His sister handed him a bottled water.

"No. Absolutely not." Aiden set the water aside. Was she serious? "We made a pact to keep this ranch going, and we all agreed we would refuse any compensation."

"I know about the pact." She sighed and leaned against the counter. "But I don't want to be your friends' charity case forever. I could work out a plan to pay them something, Aiden."

She didn't understand. Yes, she'd lost her husband. But she didn't face each day knowing she could have prevented his death. They did. Each of them. "We work on the ranch for Jace. You have to understand that. This is all we can do for him now." As free and easy as Thatch and Silas acted, Aiden knew the darkness that lurked in their memories.

That last mission haunted them every bit as much as it haunted him.

* * *

It was sad that the first girls' night Kyra ever had involved sitting around her father's study cleaning out drawers while she and Lyric drank wine.

Kyra added another log to the fire—which Lyric had taught her how to start—and sat back on the leather couch to take a break. "Well, I guess now I know where I get my tendency to keep everything." It was strange finding out that both she and her father were serious packrats.

When she'd mentally cut him out of her life all those years ago, she'd stopped wondering if she was like him, if she looked like him, acted like him, or had his mannerisms. But now, sitting in his space, getting an inside look at his life, all of those questions came flooding back.

"It's funny because my mom and I are the exact opposite." Lyric joined her on the couch. "If something doesn't bring us joy or fulfillment, we toss it. Which is why neither one of us was ever allowed in this room." Her friend laughed. "Mom had to keep the door closed. She couldn't stand the thought of all that clutter in here."

"My mom was more that way too." But not her. Whenever Kyra was faced with the prospect of throwing something away, panic would grip her. What if she needed it someday? Hence the reason she had not one but two units in storage facilities near her apartment back in Florida. "I might need you to give me some lessons on decluttering, though. I can't bring everything with me when I move to London."

"Happy to help." Lyric got up and topped off both of their wineglasses. "England is pretty far away, though.

Do you think you'll ever come back and visit Star Valley Springs?" she asked hopefully.

There was a loaded question if Kyra had ever heard one. "Oh. Uh. I'm not sure." Since the cattle drive, she hadn't been sure about a lot of things. When she'd come to Star Valley Springs, she hadn't anticipated developing real connections here. It was supposed to be simple—come and settle her dad's estate, do some work on the town, and then sell. Now she had feelings involved.

"Do you *want* to come back to visit?" her friend asked.

"I mean, I guess I kind of have to come back. I did sort of adopt Brutus, after all." When Lyric had asked how the cattle drive went, Kyra had focused mainly on the Brutus situation so she didn't have to 'fess up to kissing Aiden. "If I'm paying for his care I should probably check in on him." But coming back would mean keeping connections here, and what would that look like once she moved overseas?

"Brutus is the only one you would want to see?" her friend prompted.

She bought time by sipping her wine. "Well, there's you, of course." But could she and Lyric really rebuild their close friendship when Kyra didn't know the first thing about trusting someone?

"What about Morgan and Willow? I heard they're kind of attached to you these days. It sounds like their uncle is too, for that matter." Lyric nudged her with a knowing smile. "I know you rescued a sweet little calf on the cattle drive, but you haven't really talked much about anything else that happened."

She knew about the kiss. Maybe? Kyra studied the woman's dark eyes, trying to decide if she saw knowledge or suspicion. "I mean, a lot happened. It was a busy couple of days."

"Did you have a nice time with Aiden?" Lyric clearly wasn't going to let her off the hook.

"Yes." It came out as a helpless whine. "We had a great time together."

"You don't seem too happy about that." Her friend set down her wineglass on an end table.

"I kissed him," she lamented. "And it was a nice kiss. A really amazing, knee-weakening kiss." A kiss that had thrilled her and terrified her at the same time. And she hadn't been able to bring herself to see him or talk to him since. Even when she'd received the bid through email earlier that day, she hadn't called him to discuss the project like he'd asked her to. Instead, she'd fired off a quick response. *Everything looks great to me. Go ahead and get started as soon as possible.* So she could get the heck out Star Valley Springs.

The news about the kiss didn't seem to surprise Lyric. "And kissing him is bad because...?"

"Look." Kyra sat up taller. "I'm not like you. I don't live in the moment. I plan. I overanalyze. That's how I've survived the last ten years of my life." Planning and thinking and analyzing gave her some sense of control. "I tried. I really did. But look where enjoying the journey got me. I can't stop thinking about Aiden. But I'm supposed to be making plans to move away. And he's still dealing with a lot after what happened to Jace." The logic came flowing out, but her heart seemed stuck in a fantasy. "Nothing can happen between us." That was the bottom line. "I can't have any strings attached. Especially heartstrings."

"Okay." The woman smiled, her typical relaxed calm self, while Kyra's rapid pulse had her all worked up again.

"Do you know what this reminds me of?" her friend asked with a giggle.

"What?" Kyra didn't find the situation funny, but Lyric's laugh had always been contagious.

"Kyle Barton. Fourth grade."

"Oh, dear God." Kyra's head fell back to the cushion. She'd been pretty worked up about that boy back then too. "I'd forgotten all about him." The boy who'd kissed her on the playground and had slipped her love notes in class.

"Now *he* was a hopeless romantic." Her friend patted her knee. "That kid *loved* you."

"He did. And I loved him too." With an innocent kind of schoolgirl love. "I was an overanalyzer even back then." Kyra laughed again. After four months she'd "broken up" with the poor kid because he wanted to be an elephant trainer in the circus and she couldn't imagine a life on the road.

"I wonder if he ever found a circus to join," her friend said thoughtfully.

They both cracked up.

"Seriously, though." Kyra took a sip of wine. "I think Kyle Barton was the beginning of my romantic incompetence." Somehow she still found it easy to spill her guts to this friend. "I've never had a relationship last more than four months." Sure, she'd dated. And she'd even been close to falling in love. But she'd always found a reason to push the guy away. Somehow she knew Lyric wouldn't judge her for that.

"Relationships are hard. There's always a risk involved," her friend said wisely. "I'm not going to tell you what to do about Aiden. My advice will always be to follow your heart to happiness."

What if she didn't trust her heart?

"I'm just happy we can talk like this." Lyric held out her glass for a toast. "To friendship."

"To friendship," Kyra repeated, clinking her glass against Lyric's. As much as she was enjoying reconnecting with her friend, her gaze drifted back to all of the boxes stacked around them. "We should probably get back to work while we chat."

With that in mind, Kyra ditched her wine on the desk and headed for the exact spot she'd been avoiding. "Let's tackle the closet next."

"Sounds like a plan to me." Lyric followed her across the room.

"All right. Here goes nothing." She opened the closet doors.

"Dear God. Look at all that stuff." Lyric went back to the end table and retrieved her wineglass and then brought Kyra hers. "We're going to need this."

"I think you're right." The closet in her dad's office appeared much bigger than it had looked from the outside, and every square inch of space had been taken up with boxes. Kyra took a large sip of the cab and then set her wineglass on a nearby credenza. "This might take longer than all of the town renovation projects combined." She might be stuck here into the spring going through boxes.

"Maybe we don't have to look in all of them," Lyric suggested. She set her wine next to Kyra's and pulled a box off a shelf. "Look. This one is labeled TIME MAGAZINES." Her friend dragged the box by the door. "Pretty sure that can go in the recycling pile."

"Good. That's good." Sheesh. How would she ever get through this without Lyric's help? She was so overwhelmed by all of the stuff here it nearly paralyzed her.

"And this box." Her friend pulled down another. "This says CDs. No one needs CDs anymore."

"That's true." *Whew.* "Okay, so it seems like this closet is full of outdated treasures, then." That she could deal with. "We'll make a donation pile over there." She pointed to the couch. "And then all recycling and trash by the door."

"Good plan." Lyric dragged the CDs to the recycling pile while Kyra pulled a box off one of the higher shelves, with dust raining down on her head.

She sneezed a few times and then searched the top for a label.

KYRA.

Her name had been scrawled in the corner by the same hand that had labeled the other boxes. But this one she couldn't shove aside. She could only stare, imagining her father writing her name.

"What is it?" Lyric studied the box. "Oh."

"I don't know if I can open it." A heavy weight draped her heart. Would it be more items meant for his little girl's room?

"Would you like me to open it?" Her friend lowered to her knees.

"Yes." Kyra sank beside her. "Maybe we can open it together." She held her breath while Lyric carefully removed the tape from the center seam and pulled open the flaps.

"It's letters." Handwritten letters in envelopes. Kyra pulled out a stack and inspected the writing. They were postmarked starting from three months after her father had left. RETURN TO SENDER had been written across the front of each one in her mother's loopy handwriting. "I don't understand." Her mother had never said anything about her father writing to her. She rifled through the papers. "There are hundreds of letters in here. Hundreds." All addressed to her and postmarked. They'd been sent, but she'd never received even one of them. Kyra searched through the ones she'd dropped until she found the earliest date again. She ripped it open, tears blurring the words.

Kyra,

I'm so sorry, Peanut. If I would've known how things were going to turn out, I would've done everything differently. I should've put you first. You are the most important thing in my life and I failed you. I don't know what is going to happen but I need you to know that I love you. No matter what. Always. I love you and I'm going to try to do what is best for you now.

All my love,
Dad

Tears ran freely down her face as she clutched the paper tightly. She would've given anything to have read those words when she was ten years old. Those words might've changed things for her. They would've told her that her father hadn't left because he didn't care about her. They would've told her he hadn't forgotten about her.

Kyra set that letter aside and tore through others with

Lyric sitting quietly next to her. She read the same words over and over again. That her father loved her. That he was sorry for failing her. That he hoped he could see her someday. That he hoped she could forgive him someday. In some letters he interspersed stories about life on the ranch, about the animals, about how much he missed her. Twelve letters she read. One for each month of that first year he'd been gone. And then she couldn't read anymore. Kyra left the open box sitting there on the floor with letters spilling out and got her wine so she could sit on the couch and stare into the fire.

A few seconds later, Lyric quietly sat next to her.

Kyra didn't know how long they sat there before she asked, "Did you know about the letters?"

"No," her friend murmured. "But I'm not surprised. He still treated you like a part of our lives even though you weren't with us."

"It's not fair." What her father did—betraying his wife and his daughter, leaving to make a life with someone else. It wasn't fair what her mother did—making threats, hiding the words she'd so desperately needed to hear.

"None of this was fair to you," Lyric agreed. "Do you want me to put that box in the recycling pile?"

She knew why her friend was asking. It would be painful to comb through every single letter, to hear her father's regret echoed over and over. But that was exactly what she needed to do. "I'm going to keep the box and read the letters over time." They were her only chance to finally get to her know her father.

CHAPTER TWELVE

Kyra set down the letter she'd been reading and rubbed her eyes.

She really should shower and get dressed...maybe get out of the house for a while. After all, it had been three days since she'd discovered the box. Three days of holing up at home reading letters between binge watching romcoms and eating chocolate and ice cream for some solace in between.

Lyric had offered to stay with her while she worked her way through her dad's words, but this was something she had to do on her own. By herself. At her pace. And so far she'd made it through all but one year of letters. Her father had faithfully written to her once a month for her entire life.

The letters were full of emotion and humor and details. After the first year he had treated them more like journal entries, including his thoughts and reactions to the things that were going on in Star Valley Springs, the world, his new family. Kyra stared at the window over the kitchen sink, a fresh round of tears burning in her eyes. She knew the letters had been meant to include her in his life, but every time she read about some mountain he'd climbed with Lyric and her mother or a horseback ride they'd taken, the fissure in her heart opened a little bit more. Yes, he told her he missed her. Yes, he said he wanted to see her, that he hoped she'd be able to come and see him. But the words couldn't change anything now. She didn't know how to reconcile with a dead man.

Kyra eyed the last bundle of letters sitting on the kitchen table waiting for her. There was a reason she'd been procrastinating today. Instead of her mom's writing on these envelopes, it was hers. *Return to sender*. Those envelopes had been addressed to her at college. One for every month of her freshman year. If only she'd known he hadn't sent them out of the blue, that they were a continuation of the letters he'd sent every month for more than eight years. She might've opened them back then, and maybe she would've had some time with him…

A delicate chiming sound broke off the what-ifs. Was that the doorbell? She glanced down at her frumpy sweats and ran a hand through her tangled hair. Oh, well. The only people who would actually ring a doorbell in Star Valley Springs were the package delivery people. Before now, she hadn't even realized her father's house had a doorbell.

Pushing back from the table, Kyra dragged herself down the hall and swung open the door. "Aiden."

The sight of the cowboy standing there in his signature snug jeans with a heavy flannel coat immediately sent a jolt of energy through her, and suddenly she felt very awake.

"Hey." He seemed to carefully look her over. "You okay?"

"Yeah. Sure." She collected her bangs in her hand and pushed them off her forehead. She really should have showered today.

"You haven't returned any of my texts or calls." He stepped inside the door and glanced around as though he suspected someone might be holding her hostage. "I wanted to check in, make sure nothing was wrong."

"Right. Sorry." She closed the door. There was nowhere for her to hide now. "I've been pretty consumed with going through some of my father's things." And she hadn't felt like dealing with Aiden on top of that. She'd been hiding from complicated relationships for years. Why stop now? "What did you need from me again?"

He blinked a few times, as though lost in thought. "Uh...the shingles. I needed you to make a decision on which color."

"It doesn't really matter to me." The teapot whistled, so Kyra shuffled down the hall into the kitchen. "Whatever color they were before is fine."

"But that's the thing," Aiden said behind her. "They discontinued the slate gray. So now we need to know what else you'd like to use." He seemed to notice the pile of letters on the table but didn't say anything about them. "I have samples for all the shingles that are in stock down at the town hall right now. I can show you and we can make a decision."

"Right now?" She removed the teakettle from the stove and poured the hot water over her chamomile teabag.

"We'd like to get started. Silas and Thatch are already working to demo the old shingles." Aiden glanced at the letters again. "But if this is a bad time, you can meet us there tomorrow."

"I don't want to hold things up." Kyra left her steaming mug sitting on the counter. "But I have to change real quick." Actually, she could use a good hour to make herself presentable, but she didn't want to make Aiden wait that long. "Be right back."

"Take your time." He pulled out a stool and sat at the kitchen island.

Kyra's heart pounded as she ran up the stairs and closed the guest room door behind her. Clothes. She needed decent clothes to wear. Tearing through her suitcase, it became apparent she should do laundry as soon as possible. After settling on a pair of wrinkled jeans and her warmest sweater, she rushed into the bathroom and brushed out her hair, pulling it into a quick ponytail on her way out the door.

By the time she made it back to the kitchen she was nearly out of breath.

"I poured your tea into a travel mug." Aiden handed her a stainless steel cup. "It's cold outside. Might be nice to have a hot drink."

"Thanks." His kindness didn't help the heart palpitations she was already experiencing standing close to him. "I guess we should go. Are you driving?"

Aiden gestured for her to lead the way down the hall. "I walked. It's only a ten-minute walk."

Kyra stepped outside. The air seemed much colder than it had been the last time she'd left the house. But it was refreshing too. "I guess a walk is good for me. I haven't left the house in a few days," she admitted, taking in the scenery. It was cold, but the mountains appeared even more majestic, all bold colors and a white dusting of snow on the peaks. She inhaled deeply as they started off down the driveway. Already, the brisk fall air had lured her out of her isolation-induced haze.

"You want to talk about the letters on the table?" Aiden asked after a few seconds. "I wasn't trying to pry, but it's pretty obvious they were from your dad."

Kyra sipped her tea, letting the warmth and chamomile soothe the ache inside. "There's not much to say." A letter wouldn't have been a replacement for having a father, but at least she could've heard his voice sometimes the way she did when she read them now. "My mother made sure I never read a single one of them. She wrote 'return to sender' on all of them, and I found them sitting in a box in his closet." She'd meant to sound matter-of-fact, but a tremor worked through her voice.

At the end of the driveway they turned onto a neighborhood street, following the sidewalk toward town.

He seemed to watch her face while they walked. "How do you feel about that?" he asked quietly.

She hadn't been prepared for the question. But with Aiden the conversation never felt forced or rushed. He always seemed to give her the right amount of space, allowing her to think and consider her response. Maybe that's why he was so easy to talk to. "I wish I could ask my mom why she felt like she had to hide the letters from me." She so badly wanted to understand. Had her mother really thought Kenneth would want to leave and forget all about her? "And I feel helpless knowing my father wanted to have a relationship with me when there's nothing I can do about it now."

"Feeling helpless is the worst." Aiden shoved his hands into the pockets of his flannel coat.

Kyra checked his face. His eyes were focused ahead of them, but they hinted at sadness too. “Is that how you feel? Because of what happened to your brother-in-law, I mean?”

“Yeah.” He grunted the word in a stark admission. “I wish there was a way to change the past.”

“Me too,” Kyra murmured. Somehow sharing the sentiment made her less lonely.

They turned another corner on the residential street and met an elderly gentleman who was getting his mail.

“Hey, Robert.” Aiden paused to shake the man’s hand. “This is my friend Kyra.”

She liked hearing him call her his friend. He did seem like a friend. The closest thing she had to a friend in Star Valley Springs, other than Lyric, of course. Aiden knew more about her than most of her friends back home.

“Kenny’s girl, eh?” The man squinted while he smiled at her. “Your dad was a real good one. We sure do miss ’im.”

All of the emotion from the last few days filled her eyes again. “Thanks,” she managed.

“How’s November treating you so far?” Aiden asked Robert, as though sensing she needed a rescue.

“Can’t complain too much.” The man tucked the pile of mail under his arm. “My furnace’s acting up, though. Buzzing something awful. Noticed it again last night with temperatures getting close to freezing.”

“Sounds like it needs a cleaning. I can stop by later and give it a tune-up, change out the filter for you,” Aiden offered.

“That’d be real nice.” Robert shook his hand again. “I’ll give you a couple jars of Marge’s apple butter in return.”

"Never necessary but always appreciated." Aiden patted the man's upper arm with a fondness that touched Kyra. "I'll be by later this afternoon with a new filter."

"Thanks, Aiden." Robert turned onto his driveway and plodded to his front door. "Don't know what this town would do without you boys."

"Don't mention it." He aimed a pointer finger at the older man. "And don't forget the apple butter."

Chuckling, Robert waved goodbye, and Kyra found herself smiling. "So, if you work for apple butter and refuse to let Tess pay you to work on the ranch, how do you make enough money to live on?" Sure, she was being nosy, but she recalled Aiden being nosy a time or two as well.

"I don't need much." The man shrugged. "Silas, Thatch, and I…we have our retirement from the Navy. And we make a decent living from Cowboy Construction. That's plenty for me to live on."

"Well, it's kind of you to help people out." What would that be like? To meet someone at the mailbox and have them offer to help you with your problems? It had always been a point of pride for her mother that they'd managed on their own, but Kyra was starting to wonder how much they'd missed out on, isolating themselves from everyone.

"Don't go thinking I'm some saint." Aiden paused on the curb until a man in a passing car stopped and waved them across the street. "Things are different in Star Valley Springs. I'm not the only one helping. Everyone looks out for everyone else. That's the way life works here. This town is remote and isolated, not an easy place to live—especially in the winter. We all have to stick together."

A sense of longing pressed in against her heart. "That's something special. Not every place has that sense of community." Heck, she only knew two other tenants in her apartment complex back in Fort Myers, and that was because they'd both gotten her mail by mistake.

"Star Valley Springs is something special." Aiden stopped and gazed up to the top of the building in front of them.

Somehow they'd already made it to the town hall. Thatch and Silas were sitting on the roof, ripping off shingles and launching them into a dumpster below. "Oh, wow. They're making good progress."

"Yeah." He opened a box sitting on the ground next to the ladder. "Hopefully we can pick up the new batch of shingles in Jackson and have them on by the end of the week. Everyone's talking like there'll be snow soon. Louie said his hip has been aching, and his hip never lies."

"Snow?" Kyra scanned the royal-blue sky overhead. The sunshine made every color appear ten times brighter. "Already?"

"Thanksgiving is only three weeks away." Aiden pulled shingles out of the box and lined them all up against the building.

"I guess it is." She'd lost track of time since she'd gotten here, between the cattle drive and getting sucked into the past by her father's letters. But her time was ticking. She'd lost three days alone to reading her father's words, and she'd spent most of that time wishing she could go backward when she really needed to move forward. "I suppose I'll go to Jackson in search of a winter wardrobe to get me through December." She didn't even own a winter coat.

"No reason to do that." Aiden took out his phone and started to tap away. "I'm sure Tess has extra winter gear she'd be happy to lend you. I'll tell her to bring a box by Kenny's place tomorrow." The man paused from typing and eyed her. "Unless you're planning to stay in Star Valley Springs longer term? Then a new wardrobe would be worth the investment."

Did he want her to stay? Kyra found herself staring at his lips. He'd kissed her with such tenderness. But maybe that was how he kissed every girl. "Oh. Um. Nope. Still planning to move to London." She hadn't gotten the official job offer yet, but it should come anytime now. Hopefully. And when the offer did come in, she had to be ready to go back to Florida and prepare for the new life in London she'd been dreaming about . . . with the proceeds from a sale in her pocket. Her life had been on hold long enough.

Aiden said nothing, but he stared at her with the same intensity that had lit his eyes right before she'd kissed him by the creek.

No, no, no. Not this again. She couldn't get lost in those eyes. What good would it do her to share more and more of her heart with this man when they had no future? Getting closer to Aiden would only make it harder for her to leave. And she had to leave.

Kyra quickly stepped away from him and pointed to the brownish-grayish shingle on the end. "That color will look nice with the stone." They had to get on with this project. Three weeks until Thanksgiving and then another four weeks until Christmas. She had to stick to the plan. "And what about the other jobs? The drywall and the gazebo?"

"We'll get started on those as soon as we finish the roof." Aiden began to pack the other shingles back into the box.

"But everything can be done by Christmas. Right?" Star Valley Springs might be a special place, but it wasn't her place. Spending time here, reading the letters, kissing Aiden…it was all tricking her into a life that wasn't hers. She had things she wanted to do—dreams to chase, places to experience. She could not get stuck somewhere she didn't want to be, like she had been for the last eighteen years.

"We'll do our best to get everything done before Christmas," Aiden promised. He looked around, then stepped closer to her. "Listen, I know how it feels to grieve what should have been. But being here—in Star Valley Springs—has helped. Being part of a community has helped. I guess that's how I find meaning and purpose in the helplessness."

"I'm glad that works for you." But a small town wouldn't solve all her issues. Her parents had defined the trajectory of her life with their mistakes and their lies, and she hadn't had any say as a kid. Being in Star Valley Springs threatened to drag her backward—into the past—but she wasn't helpless. She could move forward. She could take the next step. "I have to go." She had to book her plane tickets back to Florida on Christmas Day and then she had to call Mr. Podgurski and find out when she was meeting with the developers. "Thanks for getting the roof done. Just let me know how much I owe you." Kyra sidestepped him and started off down the sidewalk.

"I could walk you home," Aiden offered behind her.

"That's okay." She cast a fleeting glance over her

shoulder. "I need some space. Time to myself to think." To protect herself from more potential heartache. "I'll see you around." Maybe she'd run into him at the café, but she couldn't spend more time alone with him. She rushed down the sidewalk and pulled out her phone after she'd safely turned the corner.

Mr. Podgurski answered on the third ring. "Kyra, good to hear from you."

"I was wondering if you've set up those meetings with the developers yet," she blurted as a greeting. "The work is moving forward, so I want to start looking at potential offers for my father's assets."

"I've been working on that," the man told her. "I asked them to submit proposals since you were wondering what each of them was hoping to accomplish with the land."

"That's perfect." She made another left turn down the neighborhood street near her father's ranch. "Then I can look them over and choose the best plan." The plan that would benefit this town the most.

"Exactly." Mr. Podgurski paused. "Hmm. It looks like I have all three of them in my in-box here. I'll forward them so you can see what you think."

"Great. Thank you so much." Kyra disconnected the call and tapped the airline app on her phone. "Let's see...one-way ticket back to Fort Myers on Christmas Day." That would be her deadline. She scrolled through the calendar and found an afternoon flight, which would give her plenty of time to get to the airport in Jackson. Inhaling deeply, she clicked the purchase button.

Now all she needed was the job offer to come through from London, and she'd be home free.

CHAPTER THIRTEEN

I told you my hip don't lie." Louie refilled Aiden's coffee mug. "I'll betcha we've got six inches on the ground before the day is done."

Aiden glanced out the windows. Heavy gray clouds had socked in the mountain peaks, and fat flakes were starting to float down onto the hood of his truck. "You're never wrong."

Since he'd moved to Star Valley Springs, he'd given up on weather forecasters and had come to rely solely on Louie's hip. The man always knew when it was going to rain or snow.

"I'm glad we finished that roof yesterday." It had taken a good ten days since they'd had to wait on the shingles to come in, but he and Silas and Thatch had worked from sunup to sundown to get it done. Not that the rush had earned him any praise from Kyra. He'd left her a message to tell her they'd finished the work, and she'd wired money into their account, but otherwise he hadn't heard anything from her, and the silence was slowly killing him. Yes, she was dealing with a lot. Reading those letters from her dad seemed to take a toll on her.

He understood that she was living in the moment and trying not to overanalyze things, but he couldn't seem to do either. He was trying to give her some space, but he found himself revisiting the past—when her lips had ignited his body—or the future—when would he see her again? *Would* he see her again? Maybe she'd hide from now until Christmas. Damn. He'd never been this messed up over a woman.

"I saw the new roof on the town hall." Louie shook his head. "Don't know why you're doing any work for that lady anyway with her fixing to sell us out."

"We still have time." He'd agreed to finishing the projects before Christmas, and he'd make sure none of them were done a day sooner. "I'm not giving up yet." He wouldn't give up on saving this town, but he also couldn't ask Kyra to give up on London. No matter how much he wanted her to stay.

"Are you guys talking about Kyra?" Lyric slipped off her coat and sat on the stool next to him.

"Yeah." He hadn't even realized the woman had been standing behind him.

"We're talkin' about how she's gonna up and sell us out," Louie grumbled. He snatched a coffee mug off the dish rack behind him and poured a cup for Lyric. "Minnie ran into her at the gas station the other day. She told me Kyra is hellbent on moving to London after the New Year." The man harrumphed. "As if London is so much better than us."

"I think it's hard for her to be here." Lyric dumped

some cream into her coffee and stirred thoughtfully. "We have to consider everything she's been through—having her dad walk out and then believing for eighteen years he didn't want to know her and then all of a sudden learning that her mother was hiding her away from him? That's a lot to process."

That was an understatement. He wished there were something he could do to take the burden off of her—to make things easier. But when he'd mentioned how much being a part of this community had helped him, she'd shut down, and he hadn't heard from her since. "I haven't seen her in over a week. How's she been?"

"She's managing okay." Lyric wrapped her hands around her mug as though warming them. "I'm checking in on her. The Ladies are keeping her fed and helping with chores. I guess we don't really have a choice but to sit back and wait to see what she decides to do after all of the work is completed."

"Sure we have a choice," Louie protested. "We can tell her exactly what she'll do to this town if she sells. All those lost livelihoods and homes after developers take over will be on her."

"We can't force her to stay." As hard as it was for him to admit it, staying might not be in Kyra's best interest. "Maybe she really will be happy in London. Who are we to take that away from her?"

Lyric nodded in agreement. "Exactly. If we beg her to stay and make her feel guilty, it won't truly be her decision."

"Well, it ain't our decision to lose our town to the millionaires either," Louie muttered. "But if you two are throwin' in the towel, there's nothin' we can do."

"We're not throwing in the towel." Aiden pushed his empty coffee mug across the bar and pulled some cash out of his wallet. "Operation Save Star Valley is still on. But it has to be more of a covert mission than an all-out offensive. We can still show her every good thing about this town. We can include her and invite her to be part of the community. And then we can let her decide what she wants." They had to let her decide. Aiden handed Louie the cash.

"No breakfast today?" The man stashed the bills into the register. "I've got one more slice of Minnie's quiche left."

"Nah." He put on his coat. "I have to go pick up Morgan and Willow. They're going to visit their grandparents in Florida for Thanksgiving next week, so I need to get in some time with them." Tess had told him he was more than welcome to tag along to her in-laws' place for the holiday, but he never could face Jace's parents after what had happened. "You'll keep checking in on Kyra?" he asked Lyric. "Let me know if I can help with anything?"

"Maybe you should check on her too." The woman shot him a teasing smile. "Ask her if you can help with anything yourself."

"Yeah, maybe." But she'd told him she needed space. And he was doing his best to respect her wishes. More than once he'd been tempted to stop by Kenny's and check on her, but then he'd remember the look on her face when she'd walked away from him. She'd been tense and hurting, and he didn't want to add one more complication to her life.

Saying goodbye to Louie and Lyric, he stepped outside. The snow had already started to come down harder, so he slipped on his gloves and brushed off the windshield of his truck. If enough snow piled up, maybe he'd be able to take the girls sledding later that afternoon.

Aiden drove out of town and couldn't stop himself from slowing as he passed by Kenny's place. There was no sign of Kyra, though her rental car was parked in front of the porch. Maybe he'd text her later to see if he could swing by after he hung out with the girls. He could still check in and give her space, right? Hell, he didn't know what to do for Kyra. What to do with his own feelings for her. So he kept driving to Tess's place.

His sister was outside sweeping the dusting of snow off the porch. "Hey." She leaned the broom against the house. "Geez, it's cold. I've lived here for twelve years, but the first snow still gets me every year."

"Me too." Not surprising, since they'd spent most of their childhood in Southern California. "Speaking of the cold, did you bring that box of winter gear to Kyra?"

"Yep. I stopped by Kenny's place last week." His sister opened the door and waved him inside. "I can't believe how much she's gotten done there. All that's left is one more room and the furniture. She said she's already made arrangements to donate it right after Christmas."

Aiden paused to stomp the snow off his boots on the entry rug and then slipped them off. The thought of Kenny's house being empty and ready to sell only added to the gloom that had chased him around lately. "How'd Kyra seem when you saw her?"

"I don't know her well." Tess pulled the girls' coats out of the closet and laid them on the bench. "But she seemed a little more reserved, almost businesslike compared to when I talked to her on the cattle drive."

"Businesslike." She'd been that way with him when they'd first met. But that kiss they'd shared in the woods was anything but professional. He shook his head to clear the memory.

"Yeah, you know? Kind of rigid and formal? Not chatty." Tess led him into the kitchen. "She seems really focused on tying up loose ends and getting out of here." His sister glared at him. "Did you piss her off or what?"

Before he could respond, Morgan and Willow came barreling in. "Uncle Aiden! You're here! What're we gonna do?"

He caught Willow and swept her up while he gathered Morgan in a one-armed hug. "I was thinking we could go Christmas shopping. The countdown is on. Your favorite holiday is almost here."

"It's not my favorite holiday." Morgan's smile disappeared, and she pushed away from him. "I don't want to go shopping."

"Me neither." Willow wriggled to get down.

He set the girl's feet carefully back on the floor. "Oh. Okay." Since when did they hate Christmas? He realized the holidays hadn't been easy since Jace had passed, but they used to be obsessed with snowmen and reindeer and Santa. "We can do something else, then." Maybe they didn't feel like shopping. "How about we go cut down a Christmas tree for your room and then decorate it with ornaments and lights?"

"No." Morgan posted her hands on her hips. "I don't even want a tree this year."

"Me neither." Willow stomped her foot.

His older niece's expression hardened even more. "Christmas is stupid."

"Yeah. Stupid," Willow echoed.

Both girls whirled and stomped down the hallway to their bedrooms, slamming the doors in a synchronized choreography.

Aiden looked to Tess for an explanation. "Uhhh... was it something I said?"

"Don't take it personally." His sister was busy scrubbing a blob of jam off the kitchen counter. "They get like this every time we're preparing to visit Jace's parents for Thanksgiving." She rinsed the rag in the sink. "It's like they remember how much Jace loved Christmas. How much fun the four of us always had. I know we try, but the last few years haven't been as magical for them as he always made the holidays seem."

A searing pain slashed across his chest. Jace should be here with his girls over the holidays. They shouldn't have to miss him. "What else can we do to make it magical? We put up Christmas lights last year..."

"A few." Tess rinsed the bowls that sat in the sink and arranged them in the dishwasher. "You remember how over-the-top he used to go with all the decorations and lights." She smiled as though the memory made her happy. "He took it to a new level every year. We have a whole section in the barn dedicated to lawn ornaments. But I bet they don't even work anymore."

"I could check." He hoped the hollowness inside of him hadn't changed his voice. No matter what he did, it would never be enough. He couldn't replace Jace. He couldn't give the girls back their father.

His sister closed the dishwasher and turned to him. "You don't have to do things like Jace did them. Part of moving on for all of us is starting new traditions." She gave his arm a pat. "They'll adjust. Oh!" She rushed to the small built-in desk on the other side of the room. "I almost forgot. I got this." She held out the same certified letter Aiden had received in the mail two days ago. Except that one had been addressed to him.

"They're presenting me with a Navy Cross for Jace." Tears lit up her eyes. "The ceremony will be next spring." She held out the letter. "The Navy Cross, Aiden. That's one of the highest honors. I'm so proud of him."

"Me too." He let his gaze fall to the floor before he gave himself away.

"You're not surprised." His sister carefully laid the letter on the counter. "You knew. You got a letter too, didn't you?"

"I got a letter and now it's in the trash."

Tess gasped. "What'd you mean it's in the trash?"

"I threw it away. I won't accept any honors." Fury thundered through him. Not at her. God, he was just so angry with himself. "I don't want it. I didn't earn it." They could give the Navy Cross to Jace because he deserved it. Aiden didn't.

"Of course you earned it." His sister's voice teetered. "Aiden, you served your country. You risked your life on every single one of those missions just like Jace did."

"Yeah, and he lost his life." The only mission that mattered was the one Aiden had failed on. That night had gotten too chaotic. He and Jace had always stuck close, no matter what they were doing. They always had eyes on each other, but when the gunfight started, Aiden had lost him. He hadn't been there to cover his brother-in-law. He'd only heard the fire and then he'd heard Jace yelling for him. He could still hear him…

"I won't let you turn down an honor you earned," Tess informed him. "You are not less of a hero than Jace because you made it home." Anger flushed his sister's face. "What about Thatch and Silas? Did they get letters too?"

"I don't know," he lied. The three of them hadn't discussed the letters, but he'd seen them sitting on their desks. They wouldn't accept the cross either. He didn't have to ask them to know that.

Tess stared at him for a few silent seconds, her jaw set. "I'm worried about you." She faced him over the kitchen island. "You're not working through your grief. I can tell. You're not the same person you were before that mission. I could set up a time for you to talk to my therapist. She says—"

"I don't care what your therapist says." They'd had this same conversation too many times. "This is who I am now." Watching his best friend die had changed him. No amount of talking about it with some stranger would somehow magically make him go back to being the person he'd been before.

"Uncle Aiden?" Willow's small voice called to him from the hallway, and his anger immediately receded.

He walked to her and knelt. "What is it, sweet girl?"

"Do you think we could maybe go get ice cream?" She placed her hand on her tummy. "I'm hungry for chocolate ice cream."

"That's the perfect thing to do today. I could use some ice cream too." Despite the regrets, despite the past, despite his helplessness to take away their grief, these girls made him smile. They made him want to try…to keep trying every single day.

CHAPTER FOURTEEN

"This is it, ladies. The last room we have to tackle." Kyra stood outside of the storage room in her father's basement with Minnie, Doris, Nelly, and Lyric all clustered around her. In the last three weeks, these women had become her saving grace. They had shown up at least every couple of days and helped her work her way through her father's house—organizing everything into piles, cleaning, even making trips to the thrift store for her. She was going to miss them when she left...

"This one's gonna be a doozy." Minnie stepped into the cavernous basement storage room that was illuminated by bare light bulbs.

"Look at all this stuff," Lyric marveled, pulling a fake pumpkin off a shelf. "Yet another room my mother avoided like the plague."

"I can see why." Kyra had half a mind to shut the door and sell all this clutter with the house, though Mr. Podgurski had advised her to make sure the house was emptied, since the structure would likely be leveled for the land.

"It looks like a lot of holiday decorations." Doris smiled fondly. "Your father did love decorating for the holidays."

Kyra looked to Lyric. "I do seem to remember him spending hours outside the week of Thanksgiving, putting up lights and lawn ornaments." All things her mother had gotten rid of only a month after he left. But she found the memories didn't sting as much as they had before she'd gotten to know her dad again. Through the letters. Through sorting out the pieces of his life in this house.

"He still spent hours out there decorating, even when I was in college." Lyric laughed. "He always wanted this place all lit up for his big Christmas party."

"Wait a minute." Minnie gasped. "We should have one last Christmas party here before you sell the place. In honor of Kenny."

"Oh, I don't know." Kyra hated to disappoint these women after all they'd done for her, but she'd likely be signing a contract soon. She hadn't chosen which offer to accept yet. She'd wanted to take her time. But with Thanksgiving right around the corner, she had to make a decision soon. "I'm leaving on Christmas Day. Remember?"

"Then we'll have the party on Christmas Eve." Nelly clapped and squealed. "Oh, I do love a good Christmas party."

"There won't be anything left in the house except the furniture." Kyra glanced around the storage room again. Assuming they could find a new home for all of this stuff, that was.

"Not to worry. We'll take care of everything," Doris assured her. "We can bring all of the food and the decorations."

"Parties are what we do best," Minnie added proudly.

Lyric's smile pretty much told Kyra there would be no getting out of this.

"All right. Sure. We can have a party here." These ladies had worked incredibly hard to help her out. If they wanted to work even harder to put on a party, who was she to stop them? It would be a great chance for her to say goodbye to all of them anyway. A wave of sadness seemed to crash over her heart. And she'd have to say goodbye to Tess and Morgan and Willow too. She'd only seen them a couple of times since the cattle drive—when Tess had stopped by occasionally to help her—but they were always full of smiles and hugs.

As much as she tried to deny the truth, the girls and Tess and the Ladies and Lyric weren't the only ones she would miss. She hadn't let herself think about Aiden or even check in on the projects he was supposed to be working on, instead moving from one task to the next to keep her mind occupied, but she couldn't avoid him forever…

"Woo-hoo, a party!" Nelly opened a large tub that had been shoved into one of the corners of the room. "Oh, lookie here. These decorations can get us started."

Everyone crowded around her, *oh*ing and *ah*ing. Kyra was about to join them, but her phone rang. She dug it out of her pocket and glanced at the screen, ready to shut the thing off, but it was a London number! "I have to take this." No one seemed to notice her rush out of the storage room, her heart pounding.

"Hello, this is Kyra Fowler," she said breathlessly into the speaker.

"Ms. Fowler. This is Alexis Walter."

Alexis Walter! The head of human resources at one of the best hospitals in London! *Be cool.* "Yes, hello, Ms. Walter." Somehow she managed to achieve a professional tone. "How are you?"

"I'm doing quite well, thank you," the woman replied cheerfully. "I wanted to get in touch and let you know to watch for an official offer. Since you said you would be out of town, everything will be sent to the email address you provided."

"Really?" A high-pitched squeak slipped through. "Wow. That's...amazing. Thank you so much. Really. I'll watch my email."

"Brilliant. I'll send all of the documents straight away and you'll have two weeks to sign the papers and formally accept the offer."

"I won't need two weeks." She'd been waiting for this opportunity to come through for three months.

After thanking the woman five more times, she finally said goodbye and started to celebrate, jumping around and squealing. She was moving to London! This was really happening!

"I'm guessing you got good news." Lyric peered through the open doorway.

"The hospital in London offered me the job!" She didn't bother trying to rein herself in with Lyric. Her friend started jumping and squealing too.

"That's so great! I knew you'd get the job."

The job. She'd gotten the job! A sudden panic flooded her excitement. "This is really happening. I have so much more to do." She started to pace. "I have to get all of the projects done in Star Valley so I can leave town free and clear." In order to complete the sale, she had to prove the work was done. To her knowledge, the only project Cowboy Construction had completed so far was the town hall's roof. "I hope Aiden is finished with the gazebo."

Lyric grimaced. "I drove by there on my way here, and it didn't even look like they'd started."

But he'd emailed her over the weekend to tell her they would start Monday. "They're supposed to be working today. Thanksgiving is in two days." And then time would speed ahead until Christmas. "I have to light a fire under those guys." It was time for her to stop hiding from Aiden. She had to make sure he got everything done in time. "Do you think you four can handle things here for an hour?"

"Are you kidding?" Lyric stepped aside so she could see into the room. "Look at those gals. They couldn't be more thrilled about this project."

Kyra laughed. "Perfect. I'm going to run to the park and check on the Cowboy Construction crew, and then I'll be back to help organize." Not that the Ladies needed her help. She usually only got in their way.

Kyra took the basement steps two at a time, nearly stumbling at the top.

"Drive safe," Lyric called after her. "The snow is starting to pile up out there."

"Good to know." Kyra bundled herself up before running out the front door and then drove at a max speed of five miles an hour all the way across town. She pulled up alongside the curb in front of the park and got out of her rental, especially grateful for the wool socks and snow boots Tess had loaned her.

Only having seen snow three times in her entire life, she had assumed she would hate Star Valley Springs once winter had set in, but in reality the snow seemed to make everything more beautiful. She'd never realized how the powdery white coating sparkled in the moonlight. She loved the way the flakes piled up on evergreen trees like fluffy white frosting. And somehow the layers of snow even softened all of the mountain peaks' roughest edges. Truthfully, winter in Star Valley Springs was every bit as beautiful as the fall.

Kyra tromped through the winter wonderland, past the playground and small pond until she could see the gazebo on the other side. There was no sign of Aiden or Silas or Thatch anywhere. No sign of anyone. Maybe because it was snowing? She moved more quickly until she got close enough to see that Lyric had been right. The gazebo hadn't been touched, even though Aiden had promised they would start the project this week. "Great." They hadn't made any progress at all. She turned around and followed her tracks back to her car. Once inside, she dug out her phone and dialed Aiden's number. His phone went straight to voice mail. "Perfect."

Kyra started up the car and blasted the heat. She had no idea where Aiden's house was, but he was most likely at the ranch anyway, especially with Tess out of town this week. Maybe he'd gotten held up taking care of the animals. She headed that direction, her tires slip-sliding their way down the frosted streets. By the time she skated into Tess's driveway and parked next to Aiden's truck, her knuckles were white and her neck was so tense she might as well have been wearing a brace. She had no business driving on these roads in these weather conditions. There had to be eight inches by now. She'd never driven in the snow. It was a wonder she hadn't ended up in a ditch somewhere.

Kyra got out of the car and carefully made her way up the porch steps. Loud thumping noises stopped her from knocking. A ladder leaned against the house a few feet away, but she couldn't see anyone. "Aiden?"

"I'm up here. On the roof." Snow crunched above her head. Kyra stepped back a few paces so she could see him.

The man stood at the peak of the steep roof, wrestling with a string of lights.

"What're you doing up there in a blizzard?" she called. Had he lost his mind? The roof had to be as slippery as the roads right now.

He answered in a string of curses that appeared to be directed at the tangle of lights. "I don't know what the hell I'm—" Aiden lost his balance and pitched forward.

The fall seemed to happen in slow motion and then, before Kyra could even move, the man was rolling down the roof.

"Oh, my God!" She made it to him the second after he landed in the snow-covered bushes. "Aiden! Are you okay?"

"I think so." He groaned and tried to sit up.

"Wait." Kyra knelt and held his shoulders in place. "What hurts? We need to check you out before you move."

"Sure...you can check me out." The man's grin quickly turned into a wince.

"Nice try." Relief swelled through her. At least he couldn't be too bad off, if he was joking around. "Can you move your arms? Your legs?"

Aiden shifted. "Yup. Everything seems to work."

"Did you hit your head on the way down?" She gazed into his eyes to check his pupils, and every part of her seemed to go soft when their gazes locked.

"I didn't hit my head." The man stared steadily into her eyes. "I cranked my shoulder, that's all. No big deal."

"Right. No big deal. You fell off a roof is all." She wasn't sure if her heart was pounding so hard from watching him fall or from being so close to him. The answer didn't matter. Kyra shifted into nurse mode and shoved her emotions aside. "Come on." She offered her arm to help him up. "Let's get you inside so I can take a look at your shoulder."

Aiden did plenty of grumbling while she helped him scramble to his feet, but once he was up he walked into the house unassisted. They both kicked off their boots and shed their winter layers.

"I think it's fine." He shrugged his right shoulder up and down with a grimace.

"Very convincing." She beckoned him through the small living room into the kitchen, where she pulled out a chair from the table. "Have a seat." Looking down at him would be much easier than looking into his eyes again while she examined him.

"The pain's not that bad," the man muttered, but he sat in the chair anyway.

Kyra palpitated along his collarbone, though she couldn't feel much underneath his flannel shirt. That thing was going to have to come off eventually, but she'd put off undressing him as long as she could. "This okay?"

Aiden tilted his head away from her hand. "Yeah. That doesn't hurt at all."

"Good. Then I don't think you broke your collarbone." She stepped back to judge the symmetry of his shoulders. "Can you raise your arm up for me?"

The man complied with an audible sigh. "It's an old injury. Nothing I haven't dealt with before." A pained expression twisted his mouth. "Rotator cuff. I'll need a new one eventually but hopefully not for a long time."

An old injury. Sustained in the line of duty?

He didn't offer more information.

"I'd like to take a closer look." Heat crept up her neck and seeped into her cheeks. "Just to make sure it's not dislocated," she added quickly. "But I can't do that with your clothes..." Was it scorching hot in that kitchen or was it just her?

Aiden fired up that grin again. "Are you asking me to take off my shirt, Kyra?"

"No." She made sure to glare at him. "I'm *telling* you to take off your shirt so I can make sure your shoulder isn't dislocated." This man generated as much snark in her as he did lust. "Trust me, you won't be smiling like that if I have to set your shoulder." She didn't know if she'd be able to set his shoulder without someone else here to help.

"Yes, ma'am." Aiden slowly unbuttoned his shirt, his grin turning sly. He went to slip it off his shoulders but stopped abruptly with another groan. "Damn."

"Need some help?" She didn't wait for him to answer.

Her hands grazed his skin to push the material away from his body, and his shoulders both straightened.

Kyra moved around to the front of him so the light would hit his shoulder. That was all she needed to look at—his shoulder. Not at his muscled chest or washboard abs or the Navy tattoos…

Focus.

"Looks like a pretty serious contusion, but it's not dislocated." Kyra traced the bruising at the top of his shoulder with her finger. She couldn't be sure, but it felt like Aiden's whole upper body tensed under her fingertips. "We need to get you to a doctor just to be safe." She shouldn't be touching him like this. Not when being this close to him made her breath catch.

"We don't have a doctor in Star Valley Springs." Gravel roughed up his voice. "It's not worth making the hour-and-a-half drive. Not in this weather."

Kyra glanced out the window. Dusk had set in, and a thick layer of snow frosted the glass. "Then I guess we'll have to use a good old home remedy." Taking her chance to put space between them, she opened Tess's freezer in search of tried-and-true frozen peas. Aha. After opening a few drawers near the sink, she located a thin towel. "What were you doing on the roof in this weather anyway?"

"I was trying to create a magical Christmas display for the girls." Aiden paused and cringed when she applied the ice to his bare shoulder. "Since I'm housesitting for them anyway, I figured I could get everything up and surprise them when they get home from Florida. But nothing's working. All the lights are tangled. I swear, I don't know how Jace did it every year."

Kyra sat across the table from him. “You don’t know how he put up Christmas lights?”

“He didn’t just put up lights.” Aiden held the makeshift icepack in place with his free hand. “He transformed this place. Last weekend Morgan told me she hates Christmas.” His eyes were downcast. “They used to love the holiday. It was their favorite time of year. Now they don’t even want to celebrate. I thought they’d be happy if the place was all lit up like it used to be when they get home Thursday night.”

The response struck her in the heart. Right when she got it in her mind to cast Aiden out of her dreams he did something like this and worked his way back in again. He was so devoted to his nieces, so tender and kind to them. And he never seemed to shy away from showing how much he loved them.

“All I really did was prove that I suck at putting up Christmas decorations. I should’ve waited until Thatch and Silas come back from Jackson.” Aiden took the frozen peas off his shoulder and tossed the bag onto the table. “You haven’t told me why you showed up here. Did you need something?”

“Oh.” After hearing about what he wanted to do for his nieces, her righteous indignation about the gazebo didn’t feel so important. “I wanted to check on the status of the gazebo project, but that’s not nearly as important as what you’re doing for the girls. We can talk about it later.”

“We’ll get back to work next week,” he promised. “And I’m not doing much for the girls. Except falling off the roof. It doesn’t look like I’ll be able to make their winter wonderland magic happen.”

“The magic has to happen.” She couldn’t let him give

up when this clearly meant so much to him. And the girls…her heart started to beat faster just thinking about the looks on their faces when they saw their house all lit up. "You need help."

"I'm beyond help," he muttered, wincing as he tried to move his shoulder.

"No one is beyond help." Kyra found another dish-towel and tied it around his shoulder to hold the ice in place. "The Ladies and Lyric and I were just cleaning out my father's storage room, and there's a ton of decorations in there I can donate to the cause. And I can help you untangle all the lights here. We can have everything organized and ready to put up by tomorrow."

"You're sure?" The man sat a little taller.

"I'm positive." They could all work together and have the surprise ready before Thanksgiving. "We'll get every-one in on this mission—Minnie and Doris and Nelly and Lyric. I'll text them right now. They can spread the word and we'll have whoever can come meet us here tomorrow with all the yard decorations they can spare." They might not be able to bring Morgan and Willow's dad back, but they could rekindle the joy he'd brought them each year with his Christmas displays.

Aiden watched her from across the table, a smile slowly taking over his face.

Oh, that grin. She'd missed the way his happy expression warmed her through. "What?" Kyra almost whispered.

"I was about ready to give up on Christmas magic," he murmured. "But you got here at the perfect time."

CHAPTER FIFTEEN

Are these Yoda Christmas lights?" Kyra reached into one of the tubs they'd hauled from the barn into Tess's house and pulled out yet another strand of uniquely shaped bulbs.

"Yep," Aiden said through a laugh. "Jace was a huge Star Wars fan. I warned you about how big his collection of decorations was."

"Yes, you did." But she still couldn't have imagined that they would have to make ten trips from the barn into the house carrying tubs and huge garbage bags protecting various lawn ornaments. They'd been at this for well over two hours and still had half the room to go through.

"If you think those lights are something, then you need to see..." The man looked around and then moved to a group of garbage bags by the fireplace. "These." He uncovered Darth Vader, R2-D2, and Yoda lighted statues all wearing Santa hats.

"Huh." Kyra had to laugh too. "And Tess was fine with storing all of this stuff?"

"No one could ever tell Jace no. Not even me. His enthusiasm was too infectious." Aiden unraveled the cord from the Yoda and plugged it in. The statue lit up all the way from the Santa hat to the light saber in its hands. "Thank God Yoda still works. These are some of the girls' favorites because their dad loved them so much."

"Then we'll make sure to put them front and center so they'll see them right away." When it came to Christmas, Kyra's mother had been a stickler for color schemes and adhering to a theme, so the hodgepodge method wasn't one Kyra had ever considered. But it was already proving to be more fun. "I'll just be standing by, trying to let go of my need for symmetry and order."

"Yeah, there was no order to Jace's method." Aiden plugged in the other statues and stood back as though admiring them. "It was like Christmas threw up in his yard. He made things work." There was the sadness pulling at Aiden's mouth again.

"I wish I could've known him." Not only because Aiden made him sound like a saint but also because she loved his daughters. Morgan and Willow were special—kind and giving and more compassionate than other kids she'd met at their age. But then again, they'd had to go through some serious pain to become so extraordinary.

Kyra continued unraveling the tangles in the Yoda lights. She didn't want to be pushy, but Aiden hadn't talked much about Jace. She sensed regret whenever Aiden mentioned him, but she didn't understand why. "How long did you know him?"

"Twenty years." He busied himself with unpacking a

tub of large colorful bulbs. "We played football together in middle school. Jace had just moved to San Diego from here, and he hated it there. All he ever wanted was to come back to his grandparents' ranch and take over someday." He had his back to her, but she could detect the emotion in his voice. "I introduced him and Tess. After graduation, Jace and I joined up together and managed to move up through the ranks. He's the only man I ever knew who was good enough to be with my sister."

Kyra's heart ached for him. From the sound of things, Jace had been more like a true brother than an in-law. She carefully set the light strand on the carpet and gave his words the space they needed. Anything she said would've sounded too trivial, and she didn't want to push too hard for more information. It was obviously difficult for him to talk about Jace.

After a few minutes of silence between them, Aiden pushed off the floor. "I could use some hot chocolate. You want some?"

"I'd love some." She couldn't even remember the last time she'd had hot chocolate. Her mother used to make it sometimes on the rare occasion that the temperature dipped below fifty degrees in Fort Myers. Kyra glanced out the window but couldn't see anything past the snow. There was more on the ground than she'd ever seen, that was for sure. And it was probably ten degrees out there now.

"Then let's take a break." Aiden beckoned her to the kitchen. "Have a seat." He pulled out a stool for her at the small kitchen island and then opened a drawer. "We've got peppermint hot chocolate, caramel hot chocolate, white hot chocolate, dark hot chocolate..." He raised his eyes to hers, waiting.

"I'm a dark chocolate girl." Without the distraction of lights to untangle, she found herself unable to look away from him while he filled a teakettle with water and set it the on the stove. Then he tidied up the kitchen, rinsing a few dishes before stashing them in the dishwasher.

"Can't forget the marshmallows." He opened the pantry next to the stove and rifled through until he pulled out a bag of mini-marshmallows.

"I don't need any, thanks. I prefer my chocolate on the bitter side as opposed to overly sweet."

He looked at her aghast. "You can't have hot chocolate without marshmallows. They add the magic. Trust me." He took two mugs out of a cabinet and dumped in the chocolate powder along with way too many marshmallows. "When they melt, they'll give the drink a nice frothy finish."

"I'll take your word for it." Kyra found herself smiling. He might not recognize it, but his enthusiasm was infectious too. Somehow he made her want to try new things, like going on a cattle drive and indulging in too many marshmallows. She watched the man hum to himself as he took the kettle off the stove and poured the steaming water into their mugs. The telltale burn of desire stirred insidc her. Forget the marshmallows. Maybe Aiden was the real indulgence.

"Give it a stir." He handed her the mug with a spoon and then sat on the stool next to her with his hot chocolate. "Taste it and tell me that's not perfection in a cup."

Kyra took a sip, the melty marshmallows sticking to her lips. "Mmmm." It really did taste better than she remembered. Or maybe the company made it taste better. "You're right. The marshmallows do add the magic."

"We have the girls to thank." Aiden turned on his stool to face her. "Morgan and Willow have reintroduced me to the magic of everything. I tried to tell them once that marshmallows would make hot chocolate too sweet and then they dumped a whole bunch into my mug and here we are."

"Here we are." Somewhere she never dreamed she would be. In Wyoming, of all places, sitting with a man who had an uncanny ability to get her to open her heart. Kyra wiped the marshmallows off her mouth with the back of her hand. "Your nieces are pretty incredible."

"They are." That look on his face—the tenderness in his eyes, the pride in his smile—made her melt like those marshmallows in her mug. "And you're a pretty incredible father figure for them too, you know," she added quietly.

Aiden seemed to freeze, holding the mug halfway to his mouth. "You think so?" he asked with uncertain hopefulness.

"Having someone like you in my life back when my dad left would've made a difference for me." Someone to make her feel protected and special the way he did for Morgan and Willow. "They're lucky to have you, Aiden. You're making a difference for them." He might not see it, but he was an important part of those girls' stories.

"They're making a difference for me too." He set the mug back on the counter. "If it weren't for them I don't know where I'd be." His grave tone implied he likely wouldn't have been in a good place if it weren't for his nieces. "I didn't know what to do with myself after...Jace." He cleared his throat. "In a way, this place saved me." Aiden directed his gaze out the ice-encrusted window over the kitchen sink.

The statement made her wonder... would London save her? Would it fill the void nothing else had ever seemed to reach? "I got the job in London." She needed to tell him. And maybe the fact that she was leaving would put the distance between them she couldn't seem to maintain. "They emailed me the official offer."

Aiden had frozen again, his eyes still focused on the windows. "That's great." He took a drink of his hot chocolate and smiled again, but this one seemed forced. "It's what you wanted, right?"

"Right." And yet telling him now, she couldn't seem to muster the same excitement that had consumed her only hours earlier. "I mean, that's what I've been working for." That was the whole reason she'd gone back to school—so she could open up more opportunities for herself abroad. But that wasn't all. "When my mom was sick, we would look at pictures of the trip we'd taken there, and she'd smile and tell me she wanted me to be as happy as I'd been on that trip again someday. She said she could see me living there, and that's when the dream really started."

"Then I'm really happy you get to go." He turned his head to look at her, and she knew the words were true. "Cheers." He held up his mug until she clinked her glass against his. "Tess said you're leaving on Christmas?"

"Yes. That's the plan." Hopefully, her voice didn't reflect the pinch of uncertainty that had crept into her thoughts.

His gaze dropped to her lips. "I probably shouldn't kiss you again if you're leaving."

He was right, yet her heartbeat picked up. "Well, in another month you won't have the opportunity. Really, this could be your last chance." What was she saying right now? The rush of energy he generated inside of her had taken over. She *wanted* him to kiss her. She wanted to revisit the rush of desire he'd made her feel. Right now she wanted him. "You know what they say, you should make the most of every opportunity." Yes, she was leaving, but why couldn't she enjoy the next month here? Why shouldn't she enjoy Aiden when he made her feel something no one else ever had?

The man's slow smile didn't make it far before his lips came for hers, bringing a moan thundering up her throat. They stood... well, she half stood and half leaned into his strong body, letting his arms come around her to hold her up. This time the kiss didn't start gently and searching. They both knew what they wanted, or maybe what they needed. His mouth was as urgent as hers. Their lips already knew a rhythm somehow, opening to each other, clinging, exploring.

Kyra breathed him in while she had the chance, tasting the chocolate in his mouth, inhaling the woodsy scent of an alluring cologne.

"You're leaving," he murmured against her lips.

"I am," she confirmed breathlessly. "But I'm here now. I'm here tonight." They were here together, and right now she wanted more. More of him. More of that adrenaline spiking inside of her. She backed him up against the refrigerator, her hands working their way under the shirt he'd put back on.

Aiden pulled back from the kiss, letting his head rest against the stainless steel while he closed his eyes. "I meant what I said earlier," he uttered. "You came at the perfect time to bring back the magic. But I'll take you home right now if you want me to."

She stood on her tiptoes and brought her lips to his ear. "I don't want to go home." She wanted to be fully immersed in the chemistry between them, even if it was only for one night.

"I don't want you to go home." Aiden brushed his lips against hers, teasing. "I want you here. With me. All night."

"That's good." She buckled her hands behind his neck. "Because I'd rather not go back out in that storm." She kissed him again, letting go of all rational thought. It had been too long since she'd given herself to passion. But maybe that was because she'd never felt passion as strong as this.

Aiden's hands went to her hips, dancing her through the kitchen into the living room, where the fire's light still glowed.

Seeing the Christmas decorations still scattered around the room reminded her of their mission. "This is your sister's house."

"Yeah, but I'm housesitting, remember?" He took her hand and tugged her down the hallway. "And the guest room is pretty nice."

"Can't wait to see it." Warmth swelled, carrying her through the door. This time there would be no interruptions, no distractions, no reason to hold back anymore. "The room is nice..." With a large king-size bed and luxurious mountain lodge–themed linens. She turned back to Aiden. "But I'm more interested in you."

"You're sure about this?" He pulled her to him, threading their fingers together, staring into her eyes.

She answered him with a wet, hot kiss.

Aiden groaned against her lips and moved his hands to her backside, lifting her against him. She wrapped her legs around his waist, and traced her lips down his neck, sucking and licking.

This time the man whimpered helplessly. "I need you. I don't think I've ever needed anyone as much as I need you."

"Yes" was all she could manage in response. Her own need was pulsing now too—in every erotic zone in her body. She hadn't even realized how much she wanted him until he touched her.

Aiden carried her to the bed and gently laid her down. He hovered over her and, with his sharp focus, he undressed her, painstakingly slowly, first pulling her sweater up and over her head and then kissing along the lace edge of her bra before easing one hand under her to unclasp it. "What're you doing to me, Kyra?" he breathed against her skin in a tortured murmur.

"I'm not sure..." She wasn't sure where any of this had come from—the fire in her, the intensity. She only knew that, as Aiden moved his mouth over her breasts, she wanted him more than she'd wanted anything ever. "Your shirt..." She pushed him up so she could work on the buttons, so there would be nothing between them, so she could feel his skin against hers.

Aiden impatiently helped and then shrugged the shirt off with a wince.

"Your shoulder." Kyra ran her fingertips over the bruising. He hadn't complained, but it had to be sore.

"Forget my shoulder." He rolled onto his back next to her and moved her on top of him so she was straddling his waist again. "I can't feel anything except for you. And I want more. I want all of you."

"So impatient," she teased, unclipping the belt buckle on his jeans. She was one to talk. Her hands fumbled with the button fly until she'd gotten them all undone, and then she scooted backward as she worked his pants and boxers down his hips. When her feet found the floor, she pulled his jeans the rest of the way off and stood over him, admiring every inch of his body—every muscle, every tattoo, every scar. There were many scars—especially across his right rib cage.

Aiden sat up, his breathing heavy. He tugged the waistband of her jeans to move her closer and then easily undid the button before pulling her pants down to her ankles. She stepped out of them, taking her time to give him a proper view of her G-string.

"My God, you're sexy." He hooked his fingers into the straps of her underwear and pulled them down, caressing her thighs on the way.

The smoldering in his eyes took away every doubt about her body, every concern over the imperfections. She'd never stood so freely in front of anyone, letting him see all of her—wanting him to see all of her. Kyra eased onto his lap again, her knees resting on the mattress on either side of him. She pressed her fingers against the largest scar right beneath his ribs.

"Shrapnel."

The word was a gift. An offering.

She pushed on his shoulders, prompting him to lie down, and then she kissed that scar. She kissed all of his scars, wishing she could take away the internalized pain that went with them.

Aiden's hands smoothed through her hair while her lips moved from one damaged place to the next, working lower and lower down his abdominals. In that moment, her heart beat for him, only for him, and all she wanted was to make him feel good. Her feet found the floor again, and she hovered over him, taking him fully into her mouth.

A sharp intake of breath shuddered through Aiden's body. His hands gripped the blanket next to him in tight fists.

She swirled her tongue and sucked in long strokes, spurred on by the moans and fast breaths stuttering through his lips. Giving him pleasure increased the pressure between her legs, making her tingle with anticipation.

"Come here." Aiden roughly reached for her, pulling her over him, and then rolled so he was on top. He started kissing her at the neck, scorching each spot he touched, and then moved down lower to her breasts.

His tongue was so warm and so wet, leaving a mark on every spot it touched. Now Kyra was the one moaning—small, uncontrollable sounds escaping her lips.

"You taste good," he murmured, trailing his tongue down low on her stomach while his hands parted her legs. "Better than anything I've ever tasted."

Kyra couldn't respond because his tongue found that spot, the one that made her arch her back and cry out. "Aiden." She gasped and panted. "God."

"You like that?" He pushed his tongue into her spot again and again, making her hips rock.

"Yes." Had she said the word? She couldn't tell. The pressure between her legs drove her to the edge, but she fought it back. "Wait." She wanted him to go over the edge with her... they had to go together.

"Let go," he commanded her, still licking and sucking. "I can make you come again."

Her body took over, making the decision for her. Aiden's tongue broke her apart, shattering her vision into a million glittery pieces, and she had no control over her own cries or the convulsions that shook the deepest parts of her.

Out of breath and boneless, Kyra tried to pull him over her, but she had no strength left. Thankfully Aiden took the hint and moved himself, first getting up to put on a condom and then easing his body over hers.

"I want you inside of me," she whispered, moving her legs apart. "Please, Aiden." She had to feel their bodies connected.

"Tell me what you like." He tenderly kissed her collar bone and pushed into her, bringing another surge of energy. She gasped louder.

"I like you." Her breathing had gone choppy again. "I like how you make me feel." Still strong and independent but also defenseless at the same time.

"I like you too," he whispered in her ear.

Kyra placed her hands on his hips and urged him deeper, rising slightly to meet his thrusts. Aiden gently pushed the hair back from her eyes and held her gaze while they moved together faster, harder. She focused on the sensations he drove into her, the feel of his warm skin, the force of his breaths coming as fast as hers. Her body had never responded so easily to someone, so freely. Aiden somehow did what he promised, brought her to the edge again. Her hands clawed at his back. "I can't wait." But she didn't want this to end, either…

"Let go," he said softly. "And I will too."

He hadn't even finished speaking when Kyra cried out again, the pleasure rocking through her.

Aiden's body strained and he convulsed over her with a husky, growling moan, holding her tightly to him. His body relaxed over hers, that powerful chest rising and falling with satiated breaths. He kissed her shoulder and rolled to his side, facing her, gazing into her eyes again.

Kyra wrapped her arms around him, holding him there, not ready for this night to end.

CHAPTER SIXTEEN

Aiden woke in a cold sweat, the gunfire still echoing in his ears. No. There was no gunfire here. No Jace lying on the ground. It had only been a dream.

And yet every time he closed his eyes, he could still see his hands covered in his best friend's blood. He'd tried to stop the bleeding. He'd tried. But there was too much. Jace's blood had covered everything. It still covered everything…

The tightening in his chest made his lungs heave. *Stop.* But the truth was he could never stop the images. They came even more frequently when he found fleeting moments of happiness—a reminder that he could never be fully happy again. Not without feeling torn by the past.

He closed his eyes again and, feeling Kyra's weight against him, turned on his side to move closer to her, to cradle her back against his chest and drape his arm over her so he could lie with her until his heart settled.

Instead of settling, his pulse continued to race, flooding

him with adrenaline, with the same panic he'd felt in his best friend's last moments. Aiden held his breath to stave off the pain and focused on Kyra instead. Jesus, she was gorgeous. And good. And compassionate. The sun peeked in through the curtains, letting in enough light that he could see the sheen on her golden hair, the faint freckles around her nose. He knew he couldn't hold on to her for very long, but he couldn't let go. Not yet. He didn't deserve her. He didn't deserve to lie here with this woman in his arms, but he could pretend. He was willing to pretend. That she wasn't leaving for a different continent, that he wasn't too haunted to give his heart to someone, that maybe he could have dreams of his own.

"Mmm." Kyra pulled his arm tighter around her and shimmied her body all the way up against his. "'Morning."

Aiden attempted to smile, but the dream still tainted his thoughts. "'Morning." Why couldn't the morning be good? Why couldn't he forget? He wanted to forget...

"What's wrong?" Kyra propped herself up and peered at his face with sleepy innocence.

"Nothing." He steered his gaze away from hers. "You're beautiful," he whispered into her hair. His hand caressed her hip, the softness of her curves and skin stirring a powerful physical craving that silenced the turmoil swirling in his brain.

"Mmmm." Her hand wandered too, finding his thigh and then moving higher to stroke him.

"Ahhh." No matter how hard he tried, he couldn't stay silent when she touched him like this. He couldn't stay silent and he sure as hell couldn't stay still.

Still lying on his side, Aiden guided Kyra's top leg

open, draping it over his. In this position, his fingers had complete access to her, rubbing against the places he already knew would make her moan. He reached his other arm under and around her so he could caress her breast at the same time.

"More," Kyra begged, already panting.

He released her for only a second so he could reach for the condoms he'd thrown on the nightstand last night and then put one on before pressing up behind her again. Kyra draped her leg back over him and, using her hand, she guided him into her to bring them together.

He called on every ounce of strength he could muster to keep his hips still and propped himself up on his elbow so he could kiss the places he could reach—her shoulder, her neck, her earlobe. Then he smoothed his hand up and over her hip, teasing her with a brush to the inner thighs before he found her clit again.

"Oh. Ohhhhhh." Kyra started to move her hips first as though she couldn't keep still. And thank God, because he couldn't either. Need pulsated though him, heightening the sensations as Kyra met his thrusts.

Hold on. He had to hold on.

"I like…making you feel good," Kyra said between gasps.

"You make me feel so good," Aiden told her, holding his finger in that one arousing spot.

"Aiden," she whimpered, tightening around him.

There was nothing like watching Kyra climax. Seeing her eyes close and her mouth open to cry out and her body arch to welcome him.

"What're you doing to me, Kyra Fowler?" he asked helplessly as he came into her, convulsing until he was spent, until he became a heap beside her. She was making him forget. At least for now. At least until the dreams came again...

"I don't know what I'm doing." Kyra rolled on her side to face him, a soft smile on her kissable lips. "But whatever it is, I like—"

The doorbell rang.

The doorbell?

The doorbell!

"Oh, my God!" Kyra shot straight up. "Aiden! What time is it?"

He squinted at the clock across the room. "Ten minutes until nine."

"No!" The woman scrambled and sent the bedcovers flying. "I texted everyone and told them to be here at nine to help decorate." She dashed in the direction of the bathroom and then back to the bed in a full panic.

"What? Nine?" Adrenaline surged, pushing him off the bed. She'd neglected to tell him they were going to have a Star Valley Springs–style wake-up call. "Okay. Okay. Everything'll be fine." Except for the fact that half the town likely stood out on Tess's front porch right now expecting him to be here alone. "You take your time getting dressed and I'll answer the door." After he cleaned himself up real quick.

The doorbell rang again, and he rushed into the bathroom, washing up in record time before throwing on the clothes he'd worn last night.

"I can't believe this. I can't believe they're all going to know." Kyra darted around collecting her clothes.

"Who cares if they know?" He clasped her hand in his and drew her to him. "Last night was worth me never hearing the end of it from Silas and Thatch." They wouldn't let him forget this. But he wouldn't want to anyway.

"That's true." She kissed him, but the doorbell rang again.

"Go, go, go." She sent him out the door with a pat on the butt and then slammed it shut.

Aiden careened down the hallway and tried to smooth out his hair before pulling the door open.

Sure enough, it seemed everyone had arrived a few minutes early. Minnie and Doris and Nelly were peering in through the living room window. Silas and Thatch were standing with Lyric at the bottom of the steps. "Hey, guys," he said casually. "Thanks for coming."

"Were you still sleeping?" Silas marched up the porch steps. "At nine o'clock?"

"Uh, yeah." He did his best not to look too guilty. "We were up pretty late sorting out some old decorations from the barn."

"We? As in you *and* Kyra were up late? Together?" Minnie shuffled to the front door and tried to peer behind him.

"Uh, yeah..." He had to play this cool, so they didn't see through him. "She didn't want to drive home in that storm so she slept in the guest room and I slept on the couch. I think she's still sleeping, actually. I haven't seen her yet this morning."

Thatch's and Silas's amused expressions both called bullshit, but thankfully his friends didn't make any off-color comments in the presence of the Ladies. They knew better.

"We brought pastries!" Doris held up a basket in her hands.

"And coffee from the café," Nelly added, holding up the cardboard coffee takeout container. "No offense, but we didn't think you'd have breakfast ready for everyone."

"No offense taken." He stepped aside so the Ladies could do their thing and set up in the kitchen. "I hadn't even thought to provide breakfast, but as usual your thoughtfulness came through."

The compliment made all three of the ladies beam. "You're a charmer." Minnie pointed at him on her way past. "It's a wonder Kyra managed to stay in the guest room all night with you right outside the door on the couch."

Yes, that was a wonder.

"More people are on the way." Lyric stepped inside and stomped the snow off her boots. "Wait until you see how many decorations we've got to create a magical Christmas wonderland for the girls. It's going to be epic."

"I can't wait." He was more excited to see the girls' expressions when they drove in from the airport tomorrow night than he'd ever been for Christmas itself.

Seeing that Silas and Thatch still hovered just outside the front door, targeting him with questioning stares, Aiden decided to follow Lyric into the kitchen. He couldn't deal with those two right now. He'd never been able to lie to them.

"Here are the plates." Minnie started to unpack a cloth grocery bag. "And cups for the coffee too."

"You three always think of everything." Aiden found some napkins and laid them out.

"Well, I'm starving." Silas took a plate and a pastry, smirking at Aiden as he passed by. "What about you, bro? Did you work up an appetite organizing all of those Christmas decorations last night?"

"Yeah," Thatch added. "I bet you're *starving* this morning."

Lyric hid her laugh behind a napkin while Aiden tried to silently threaten them with his eyes.

"Now what is so funny?" Doris demanded. "I don't understand. Why would he have worked up an appetite organizing Christmas decorations?"

"They're giving me a hard time," Aiden told her. He directed a glare over the woman's shoulder to shut up Dumb and Dumber. "They always give me a hard time."

Silas's wide grin made Aiden brace himself.

Uh-oh.

"I'll bet last night was a real *hard* time—"

"Good morning." Kyra walked in, and Silas instantly snapped his trap shut. Good thing or Aiden would've shut it for him.

"Sorry I wasn't ready when you all got here. I'm moving slowly this morning." A pinkish hue lit up her cheeks. "I didn't sleep great on the couch. It was pretty lumpy."

"Oh!" Doris's eyes went wide, and Minnie snickered from behind her napkin.

"You slept on the couch?" Nelly was the only one who looked confused. Everyone else in the room was grinning from ear to ear. "I thought Aiden slept on the couch."

Kyra's mouth dropped open in a horrified expression, but Minnie covered for them.

"No, no, dear." The woman clucked, coming alongside Nelly. "You must've heard wrong. Aiden definitely said Kyra slept on the couch."

"Oh my. This darn hearing aid." Nelly shook her head and fiddled with the hardware behind her ear.

Everyone else nodded along with Minnie, most likely to protect Kyra from the fact that they all knew the truth.

Aiden made a mental note to send the woman flowers later.

"Now everyone eat." Minnie ushered Kyra to the pastries and coffee. "We've got a lot of work to do today. There'll be no working tomorrow. Only feasting during our Thanksgiving Day celebration at the café." She poured Kyra a mug of coffee. "You're planning to come, I hope."

"Um, yes. I think I should be there." She peeked at Aiden, and he smiled back at her. Maybe they could lounge in bed longer tomorrow morning and then go to the feast together…

He shook off the thought. They'd said one night. Kyra was leaving in a month. And he didn't want to stand in the way of her dreams. He couldn't let himself forget that.

"I was also thinking we should have a surprise party here tomorrow night." Kyra sat at the table with Lyric. "Wouldn't it be fun if we were all here when the girls got home?"

"I love that idea." Aiden had to stop himself from walking over to caress her shoulders. It would be too easy for him to touch her now after they'd broken down every barrier between them. It would be too easy to keep touching her and forget where he stood. He was only temporary in her life. Nothing between them could be permanent. "We could break Kenny's old sleigh out of the barn and do horse-drawn sleigh rides."

"Oh, yes. This town needs another party! We should have as many parties as we can before Kyra leaves."

Minnie handed plates to Nelly and Doris, seeming not to notice the collective pause in the room.

Aiden met Silas's eyes, and he could hear his friend's thoughts. They'd been reading each other under the worst of circumstances for years. *You can stop her from leaving*, Silas's expression seemed to say. And maybe Aiden could. But he wouldn't.

"We'll miss you so much, dear," Nelly murmured glumly.

"But we're excited for your next adventure," Lyric insisted, prodding the rest of the group to agree with a nod.

"I'll miss you all too." Kyra looked at him, her cheeks flaming red, and she went wide-eyed like she was afraid someone would discover their secret. Their friends might've found out they'd spent the night together, but no one else could possibly understand what had happened between them last night. Aiden didn't even know how to explain it.

All he knew was when he looked into the woman's eyes, something inside of him shifted. Kyra shined a light into his darkness. She made him wish he could be a different man—healed and whole again so he could move Heaven and earth to make her happy.

Aiden snuck into the barn, where Kyra was fashioning evergreen branches into wreaths. Alone. He finally had her alone. He'd had his eyes on her all morning while they'd worked, but this was the first time he'd managed to talk to her. "Hey."

Kyra whirled. "You scared me." Her cheeks were bright from the cold, and she looked extra lovely in the red beanie she wore on her head.

"Sorry." He tried to look apologetic. "I've been dying to do this all morning." After a quick glance at the door he pulled her in for a long, extra-sensual kiss. Why couldn't one night turn into two? Or three? He knew she'd have to leave eventually, but he had a hard time remembering that when he looked at her.

Kyra leaned into him, eagerly kissing him back. "Do you really think we fooled them all this morning?" Hopefulness widened her eyes.

"Not a chance." But he didn't care that everyone knew they'd spent the night together. He didn't care how obvious his feelings were for her. "Well, except for Nelly. I don't think she has a clue."

Kyra giggled. "Sweet Nelly. I'm glad we didn't taint her innocence."

"Hey, you two." Silas strode into the barn, and Kyra lurched away from Aiden.

"Hi!" Her voice was overly shrill.

"Do you mind?" Aiden had no problem directing his friend right back outside. "We were talking."

"I'm only here on assignment from Minnie." His friend raised his hands and took a step back. "She sent me to find out if the wreaths are ready to hang on the porch."

"Yep. They're all done. In fact, I'll take them to her right away." Kyra gathered up the evergreen decorations in her arms and then got out of there, but not before Aiden saw the fierce blush on her cheeks. Damn. Now he'd probably have to wait three more hours before he could get her alone again.

"You're taking this Operation Save Star Valley Springs much farther than I thought you would." Silas crossed his arms and gave Aiden a silent interrogation.

"What's that supposed to mean?" He stared his friend down. Out of the three of them, he and Silas had always sparred the most.

"I thought you said you weren't going to seduce her."

"I'm not." Defensiveness churned his gut. "I mean . . . I didn't intend for anything to happen between us last night." He hadn't meant to sleep with her, but he hadn't been able to stop himself either. "She's leaving. She's already made the decision. She'll sell all of her holdings in Star Valley Springs and move to London."

The information seemed to surprise Silas. "You said you wouldn't let that happen. What about Operation Save Star Valley Springs? What about convincing her to keep Kenny's properties?"

That was before he'd known her. Now that he knew what London meant to her, he couldn't take it away from her. "I can't stop her." He had to let her go. That was the best thing for Kyra. And it was the best thing for him too.

"You can't stop her or you won't stop her?" Silas pressed. "Come on, man. Don't deny that you're falling in love with her. I can see it all over you. You've never looked at any woman like that."

His shoulders, which had been light and unburdened earlier, turned to lead. "You know why I can't be with her." Silas and Thatch carried the burden of their pasts with them the same way he did. Look at their track records for relationships. One-night stands and no commitments. They suffered from the same afflictions as he did. Regret. Guilt. You couldn't bring those things into a relationship and expect it to work.

"But you being with her might convince her to stay

here," Silas argued. "Doesn't that matter? What if you could get out of your own head and give her a reason to stay?"

His head wasn't the problem. "She would never be first." Jace would always be first in his life. Jace's family would always be first. That was the way it had to be. "Kyra deserves more than that." She deserved more than him. When he was with her—when he was holding her and kissing her—he could pretend, but he couldn't pretend now with Silas.

"So whatever this is between you two, you're just going to walk away?"

The question hung heavy in the air between them. Aiden couldn't answer him. He didn't have an answer. He couldn't stand the thought of Kyra leaving, and he couldn't ask her to stay when he had nothing to offer.

"What if this is your shot to have something real?" An uncharacteristic desperation filled the words. It almost sounded like his friend was grasping at hope too. "Don't you think something as good as what could be between you and Kyra would be enough to wipe out all the shit we've been through? Maybe love like that could save you, man. Maybe it could save me if I found it too."

That was too much of a burden to put on someone he cared about. "I can't ask her to save me."

Not even if it meant saving this town.

CHAPTER SEVENTEEN

"This is quite the work of art." Lyric joined Kyra in the middle of the driveway, where she'd stood for the last five minutes, assessing the day's efforts.

Almost every inch of Tess's ranch house had been covered in lights—a display to rival Chevy Chase's in *Christmas Vacation.* All around the house, they'd placed the lawn ornaments people in town had brought with them for the cause—including two massive blow-up snow globes powered by a generator, a Christmas train that actually ran back and forth on tracks, a cluster of lighted deer and other woodland creatures near the garage, the Star Wars characters lined up in front of the porch, miniature Christmas trees lining the driveway, and a snowman family by the mailbox. At the entrance to the driveway, Aiden, Silas, and Thatch had fashioned an arched tunnel of blinking lights that were strung from tree to tree.

"It's almost perfect." But there was one thing she needed to change. Kyra plowed through the snow to get to the front porch. "Can you help me move these Yoda lights to the outside of the porch?" Louie had accidentally hung them on the inside, and they were hardly visible.

"Of course." Lyric retrieved the stepladder from its position up against the house, and they worked together to move the strands.

"Sounds like things are going well for Santa and his helpers up on the roof," her friend joked.

"I'm glad someone is up there with Aiden this time." He and Silas and Thatch were putting on the finishing touch—Santa in his sleigh and nine reindeer statues secured with tethers. Everyone else had already gone home for the night, but she wouldn't let the man's friends leave until they were done supervising his roof work. His shoulder didn't seem to bother him too much, but they didn't need him taking any more tumbles.

Kyra finished working on the last strand of lights and then climbed down the ladder.

"Are we still on for tonight?" Lyric asked watching her closely.

Aiden had been right. Everyone totally knew they'd spent the night together. They shouldn't have even bothered trying to pretend. They might as well have answered the door together, still naked and wrapped up in the guest room comforter. "Tonight?" She tried to remember what day it was—a difficult thing to do since Aiden had turned her world upside down.

"The Christmas movie marathon. Remember?" Her friend nudged her gently in the ribs. "We were going to get takeout from the café and watch the classics all night?"

"That's right!" Kyra folded up the stepladder, overwhelmed once again with gratitude that she had gotten her best friend back. "Of course we're still on for tonight."

"Are you sure you don't have something more important to do?" Lyric asked with feigned innocence. "Because we can take a rain check. I don't want to stand in the way of any secret rendezvous with a certain cowboy."

"I'm sure." As much as she'd enjoyed her night with Aiden, she wouldn't give up the opportunity to spend as much time with Lyric as she could before she left for London. Heaviness pressed against her heart, but she wouldn't let herself think about leaving right now. "I've been looking forward to our movie night."

Watching movies and eating snacks together had been one of their favorite activities back in the day. Until she'd reconnected with Lyric, Kyra hadn't realized how much she'd missed having someone to talk to, to laugh with, to just be herself with. "Why don't you come over around seven?" That would give them an hour to finish up here... and maybe give her a few minutes alone with Aiden too.

"Sounds like a plan." Lyric tilted her head to the side and squinted at her apologetically. "You know we're going to have to talk about what happened with you and Aiden last night, right?" she whispered. "I have many questions."

"I doubt I have the answers." Kyra peeked around the house to make sure Aiden wasn't coming down the ladder and eavesdropping. "Honestly, it's like my heart completely takes over my logical brain when I'm with him. One minute we were drinking hot chocolate and the next I was pushing him up against the refrigerator to kiss him." She'd never been so bold with a man. But then again, she'd never wanted any of the guys she'd dated in quite the same way she wanted Aiden.

"In case you weren't aware, that's a good sign," her friend assured her. "You want to be with someone who makes you feel bold and safe instead of someone who makes you weak and insecure. Trust me." Lyric's gaze fell to the ground only for a brief second, but it was enough to make Kyra wonder about her dating history. Had she been with a man who'd made her feel weak and insecure? They would have a lot to talk about later...

"Ready for the big reveal, you two?" Aiden climbed down the ladder, followed by Thatch and Silas.

"We're ready." Kyra shivered but it wasn't from the cold. She couldn't get within five feet of this man without every part of her quivering. He always brought warmth flooding through her, carrying away her doubts and hesitations. He made her feel like she could tell him anything and he would hear beyond her words.

"Silas, Thatch, to the electrical box." Aiden dramatically pointed to the complicated-looking panel they'd set up earlier.

"Come on." He took Kyra's hand and led her away from the house, beckoning Lyric to come too. "We have to stand back to get the full effect."

They stopped halfway down the drive, but Aiden didn't let go of her hand. He squeezed it tightly in his while he counted down. "Five, four, three, two, one..."

Right on cue, Silas and Thatch turned on the lights.

"Wow," Kyra breathed, taking in all of the different colors flickering against the snow. Even though it wasn't fully dark, the house came to life with Christmas magic.

"I'm not sure where to look first," Lyric mused, panning her head from side to side.

"Yeah, it's a little busy." Aiden grinned. "But I think Morgan and Willow are gonna like it."

"Morgan and Willow are going to *love* this." Kyra was eager to see the looks on the girls' faces when they came home to this wonderland.

"This will be the best display in all of Star Valley, that's for sure." Lyric took a few pictures on her phone. "I can't wait to see how they react when they get home tomorrow."

"We'll have the camera rolling," Thatch said. "But man, after all that work, I could use a beer at the café. Who's in?"

"I'd love a beer." Lyric pulled her car keys out of her pocket.

"Sounds perfect. I'm in too." Silas looked to Kyra and Aiden.

"I've still gotta feed the animals tonight," Aiden said, squeezing her hand again. "Next time."

"I'll stay and help and then I'll meet you at my house," Kyra told Lyric. Then she quickly amended her mistake. "I mean at my dad's house." She couldn't get too attached to any of this—the house, the town, her new friends. Her gaze found Aiden, and she knew it was too late. Every day she told herself she had to keep her eyes on the prize—London. Moving had to be her singular focus. But even after overanalyzing the three developers' proposals for her father's various properties, she still hadn't committed to a sale. Mr. Podgurski had told her to take her time, but he'd been checking in with her every other day.

"See you at seven. Don't be late." Her friend offered

up a snarky little wave and then tromped to her car with Silas and Thatch following behind.

"You're too busy to hang out tonight?" Aiden turned her to him and settled his hands on her hips.

"I am, actually." Even with this man tempting her the way he did. "Lyric and I are doing a girls' night in." And she needed that time with her friend. "Even though we were apart for so long it feels like I've known her my whole life."

"Everyone should have a friend like that." He brushed a fleeting kiss across her lips. "I'll miss you." His hands fell away from her. "But I guess it's better that you're busy."

Better? What did he mean by better? "I don't understand." She searched his eyes but he looked away. "Don't you want to spend the night with me again?" Because the man had her heart revving simply by putting his hands on her hips.

"I do. I would love to spend the night with you again. And again. And again." He looked at her, but sadness seemed to weight his gaze. "You're leaving."

"Not for a month," she reminded him. "That's over thirty days from now. We could have a lot of fun in thirty days. Let's focus on that." It used to be that looking toward the future had gotten her through—after her dad left, when her mom got sick. She'd learned how to focus on what would come next so she could remember the pain wouldn't last forever.

But for the next thirty days, she needed to take Lyric's advice and learn how to focus on the present.

* * *

When Kyra had typed *easiest Thanksgiving dishes to make* in her search engine, mashed potatoes had topped the list, but it appeared the internet had lied yet again.

She'd followed the directions perfectly, and all she had to show for her labor was a pot of messy, lumpy, ugly half-mashed potatoes that looked nothing like the creamy dish in the picture. She sucked at cooking. She'd always sucked at cooking, but she'd still wanted to contribute something to the big feast at the café. Lyric had made a pumpkin-spice cheesecake, the showoff. Silas was apparently bringing his famous oven-roasted parmesan green beans. Rumor had it that overachiever Thatch had made cornbread from scratch, and Aiden had mentioned on the text he'd sent last night that he was making his grandmother's famous rosemary stuffing. He had proceeded to send her a picture of himself wearing only an apron and nothing else, which she'd saved to her phone.

Kyra stabbed the potato masher into the pot again, but she couldn't get rid of the lumps. These people took their Thanksgiving meal seriously, and all she had to add to the table was this sorry excuse for potatoes.

The doorbell rang, and she checked the clock on the stove. *Crap.* Aiden was fifteen minutes early to pick her up. Sighing out a morningful of frustration, Kyra hurried to answer it. "I hope no one wants mashed potatoes, because I'm not bringing them," she said by way of greeting.

"Uh-oh. What happened?" The man stepped inside, smelling as good as the forest after a rainstorm. She liked his dark jeans and his rust-colored sweater, though she preferred seeing him wear the apron.

"I have no idea what happened." Kyra stormed back into

the kitchen, humiliation prickling her neck. Who couldn't make mashed potatoes correctly? She'd wanted to make something people would enjoy...not something people would be secretly dumping in the trash after dinner.

"They aren't right. They're lumpy and they're way too thick even though I added a half cup of milk like the recipe said." She might as well admit the truth. "I've never made mashed potatoes." She'd never made anything that didn't come already cooked or in a box, truthfully. Her mother had worked long hours, so they'd done a lot of frozen meals.

"You've never made mashed potatoes?" Aiden peered into the pot and made a face.

"No." Kyra crossed her arms and leaned against the counter. "My mom and I didn't do this. We didn't host huge celebrations with tons of people. We were on our own, so we went out most of the time. My childhood wasn't like everyone else's with a grandma who'd wake up before dawn on holidays to roll out the pie crusts." She'd always envied the kids who came back to school the Monday after Thanksgiving with tales of family gatherings and huge turkeys and a dessert table that offered bottomless pumpkin pie. "I don't think I want to go." She couldn't face these people.

Aiden came for her, his arms outstretched. "You're not on your own anymore." He pulled her against him, instantly calming her inner storm. "And the potatoes are fine. They're not done, that's all. I can help you finish them."

"Really?" She peered up at his face to see if he was serious.

"Sure." He planted a kiss on her lips and released her.

"We're going to need the milk, butter, and cream cheese from the refrigerator stat."

"All right." Kyra collected the items from the refrigerator and brought them to the counter next to the stove.

Aiden rolled up his sleeves and turned on the burner under the pot. "They need to cook a bit more, and the recipes never tell you this, but you have to almost double the butter and milk the recipe calls for to make them creamy." He added a generous helping of each ingredient to the pot.

"So you're like a professional mashed-potato maker, then," she teased, watching him work.

"Pretty much." Aiden grabbed the masher and started to stir. "I always made them for the guys in my platoon. The trick is to bake them after you mash them too." He used the masher to break up the lumps while the potatoes simmered on the stove. "See? They're smoothing out already."

"Amazing." Kyra found herself smiling, all of her earlier frustration a distant memory. "You're amazing." Seriously. An ex–Navy SEAL who loved kids and cooked and looked damn good in an apron.

"I have flaws. Trust me." His smile had evened out. "I have plenty of flaws."

"That's good, because so do I." She nudged her shoulder against his. "And I'm not looking for perfection."

Aiden set down the masher and fully faced her. "What are you looking for?" he asked quietly.

She'd thought she'd known. She'd thought she had her whole future lined up, but the doubts kept creeping in. She'd spent a half hour staring at the paperwork from the hospital in London earlier, and she hadn't been able to sign anything. "I think I'm still figuring out what I'm looking for."

Aiden nodded, giving her space before speaking. "Well, you know you'll always have a place here. No matter where you go. Star Valley can be a place you come back to."

"Maybe." But living in London would make visiting difficult. Kyra blew out a sigh. She was confused, that was all. The last few days had been eventful, to say the least. "I mean, sure. I'll come back and visit sometimes." Maybe once a year or every other. She smiled at him to cover her doubts. *Live in the moment.* "We should finish the potatoes and get going."

"Right. The potatoes." Aiden turned back to the stove and finished mashing the potatoes. He opened a cabinet and found a casserole dish. "This is when the real magic happens." Using a spatula, he smoothed the potatoes in the dish and then put on a pair of oven mitts before popping the food into the oven. "We'll broil them for a few minutes and then we'll be ready to go."

A few minutes, huh? Kyra stood back, admiring him. "Who would've thought oven mitts could be so sexy on a man?"

"You like them?" He kept them on and reached for her, putting his hands on her hips to draw her close. "I missed you last night." He brushed a kiss across her lips.

"I missed you too," she whispered in his ear. "Especially after I got that apron picture."

"I'm happy to put it on for you anytime." He frowned. "Actually, scratch that. Tess is getting home tonight, and she probably wouldn't appreciate me wearing her apron that way."

Kyra loved how he always made her laugh. "Probably not."

He pulled her closer. "But we can hang out after the big Christmas display reveal tonight. If you want."

"I want." She pressed her lips to his. "I really want." Kissing him made her want everything.

The timer on the oven dinged. "I guess that's our cue." It took every ounce of willpower Kyra had to tear herself away from the man. "We'd better head over to the café before everyone gets the idea that we're in bed again."

"Yeah, about that." Aiden opened the oven. "For future reference, I'm the one who would be sleeping on the couch, because I'm a gentleman like that."

"You were quite the gentleman that night." She pinched his butt as he bent over to pull the potatoes out of the oven.

"You haven't seen anything yet." He set down the dish and then whirled to capture her in his arms, dipping her low and kissing her while they both laughed.

Had she ever had this much fun with a man?

Aiden set her back upright. "Stay tuned for more of my moves later tonight."

"Can't wait." Kyra got out some towels and wrapped them around the casserole dish. The man hadn't been kidding. The potatoes now looked perfect. "I can't wait to show these off." Kyra led the way out the door, and they drove to the café in Aiden's truck.

"I think we're the last ones here," she commented, scanning the full parking lot. "How many people are coming?"

"This year I think it's thirty-four." He retrieved the potatoes and stuffing from the seat behind them and pushed open the door. “Last year we had fifty. Louie and Minnie open the celebration up to anyone in town who isn’t traveling or having a bunch of family and friends over. Since Tess and the girls go visit their other side of the family, I come every year.”

“How fun.” She held the door to the café open for him and then stepped inside. “Wow.” All the tables in the restaurant had been pushed together, and they’d been set with beautiful china plates and fancy silverware and crystal goblets. Pumpkins and squash and colorful foliage were interspersed at the center of the tables, dressing them up with the beauty of fall.

“Told you it was a big deal.” Aiden brought the food to the bar and shook hands with Silas and Thatch.

“Kyra, we’re so happy you came.” Minnie rushed out from the kitchen and hugged her tightly. “I caught a glimpse of your mashed potatoes. They look divine!”

“I know I can’t wait to try them.” Aiden winked at her from the bar.

“Thank you for having me. Aiden and I made the potatoes together.” She had to give the man credit. He’d rescued her again. “This place looks absolutely incredible.” The crowd milled around the tables, drinking wine while they chatted and laughed. Each face seemed familiar, though Kyra didn’t know everyone’s name.

“It’s one of our favorite days of the year.” Minnie waved her husband over. “Say hi to Kyra, doll. It’s her first Thanksgiving in Star Valley Springs.”

Louie handed Aiden a beer and then tipped his cowboy hat to her. “Happy Thanksgiving, ma’am.”

“Thanks. Happy Thanksgiving to you too.” She’d never talked to Louie much, only receiving a polite hello when she came by the café, and she wasn't sure what to make of the man. Minnie was warm and friendly, but her husband was hard to read. "This has to be the best Thanksgiving celebration I've ever been to." In reality it was the only true Thanksgiving feast she'd ever been to.

"Glad you like it." Louie put his arm around his wife.

"It's a yearly tradition," the woman said proudly. "But I suppose you won't be here next year. We're going to miss you when you go off to London."

"I'm trying not to think about that now." But leaving was all she'd thought about last night after Lyric had gone home. Kyra had no one in London. Back in Florida, when she'd been making plans for her future, having no one hadn't mattered. It wouldn't have been any different than her life back in Fort Myers.

"Have you talked to any developers yet?" Louie asked grimly.

"Oh. Um, no. Not directly." But she would have to choose one of those proposals sitting in her in-box sooner rather than later. "I wanted to wait until all of the projects were farther along."

"We're planning to get the gazebo done next week." Aiden joined them. "And the week after, it shouldn't be any trouble to re-drywall the antique store."

"Right." She tried to smile. "That's great." Three days ago she'd been upset that the man hadn't touched the gazebo, but now she wouldn't mind if he took his time. "I guess I should focus on preparing for the sale, then."

"Just don't let those developers ruin this town," Louie muttered. "You know what'll happen when those guys move in."

"Now, Lou." Minnie grabbed her husband's arm.

"I don't know what'll happen, actually." Kyra looked from Minnie to Aiden to Louie again. "I mean, I'm assuming they'll build new homes and bring in some new businesses." At least that's what each of the proposals outlined. "But that's good, right? More businesses will attract more tourists who'll eat at the café and stay at the hotel."

"Yeah and higher taxes and more traffic," the man grumbled. "Development'll change this community, you mark my words. When those big resorts move in here, all of us little guys'll have to move out. That's the way it works. A buddy of mine used to own an old hotel on the outskirts of Jackson, and those big fancy resorts ran him right out of business."

"All right, now." Minnie patted her husband's shoulder. "That's enough. You've said your piece. Today is all about focusing on what we're grateful for." The woman prodded her husband away. "I think it's time to cut the turkey."

"I don't understand." Kyra pulled Aiden to a quiet corner. "Why didn't you tell me everyone thinks the developers will ruin this town?" Louie clearly had plenty to say on the subject, and yet this was the first she'd heard of it.

"I didn't want to influence your decision," he said. "You should be free to go to London and chase your dreams."

But what would her dreams cost Minnie and Louie? What would her dreams cost all of the other small local businesses? "I need the money." To start a new life, to move forward. She was still paying off her school debts as it was.

"I know you do." He held her hand. "This isn't your

problem, Kyra. Yes, things will change, but we'll manage. Your dad would've wanted you to use what he gave you to live your best life."

Kyra scanned the faces gathered around the giant table. This town had welcomed her into their community, even though they knew she didn't plan to stay. They'd shown up for her every time she needed them. They'd made her feel like she belonged.

For such a long time she'd held on to London, but maybe she needed to rethink what living her best life meant.

CHAPTER EIGHTEEN

Let's put that bench here." Aiden pointed to the other side of the fire ring, directing Silas and Thatch to set the thing down.

"You sure?" Thatch slanted his head and narrowed his eyes. "Because we've moved this thing three times now, and I'm about ready to set it on your foot."

"What're you whining about?" He gestured for them to lower the bench. "I just heard you bragging to Lyric about how much you supposedly *work out*." Aiden enclosed those last two words in air quotes. "Carrying a bench around should be no problem."

"Carrying the bench isn't the problem. I was getting somewhere with Lyric," his friend insisted. "Five more minutes with her and I would've asked her out."

"Uh-huh." Silas glanced at Aiden. "She only rolled her eyes at him twice, so they were definitely getting *somewhere*."

"Nothing's stopping you from asking her out." Except

they all knew she would say no. As far as Aiden knew, Lyric didn't date. And she also seemed to have Thatch's number. Everyone in town knew Thatch and Silas made the most of bachelorhood when they partied in Jackson. "On second thought, I need your help to hitch up the horses to the sleigh. Besides...Lyric is busy right now." She and Kyra were in the kitchen helping the Ladies organize the various desserts Minnie and Louie had brought after they were left over from the feast.

He would've liked to take a quick break to talk with Kyra since they'd hardly had a second alone after the feast, but dusk had settled and Tess should be driving in within the half hour. He'd told her about the surprise, so she'd been texting him their progress. "Let's go. I want the sleigh ready before the girls drive in."

They tromped through the snow to the barn, where he'd parked Kenny's old sleigh. He'd offered to buy the thing from the man's estate, but Kyra wouldn't hear of it. She'd wanted to give it to Tess and the girls. "We'll use Pip and Chip." The two thoroughbreds had the best temperaments in the stable other than Blondie, but after that stunt she'd pulled with Kyra, that horse was grounded.

"Sounds good. I've got them." Thatch opened the horses' gates and led them to the lead on the sleigh.

"Kyra sure seemed to enjoy the Thanksgiving," Silas commented casually while he helped attach the harnesses.

"She did." But after her encounter with Louie, she'd also been subdued all afternoon. "I think she feels bad about selling, but she also needs the money."

"She might not need the money if she moved here instead of to London," Thatch pointed out. "Maybe she wants to stay."

Over the last two days, there'd been moments when Aiden had pictured what the future could look like if Kyra stayed. How he'd wake up with her in his arms every morning. How they'd take horseback rides up to that perfect spot in the woods where she'd kissed him by the creek. How'd they'd cook dinner and share the meal and then sit on the couch watching a cozy fire crackle. But then when he was alone again, the shadows of his past would descend on him once more, shrouding that hope in darkness. Ever since Kyra had arrived, his own internal battle between shame and peace had only intensified.

He'd left the war in the Middle East only to come home to a war within himself.

"I don't want to hurt her." The dark memories took up too much space inside of him, and he wasn't sure there was enough room left for him to love Kyra the way she deserved. "I won't get close enough to hurt her." Aiden called out his friends with a long, steady glare. They fought their own battles too, privately, quietly. They might not talk about the struggle under the surface, but they shared it all the same.

Silas was the first to nod. "We'll have to find another way to save the town, then."

"Yeah. We can improvise, come up with a new game plan." Thatch stretched the reins over the sleigh's bench seat.

A text dinged in on Aiden's phone, and he embraced the distraction. "Tess is ten minutes out, people. Let's move."

They all climbed into the sleigh, and Aiden steered the horses out onto the driveway, parking them between the house and the firepit. Everyone had come back outside, and Aiden found himself searching for Kyra. She waved and met him as he climbed down.

"The sleigh looks great." She petted Chip.

Aiden moved alongside of her and snuck an arm around her waist. Since she was leaving in a month, he could let himself touch her. He could let himself get close. "Your dad used to do sleigh rides at his annual Christmas party. Everyone loved them." He couldn't wait to see the looks on Morgan's and Willow's faces when they noticed the sleigh.

"I wish I could've taken a ride with him." She turned into him so they were face-to-face. "I wish I could've known my dad."

"I think you would've loved him." When they had more time alone later he could tell her some stories about Kenny. "And he loved you. That much was obvious."

She hugged him tightly. "Thank you for always knowing what I need to hear."

"There!" Minnie pointed to the road. "That's Tess's car! They're here!"

Sure enough, Tess's SUV drove along the fence.

"Thatch and Silas, go hit the lights." It was just past sunset, but hopefully the display would still look as impressive as if it were pitch-black outside.

"On it." Thatch took his position alongside Silas.

Everyone else gathered around the fire while Aiden pulled Kyra to the front of the group. "You should stand with me. This never would've come together if it hadn't been for you."

She shook her head, deflecting the compliment. "I don't know about that."

"Really." He squeezed her hand. "Thank you. This

means everything to me, and it will mean everything to Tess and the girls too."

"You're welcome," she said softly.

Two seconds before Tess turned onto the driveway, Thatch and Silas fired up the lights. Right away, Tess's car slowed. The windows rolled down, and he could hear the girls inside.

"What's going on?" Willow asked.

"Look at all the lights!" Morgan stuck her head out. "Oh wow! A train! And look, Willow—Santa's on our roof!"

"Santa!" His younger niece peeked her head out too.

The girls both marveled at all the sights while Tess parked her SUV near the firepit.

"Uncle Aiden!" The doors flew open, and Morgan made it to him first. "Did you do this? I can't believe it! This is just like when Dad was here! We even have the Yoda lights!"

"Surprise." He picked her up and hugged her and then opened his other arm for Willow.

"It's beautiful," his younger niece whispered.

"Hi, Minnie! Hi, Louie! Hi, Lyric!" Morgan made it a point to wave and greet each person standing around the fire. "Kyra!" She scrambled to get down and hugged the woman standing next to him. "Did you help?"

"She did most of the work." He would've given up after the roof debacle if it hadn't been for Kyra.

"I didn't do all the work," Kyra corrected. "So many people in town helped. Everyone here but also tons of people who couldn't be here tonight. We had so much fun creating a magical Christmas wonderland for you."

"I love it!" Morgan hugged her again. "It's the best gift ever!" His niece looked past the fire. "Oh wow, wow, wow! You even have the sleigh here!"

"With Pip and Chip!" Willow added, squeezing his neck.

"I can't believe this." Tess finally joined them, wiping away tears. "I mean, I know you said you decorated the house, but this is way more than I imagined. I don't even know how you could've pulled this off."

"It was all hands on deck, that's for sure." Seeing his sister's emotion choked him up too.

"Jace would've loved this." Her tears spilled over again.

"Yeah. He would've." He lowered Willow back to the ground. But his brother-in-law wasn't here. Jace couldn't see the joy light up his little girls' faces. He couldn't kiss away his wife's tears. Once again the paralyzing weight of guilt held Aiden captive.

"Welcome home, Tess." Silas approached and gave her a hug, and she cried on his shoulder for a minute.

Morgan and Willow didn't seem to notice, though. They were pulling on Aiden's hands. "Can we go for a sleigh ride right now?" his older niece begged.

"Pleeeeeeaaase," Willow added.

Aiden masked his internal chaos with a smile. "You bet. Let's go."

"I'll start preparing the marshmallows for s'mores," Minnie said, breaking the sullen silence around the fire-pit. They all missed Jace. He would forever be their missing piece.

"Everything'll be all ready for you when you get back," Nelly added, already scurrying to the table they'd set up earlier.

"Woo-hoo!" The girls took off cheering. Halfway to the sleigh, Morgan paused. "Can Kyra come with us?"

He looked at the woman standing next to him. She was wiping away tears too.

"I would love to go on a sleigh ride with you." Kyra hurried to join the girls ahead of him.

Aiden followed them to the horses, fighting the temptation to detach, to wallow in his regrets. He had to fight. For the girls. For Kyra.

"Sleigh rides are the best." Morgan climbed right up into the sleigh while Willow held out her arms to Aiden. He set her on the bench and then gave Kyra his hand to help her climb up. When they were all settled and covered with a blanket, Aiden pulled himself up to the driver's seat and took the reins.

"Oh, wait." Kyra pulled out her phone. "We need some Christmas music." She fired up "Winter Wonderland," and both girls started to sing along.

"Come on, Uncle Aiden." Morgan tapped his shoulder. "I can't hear you."

"Sorry." He hummed as he urged the horses to get moving, but he still couldn't shake the heaviness weighing against his heart. The girls didn't know what he knew. They were too young to understand, but would they someday? Would they want to know the truth about what had happened the night their father died? Would they someday resent him for coming back in one piece when their father hadn't made it?

He tried to tune out the questions while he drove the sleigh, taking the girls by each Christmas decoration so they could see them up close. They sang and chattered about all of the different displays and begged him to take them through the tunnel of lights six times. After the last trip through the tunnel, Morgan announced she was ready for s'mores, so Aiden steered the horses back near the fire. He helped the girls down, and they ran off to roast their marshmallows, but Kyra stayed seated on the bench.

Aiden climbed up and sat next to her. "You okay?"

"I'm good." She turned her face to his, a soft smile brightening her eyes in the twilight. "But you're not." Her eyes searched his. "You seem... quiet."

"I'm good too," he lied. He had moments of good. More over the last few days with her, but they never lasted long enough.

Kyra's unrelenting stare told him she saw through his smile. "This celebration is hard for you. Without Jace."

Every celebration was hard. But Aiden shifted his gaze to where his friends and family had gathered around the fire. "I'll get through it." He'd learned how to detach from his emotions to dull the pain.

"I wish you would talk to me." She tugged on his coat until he faced her again. "Or talk to someone. You've been through trauma and you're hurting. I could find you resources if you want. There are counselors and therapists who specialize in PTSD..."

"I'm okay." He took her hands in his. He wanted to be okay. He didn't want to have to retrace his steps back in time only to find he could never be the same man he'd been before they'd gone on that last mission. Once she left, his life could go back to the way it had been before. "And I do talk to you." He'd told her more about losing Jace than he'd told anyone else. Aiden leaned forward to kiss away the concerns on her face. Her soft lips brought him a temporary reprieve, stirring up a hunger for more of her.

But Kyra pulled back. "I've been thinking about London. I'm not sure I want to go."

"Really?" His body tensed. At first, all he wanted was for Kyra to hold on to the land—to stay connected to Star Valley Springs so they could save the town. But now . . . she made him feel too much. She made him want things he couldn't have. "Moving to London is your dream."

"It was. Or still is, I guess." She stared down at her mitten-clad hands. "I don't know." She glanced at the group gathered around the fire. "I hate to think about Star Valley Springs changing after I sell. This is a special place."

"It is, but you can't stay out of guilt. Trust me. That's no way to live your life." Guilt offered no freedom, and what Kyra deserved most of all was freedom to live her dreams.

She raised her eyes back to his. "Do you want me to leave?" she asked directly.

Yes. Because if she left he wouldn't have to see what he was missing out on every day. He wouldn't have to pretend he didn't want her. If she left they would have thirty days to enjoy each other without the commitment he could never make. A mounting panic tightened his throat. "I want you to do what's best for you." That was the most honest answer he could offer.

All he knew was that she couldn't stay for him.

CHAPTER NINETEEN

Namaste." Lyric ended the yoga session with the typical closing salutation at the front of the studio, but Kyra didn't move.

While the other participants in the class slowly stood, rolled up their mats, and exited the room, she stayed in her corpse pose, staring up at the fancy chandeliers dangling from the spa's gold-tiled ceiling.

Inhale. Exhale. Her body remained in a state of relaxation after concentrating on holding poses for the last hour, but tension still knotted her heart and mind. Two weeks ago, her path had seemed clear, but right now the employment contract from London still sat unsigned on her father's kitchen table and the land proposals still cluttered up her in-box. Coming on this girls' weekend to Jackson was supposed to help her make some decisions, but so far she still didn't know what to do.

"Would you like some water?" Her friend sat down next to her and handed her a water bottle.

"Thanks." She pushed to a sitting position and took a long drink. "That was a great class. It actually helped me stop overanalyzing everything." At least for an hour…

"Did you have any epiphanies when we were doing the meditation?" Lyric pulled her legs into a butterfly stretch and straightened her posture.

"Um, no." She'd never been good at clearing her mind. "I've been over the pros and cons of selling about fifty times." Walking around Jackson yesterday had only served to prove Louie right. Many of the shops and restaurants were part of chains—and as beautiful as the town was, the commercialism and extravagance didn't have the charm she'd come to love in Star Valley Springs.

"Tell me to go to London." That's what everyone else had been telling her. Even Aiden. He seemed to be holding on to her dream tighter than she was. "That's the logical thing to do, right?"

Lyric gave a small shrug and lengthened her legs out in front of her, reaching for her feet in another stretch. "I think dreams change as we do. At least mine have." She inhaled deeply, closing her eyes, and then slowly exhaled. After a relaxed pause she looked at Kyra. "Believe it or not I used to plan things out too. When I left for college in Colorado, I had my future set. I wanted to get my business degree, get married, find a great job, and have a family." She counted each of those items out on her fingers.

Kyra let her jaw drop. Lyric had wanted a *business* degree? Clearly her life had changed course somewhere along the way. "What happened?"

"I did almost all of those things," her friend said. "I graduated with a degree in business, got a great job, and got married."

A shocked gasp snuck out. Lyric had been *married*?

"Let's just say the grass wasn't greener after I checked all my boxes." Her friend's jaw tightened. "In trying to stick to my plan I overlooked certain things about my husband that should've been red flags."

Kyra held her breath, her heart aching. Over the last month, Lyric had hinted at having difficult experiences with men, but she'd never shared any specifics. She waited, wanting to comfort her but also wanting to give her the space to speak.

"Pierce turned out to be controlling and jealous." Her friend hugged her knees to her chest. "For the first year of our marriage he would track me on my phone. If I was running late, he would show up wherever I was and demand that I leave with him. He didn't want me talking to my family or other friends. He told me he was all I needed." She paused as though staving off emotion.

Forget fighting the tears. Kyra let them fall. But she still wouldn't speak. She wouldn't interrupt, no matter how much she wanted to hug Lyric right now.

"And then one night he grabbed me and threw me down onto the floor, breaking my arm." Lyric touched a thin scar that ran down the back of her forearm. "That was the night my whole life—and all of my dreams—imploded."

The tears had become a steady stream down Kyra's cheeks. "I didn't know," she whispered. If she'd known, she would've been there for her friend. She would've helped her pick up the pieces. "I wish I could've been there for you."

"I didn't let anyone be there for me." Lyric brushed away a few tears. "No one knew what was going on until

I called my mom from the hospital. She and Kenny came to pick me up the next day."

"I'm so sorry you had to live through that." But she was glad that her father had been there to help, that Lyric had someone in her corner to call on when things had gotten tough.

"It was painful," her friend acknowledged. "And it took me a long time to process everything I'd been through." Her lovely smile came back. "I'll never forget what your father told me that day. He said, 'Lyric... starting today—starting right now—you can make your life anything you want it to be. You're free.'"

Two words. Such a simple sentence but so profound. "I don't think I've ever felt free," Kyra admitted. She'd lived under the weight of her father's abandonment and her mother's expectations and illness and her own obsession with getting all of the boxes checked off with her degrees and career so she could finally start her real life.

"Kyra..." Lyric took her hand. "Starting today—starting right now—you can make your life anything you want it to be. You're free."

"I'm free." She might never get to spend time with her father, but maybe in bringing her to Star Valley Springs he'd rescued her the same way he'd rescued Lyric that day. Being welcomed into the community by the Ladies and Tess and the girls and Aiden and Silas and Thatch had shown her a different kind of life—one surrounded with the love of a family.

Maybe that had been what her father intended in leaving this place to her all along.

* * *

Aiden fought the pain in his shoulders and pumped the barbell up and down over his chest, the sweat pouring off of him. But no matter how many reps he did on the weight bench he couldn't seem to work off the angst that had been clinging to him ever since Kyra said she might not go to London.

On the other side of the office, Silas and Thatch both sat at their desks engaging in more friendly Battleship fire.

"You two get those bids done for Neptune Ranch?" he grunted, cranking out a few more chest presses. It wouldn't kill them to get a little work done in between games, would it? He'd finished all of his tasks and then some.

"Almost." Silas made a sound that mimicked an explosion. "That's it. Kicked your ass again, Thatch. You want to go best out of three?"

"Enough with the Battleship." Aiden hoisted the barbell back onto the rack and sat up, wiping his face with a towel. "How about you start earning your paycheck?"

"And how about you tell us why you've been such an ass lately?" Silas leaned back in his chair and crossed his arms with a smirk. "Never mind. We already know." He shot a glance over to Thatch.

"How many days has it been since you've seen Kyra?" Thatch asked innocently, tossing a football to Aiden.

He caught the pass. Five days and three hours. Not that he was counting. "I don't know. She's been in Jackson with Lyric."

"Almost a week, right?" Silas shook his head. "If he's this pissed off after a few days, we'd all better run for cover when she leaves for good."

"Shut the hell up." Aiden threw the football onto the

ground. Yes, he was taking out his frustration over his own issues on his best friends, but he also knew they were strong enough to handle it. "It's not too much to ask for you guys to put in a little more effort around—"

Their office door creaked open. "Aiden, Silas, Thatcher?"

No way. Aiden gaped as their old Navy lieutenant walked in.

They all three scrambled to their feet the same way they used to when he'd walk in on their card games.

"Lieutenant Wakefield." He still couldn't believe the man was standing here. Aiden heard from him from time to time, but he hadn't seen him in two years.

"Relax, you three." The guy had a quick, easy smile.

Aiden tried, but it was hard to relax when they'd spent most of their careers walking on eggshells around the man.

"Your sister told me I could find you out here." Wakefield walked to the center of the room but kept his attention on Aiden. "I'm glad I finally met Tess and your nieces."

Aiden wasn't sure he could say the same. He'd always respected the man, but seeing him standing in his world now brought the past he'd tried to forget back into focus again. "What're you doing here?"

"I had some vacation time coming and brought the fam to Jackson. While I was here I wanted to make sure you three got your letters." His stern gaze wasn't all that different than it had been years ago. "And then I wanted to make sure you weren't getting any ideas about declining the honors you rightfully earned."

Aiden traded looks with Silas and Thatch. They still

hadn't discussed the official letters. They didn't need to discuss them. Aiden didn't have to ask them questions to know how they felt about the Navy Cross.

"All due respect, sir..." Aiden couldn't seem to find an at-ease posture. "You can't force us to accept any honors."

"It doesn't feel right, that's all," Silas added. "Jace should be front and center for that ceremony. Not us."

"Not that we don't appreciate the gesture." Thatch walked around his desk. "We just can't accept it. We can't."

Their reactions didn't appear to surprise him. Knowing Wakefield, he'd prepared for this exact scenario. "You four were the heart and soul of the team. Together. You deserve to stand up there, shoulder to shoulder, the same way you fought." Their old boss still had quite the commanding presence. "You don't stand up there for yourselves. You stand up there for the brotherhood. You stand up there for Jace because he can't stand up there himself."

Exactly. Jace couldn't stand up there. He couldn't accept his own medal. And Aiden wasn't worthy to stand in his place. "I don't want the Navy Cross." Aiden couldn't face all of those people, the photo ops, and the fanfare. He couldn't even face Commander Wakefield right now without the man's very presence dredging up feelings he'd rather avoid. "How can I accept a fucking award when there are two little girls in that house who'll never see their father again? When my sister now carries the weight of the world on her shoulders?" His throat burned. "It should've been me."

It was the first time he'd spoken those words aloud, but

Thatch and Silas would understand. They were there that day, and they saw the damage Jace's absence had done on a daily basis too.

Before Wakefield could argue with him again, Aiden stomped past him, out the door.

The icy wind bit at his face, pelting him with snowflakes. He hadn't even made it to the driveway when he heard the footsteps behind him.

"Stop." Wakefield still had his booming voice too.

He wanted to run, but his training wouldn't allow him to disrespect a naval lieutenant. So he halted his steps, refusing to turn around.

"You've read the investigation, Steele." Lieutenant Wakefield walked into his line of vision. "You know that what happened to Jace on that mission wasn't your fault."

"It's not about who's at fault." He'd read the report. Jace had been at the wrong place at the wrong time. They hadn't been able to see anything. It had been too dark, and he'd stepped outside their cover. But none of those details mattered. Didn't the man understand? "I came home and he didn't. That's all I can seem to remember." That's what he had to live with. Anytime something good happened to him that guilt came rising to the surface.

"You know survivors' guilt is a form of PTSD." Wakefield waited until Aiden looked at him. "We went over that when you were discharged. You need to talk to someone, Steele. You need to work through this." The man pulled his phone out of the pocket of his suit. "I'm texting you some numbers. Resources. Start by making some calls."

The man made it sound so easy. *Talk to someone. Get*

counseling. What if he did? What if he talked about the past, about how Jace's death haunted his every waking moment? What if he talked about the nightmares that only seemed to come on when he let himself enjoy life, and then nothing changed?

He couldn't face the possibility that he was beyond help. "I don't need to talk." He'd gotten along fine before Kyra had arrived. Before she'd made him feel something. Talking wouldn't help him. He had to go back to focusing only on his sister and nieces so he didn't want something he could never have.

Wakefield silently regarded him for what seemed like an eternity.

Aiden braced for a lecture, but instead the man shrugged. "No one can force you to get help. But those resources will be there whenever you're ready." Wakefield approached him and held out his hand. "Think about the ceremony. I'd like to see you there."

Aiden went through the motions of the obligatory handshake. "Thanks for coming all this way, sir." Even if it had been a waste of his time.

After a brisk goodbye, the man got into his SUV and pulled away, leaving Aiden to fight off an attack of anger and regret and hopelessness.

"Uncle Aiden!" He didn't know how long he'd been standing there in the cold when the front door opened and Morgan burst out. "Kyra's coming over to bake cookies with us! Look!" She pointed to the road. "There she is!"

"Yeah. There she is." His voice had gone robotic, as cold and hollow as the inside of him. Aiden let the numbness take over. All he wanted to do was retreat to his office to lose himself in the mundane tasks—the bids they'd promised and the materials they needed to order for upcoming projects—but Kyra waved at him from behind the wheel of her car. He raised his hand to wave back.

She parked near the garage and climbed out of the car wearing a smile that stopped his heart. "Hey, you two."

"Wait until you see the cookies we're going to make." Morgan bounded down the steps. "There's chocolate and some with yummy frosting and sprinkles!"

"Sounds delicious." The woman paused in front of the steps. "Why don't you go tell your mom I'm here and I'll be right in?"

"Okay!" Morgan disappeared inside the house, but her shout carried. "Mooom! Kyra's here but she needs to talk to Uncle Aiden before we bake cookies!"

Kyra laughed and then started to walk toward him. "Hey. How's it going?"

"Things are fine." He fought the instinct to reach for her, unable to move, unable to stop the panic ringing in his ears. *Don't get too close*... "Did you and Lyric have a good trip?"

"We had a great trip." She eased her body up against his, seeming not to notice how rigid his shoulders had gotten.

"In fact, there's something I need to talk to you about," she murmured mysteriously.

"Oh." He stepped back to distance himself. From her. From feeling. "Now's not a great time." He had to get away. He wanted to forget how good it made him feel when he touched his lips to hers, when he pulled her close and listened to the rhythm of her breathing. Right now he wanted to forget everything. "Silas and Thatch and I need to have a meeting."

"That's fine." Kyra studied his face. "Maybe we can talk later? After the tree lighting ceremony tonight?"

"Sure. Yeah." Just not now. He couldn't be with her right now. He was too messed up.

CHAPTER TWENTY

I've never been to a tree lighting ceremony before." Kyra undid her seatbelt and got out of Lyric's car.

"It's basically yet another excuse to get together," her friend informed her with a laugh. "Around here people get restless in the winter. They'll look for any reason to get out of the house." She gestured to the crowds that had started to gather around the newly restored gazebo. "Some of them have probably been here for an hour already."

"We should've come earlier." Kyra couldn't stop smiling. She'd just walked into a Norman Rockwell painting. Children ran around chasing and throwing snowballs, all bundled up in their cold-weather gear. Their moms and dads stood in clusters with travel mugs chatting easily with one another. "I love it here." Since she'd decided to stay she no longer felt torn. "This is where I want to be."

"Wait. Seriously?" Lyric grabbed her shoulder. "Are you staying in Star Valley?"

Oops. She was going to wait to make that announcement until everyone had arrived. The friends she met had made such a difference for her. She wanted them all to be together when she told them her plans. But after reconnecting with Lyric, and remembering what it felt like to have a best friend, it felt right that Lyric was hearing her news first. "I'm staying." She'd made the decision minutes after she'd returned home from Jackson. The house no longer felt like her father's. It had become her home, and she had no reservations.

"Kyra." Lyric got all weepy as she hugged her. "I never thought, I mean I had hoped, but I know how much you wanted to go to London—"

"I can visit London anytime." She would travel there on vacation to see the sights again someday. And with her degree, she could find a job somewhere nearby. "But I want to build my life in a community. With people I care about."

"What's going on?" Tess had snuck up behind them with the girls. "Is everything okay?" Aiden's sister looked back and forth between them.

Now Kyra was crying a little too. But she couldn't tell Tess about her decision before she told Aiden. When she'd talked to him at the ranch earlier, he'd seemed distracted, so she'd decided it would be best to wait until she saw him here.

"Kyra! Did you know there's gonna be a new hot chocolate bar in the gazebo tonight?" Morgan seemed oblivious to the emotion. "They're gonna have whipped cream and sprinkles and—"

"Extra marshmallows?" Kyra guessed. That hot chocolate Aiden had made her was still the best thing she'd ever tasted.

"Yes!" Morgan raised a delicate eyebrow at her. "How'd you know?"

"It was a guess." She knelt down so she could bring Willow into the conversation. "And what are you going to have on your hot chocolate, sweetheart?"

"I like marshmallows too!" the girl belted out.

"And candy canes. Willow loves candy canes." Aiden's voice stood Kyra upright.

"Hey." She realized her voice was an octave too high, but it couldn't be helped with the sudden acceleration in her pulse.

"Hi." Aiden locked his gaze on her, but before she could move closer to him Silas and Thatch showed up.

"Let's get this party started." Silas checked his phone. "I gotta get home and catch the football game."

"Football shmootball." Minnie approached from the direction of the gazebo, holding on to her husband's hand. "This is an important town event. You can record the game. Should we move closer to the tree?"

"Hold on." Tess still looked concerned. "I want to know why you were crying," she said to Lyric and Kyra. "Is something wrong? Can we help?"

"It's nothing bad. They were happy tears." Lyric bobbed her head in an encouraging nod.

This hadn't exactly been the plan, but now was as good a time as any to tell them. "I have news, and I wanted you all to hear it together." She was too excited to keep them in suspense. "I've decided to stay in Star Valley Springs and hold on to the land my father left me. At least into the spring, depending on where I can find a job. But hopefully longer."

"Yes!" Morgan hugged her and then let go and looked up at her. "Is it because you love my uncle?"

Kyra's eyes went wide.

"No." Aiden wasn't smiling. "That's not why. That can't be why. Surely that's not why."

She didn't have time to respond before Minnie ambushed her with a hug. "I can't believe it! This is amazing! Operation Save Star Valley Springs worked!"

Kyra broke away from her. "Operation *what*?"

Minnie waved a hand through the air. "Oh, it was nothing. We hatched a little plan to show you how wonderful this town is. And now you're staying." She smiled nervously. "So everything's okay."

No. Everything was not okay. "A *plan*? What kind of plan?" She scanned their faces. Silas and Thatch shared a concerned look. Louie all of a sudden seemed very interested in his phone. Tess and Lyric both stared at the ground. And Aiden's face was turning redder by the minute. Clearly the man had something to hide. "*What plan*?" she asked again, her voice shaky.

"Hey, girls." Tess knelt down to Morgan and Willow. "Why don't you go get some hot chocolate in the gazebo before they light the tree?"

"Yes! Hot chocolate! Marshmallows!" They both ran away from the sudden awkwardness that had fallen over the group.

"What's Operation Save Star Valley Springs?" Kyra demanded. There were too many guilty expressions around this circle. Something had been going on behind her back, and she wanted to know what.

"It wasn't an operation, per se." Louie jammed his hands into his pockets. "It was just an agreement that we would all help you get acquainted with the town is all. So you could see the value in keeping things the way they are."

"That's all this was?" Disbelief jammed her throat and weakened her voice. "The kindness and the help and the friendship?" And the nights she'd spent with Aiden? Good lord, she'd been such a fool to believe any of this—any of *them*—were real. "This was all an effort to convince me not to sell Star Valley Springs?"

"No, no, no." Minnie's hands fretted together in front of her waist. "That's not true at all. It was a silly mission. We would've helped and shown you kindness anyway. That's what we do here."

Then why would no one—including Aiden—look her in the eyes right now?

They'd all been plotting behind her back the entire time. Kyra focused her full attention on Aiden. "Is that what all this was about?" He knew what she meant. She could tell by the way his eyes darted around. He didn't want to look at her. But he'd been more than willing to sleep with her. Maybe that's why he'd been so closed off when she'd seen him earlier. Maybe he'd suddenly had an attack of conscience about fooling her. She took his shoulders in her hands and forced him to look at her, asking the silent question. *Did you seduce me to convince me to stay here?* "I need to know."

He closed his eyes for a brief second, and when he opened them they were as cold as steel. "Yes. The whole Operation Save Star Valley Springs was my idea. I wanted to keep you from selling. That's all I wanted."

Tess gasped. "Aiden..."

Kyra couldn't seem to make any sounds, to breathe past the stabbing pain. She braced herself against it, against the sadness that threatened to overwhelm her. She had been ready to give up everything—her plans, her hopes, her dreams. That's how much she'd come to care for this man in two months. That's how much she'd come to care for this whole town. She'd actually started to see her future differently—with a family, with friends, with a community she'd grown to love. Who knew if they would've ended up together, but she'd wanted to stay and see. She'd wanted to hope...

And he'd just ripped away the possibility with one sentence.

"Okay," she barely managed to whisper. "Okay." Teetering on the edge of despair, Kyra turned her back on all of them before any tears could fall and marched blindly through the knee-deep snow, her boots clumsy and dragging. She moved as quickly as she could across the park and was almost jogging by the time she made it to the sidewalk.

"Wait! Kyra!" Lyric came alongside of her wheezing like she was out of breath. "Please stop."

"Did you know?" She slowed but refused to stop. She had to get away from all of them. "Were you in on it too?"

"I truly don't think anyone intended you harm." She tugged on Kyra's arm. "Yes, I heard about the plan. But I didn't put any stock in it. The way they all took care of you...that's what they'd done for me since Kenny died and my mom moved away. That's what they would've done for you anyway. That's what they do for everyone who's hurting."

"I wasn't hurting." Kyra stopped and spun to face her. "I was fine until I came here." The words edged toward a shout. "He tricked me." Maybe the rest of them hadn't intended to manipulate her. Maybe they would've treated her the same no matter what. But Aiden had admitted his intentions in front of everyone. "He tricked me into thinking he had feelings for me. Oh, my God. I totally fell for his whole act."

She started to walk again, the images of the night they'd spent together flashing through her mind, the kisses, the intimate moments. Her stomach clenched.

"I don't know why Aiden said that." Lyric stopped her again. "But I don't believe him. There's no way he was pretending. I saw you two together."

"He fooled everyone, then." He couldn't possibly care about her. If he did—if he cared about her at all—he wouldn't have been able to stand there with that cold look in his eyes and shatter her.

Now that the shock and anger were receding, her tears started to fall. Sadness suddenly weighted every bone in her body. There was no way she'd be able to walk all the way home. "Can you drive me back to my father's house?" She angrily swiped away her tears. "I need to get out of here."

"Come on." Lyric slipped an arm around her waist and led Kyra to the car. They drove in silence for a few moments, everything passing by in a blur.

"I'm sorry." Her friend's voice wavered. "Truly. I hope you know I wasn't pretending to be your friend. I guess I should've told you they didn't want you to sell, but—"

"It's okay." Kyra closed her eyes, trying to shut down the tears. "I know you. You're genuine and kindhearted." This wasn't Lyric's fault. "Almost everyone in this town is genuine." And she'd thought Aiden was too. Had she imagined the tenderness he'd shown when he'd kissed her? Had she read too much into the way his expression would intensify when he looked into her eyes?

"For what it's worth, I've never seen Aiden as happy as he was when you were around." Lyric stopped the car. "I mean, his whole demeanor changed. He smiled. His face lit up. I'm not sure I'd ever heard him laugh before you showed up in town."

Kyra opened her eyes and found herself staring at her father's house. But she stayed right where she was. "Then why did he intentionally hurt me?"

"There's no excuse for what he did," Lyric said. "None whatsoever. He was a jerk back there."

Jerk didn't exactly describe his behavior. He'd been indifferent and emotionless. His apathy toward her had hurt worse than the words he'd spoken.

"But trauma changes a person." Her friend shut off the engine. "Especially when it's not dealt with. Thankfully, my mom and Kenny convinced me to go to therapy after my divorce. Without that I wouldn't have healed."

Aiden hadn't healed. She wasn't even sure he'd begun the process. "I know he's still struggling." She'd seen the evidence of PSTD. And it made sense that he would try to push her away. "I care for him, but I can't fix him. I can't make him heal."

No one could help Aiden until he wanted to help himself.

CHAPTER TWENTY-ONE

Oh, dear. I'm so sorry."

Leave it to Minnie to apologize for something that wasn't her fault. She hadn't done anything wrong. Aiden, on the other hand? He'd screwed up everything. If he would've kept his hands off Kyra from the very beginning, she wouldn't be hurting right now. This whole shit show was on him. "I should go talk to her. Try to explain..."

"She's gone," Tess said, her jaw clenched. "I saw her in Lyric's car. What in the he—"

"Look at my hot chocolate!" Morgan held up her cup and walked into the center of their circle. "Marshmallows, sprinkles, whipped cream..." She took a sip. "I think this is even better than the hot chocolate you make, Uncle Aiden."

"Probably." He couldn't even crack a smile right now.

Willow shuffled next to her sister, holding her own cup while she looked around the circle. "Where's Kyra and Lyric?"

Everyone seemed to look to Aiden for the answer. "They had to go." A more honest answer would've been that he made Kyra go. He'd *wanted* her to go so he wouldn't have to face up to his demons. That was the truth.

"I thought Kyra was going to watch the tree lighting with us." Morgan pouted. "She didn't even say goodbye."

"I think she wasn't feeling very well." Tess patted her daughter's shoulder while she glared at Aiden.

Yes. He understood. He'd run her off. And now he felt even worse than he had when Wakefield had stopped by earlier.

"It looks like they're about to start over by the gazebo." Louie slipped his arm around his wife and they walked away.

"I can't wait to see the tree all pretty," Willow said, taking her mom's hand.

"It'll be so much fun." Tess reached for Morgan's hand, then turned her back on Aiden. He deserved to be shut out of this celebration.

"We can take a picture for Kyra," Morgan offered. "On your phone. Right, mom? Then we can send it to her and tell her we miss her."

"Sure we can." Tess shot one last look of pure disgust over her shoulder at Aiden. But she couldn't make him feel any worse than he already did.

"Well, that was awkward." Silas watched Tess walk away. "Your sister might actually kill you for doing that to Kyra."

"What the hell were you thinking?" Thatch added. "Humiliating her in front of everyone like that? I thought you were better than that."

"Well, I'm not." And that was exactly why Kyra should

move on. "I didn't mean to hurt her." But on some level he knew he would hurt her eventually. That was exactly why she'd be better off leaving him behind.

"Then you gotta go apologize. Like *now*." Thatch emphasized his words with a shove to Aiden's shoulder. "Follow her home and tell her the truth."

"No, no, no." Silas stepped in front of Thatch. "She's not gonna want to see you right now. Trust me. You need to send flowers first. A hell of a lot of flowers. And maybe chocolate too. Then tell her you lost your head and you'll do whatever it takes to make this up to her."

"I'm not going to do any of that." It was too late. "The best way to make it up to her is to stay the hell away from her."

"Uncle Aiden! You're going to miss the tree lighting!" Morgan frantically waved to him from where she stood with her mom. He trudged in their direction. If he hadn't ridden with Tess and the girls, he'd be on his way home now too.

Instead of going home, he stood with the girls and watched the Christmas tree the Ladies had meticulously decorated light up row by row. When Willow couldn't see, Aiden picked her up and set her on his shoulders. Usually watching his nieces so enthralled with the festivities pulled him out of whatever mood he might be in, but not even their laughs and chatter could pull him out of this mess he'd made.

On the way back to the ranch, Tess said nothing to him, but the girls filled in the silence. "The Christmas tree wasn't as pretty as our lights," Willow said as they drove under the tunnel at the entrance to the driveway.

"But it was still fun because we were all together," Morgan insisted. "Except for Kyra. It's too bad she's not feeling good." She gasped the way she always did when she got an idea. "We could make a card, Willow. Or a lot of cards to help her feel better."

"I think that's an excellent idea." Tess pulled into the garage, and they all piled out of the car.

"I guess I'll head home." Aiden started to hug his nieces.

"Oh, no you don't." Tess pointed to the door that led into the house. "We have some things to discuss."

"Uh-oh." Morgan stared up at him wide-eyed. "That's what she always says to me when I'm about to get in trouble."

"Thanks for the warning," he muttered, following Willow into the house. Not that he needed a warning. Tess's fury had been radiating from her in waves all night.

"Why don't you girls go make your cards for Kyra at the desk in the office?" His sister helped them get their coats off.

"I'm going to draw a picture of Brutus for her." Willow kicked off her boots.

"That's a great idea." Morgan took off her hat and tossed it on the floor. "I'll draw a picture of the sleigh. She liked the sleigh." His niece turned to him. "Maybe we can take her on another sleigh ride when she's all better."

"Maybe." He moved on into the living room and sat on the couch while the girls bounded down the hallway.

Tess waited until the door closed, and then she sat on the couch next to him. "What the hell is wrong with you?"

"I know. I screwed up." He wouldn't even try to make excuses. "I panicked. She can't stay here for me. I'm too much of a mess."

His sister looked at him the same way she used to

when he'd get caught sneaking out of the house back in the day—like she couldn't believe he was actually that stupid. "Maybe she wasn't staying for you. Maybe she was staying because she's actually happy here. Did you ever think of that? And now you've gone and taken that away from her. Ugh." Her hands covered her face as though she couldn't even bear to look at him. "The worst part is you totally lied to her, Aiden. You *do* care about her. I can see how much you care about her." She threw up her hands. "Everyone else can see how much you care about her. You're the only one who's denying it."

"I don't deserve her." So it didn't matter how much he cared about her.

"Wakefield called me on his way out of town." His sister bit into her lower lip, the sternness on her face crumbling. "He told me what you said. About how you should've died instead of Jace. Is that really how you feel? That you shouldn't be here?" The strength in her gaze wouldn't allow him to lie.

"Sometimes." He rushed to explain. "He had everything to live for, Tess. He had you and he had the girls. I didn't have anyone counting on me."

Tess inhaled deeply, her eyes filling with tears. "We all know what this is, Aiden. The PTSD won't go away if you ignore it. Wakefield asked me if you've been self-medicating. With alcohol or drugs."

"You know I haven't." He self-medicated by living for Morgan and Willow, by making sure they had what they needed, by doing work for his sister around the ranch.

"He said he gave you numbers for counselors who specialize in PTSD." She waited until he acknowledged the statement with a nod. "You need to call them."

He let his head tip back so he could stare at the ceiling. "Maybe I do."

"Aiden." Her voice raised. "You *need* to call. I can't lose you too."

He moved closer to her. "You're not going to lose me, Tess. I promise."

"There's something I want you to read." She shifted on the couch and pulled a folded piece of paper out of her pocket. "I should've shown you this a long time ago."

Before she handed him the note, he knew what it was. He could see Jace's chicken scratch bleeding through the paper. It was his last goodbye. They all wrote them. Letters for their loved ones in case they didn't come home. Aiden still had the letters he'd written for his parents and for Tess. "I shouldn't read this." Jace's words weren't meant for him. And, even if they were, he wasn't sure he *could* read them...

"Yes. You should." Tess shoved the paper into his hand. "You need to read it as much as I needed to read it. As much as I still need to read it from time to time. That's why I always carry it with me. As a reminder."

Holding his breath, he unfolded the paper and smoothed out the wrinkles.

My beautiful Tess,

Hopefully you'll never have to read these words, but I had to write them just in case. There is nothing I want more than to spend my entire life with you—loving you, raising our babies with you, growing old with you. But if you're reading this, that means I'm gone and our life together was cut too short.

I'm sorry we didn't get to realize our dreams together. I'm sorry it was time for me to go. I want you to know the love I have for you is stronger than death. It will live on forever, even if we're not together. I hope you feel it even now in your grief. I hope my love for you will carry you through this part and make you strong.

You have to live for both of us now, babe, and that means you'll have to live big. That means you have to make the most of every opportunity, especially when it comes to love. Love is the only thing in this world worth living and dying for. You and Morgan and Willow taught me that. You three made me understand, and I would lay down my life over and over again if it meant my girls could be safe and happy.

I know you're not happy now. I know you might feel like you'll never be happy again. But don't think that closing yourself off to love will mean you're honoring my memory. Our girls are watching you, babe. They need to see that love is worth whatever it costs—that's it's worth fighting for over and over and over again, even if you lose it. So I'm telling you to embrace those feelings when they come again. I know they'll come again because you are brave and passionate and you deserve to be loved.

I have never doubted your love for me. Not once. Your love changed me. It made me who I am. You can't hide your beautiful heart away. No matter how much you might want to. You have to continue opening your heart so our girls know they can open theirs too. I want you to embrace life, embrace love, embrace anything and everything that brings you joy no matter what anyone else says or thinks.

Your best days are still ahead of you, my love. Live them to the fullest.

All my love,
Jace

Aiden read the words again. And then a third time with his eyes burning. Even now his brother-in-law was wiser than anyone else he knew.

"I don't know if I'll ever fall in love with anyone else," Tess said, catching a few tears with her shirtsleeve. "But I have to stay open. If I feel like there could be potential, I owe it to Jace and the girls and myself to try. And so do you, Aiden. The girls are watching both of us. We have to show them how to live life to the fullest. That's what Jace would want."

He carefully folded the letter and handed it back to her. "I know." In his head he knew, but he couldn't tell that to the broken pieces of his heart.

"You're not living." Tess reached up and turned his face to hers. "You're doing penance. You're shutting out every good thing except for the girls and me. That's not what Jace would want either. That's not what he asked you to do."

No. If his brother-in-law could talk to him right now, Aiden had no doubt he'd get an earful. "I'll call."

It was time.

CHAPTER TWENTY-TWO

Kyra walked to the window in her hotel room, looking out over the snowy city streets in Jackson. The gloomy clouds sagging over the mountain peaks in the distance fit her mood perfectly.

When she'd informed Mr. Podgurski that she needed to meet with each of the developers in person before she made her decision on a sale, he'd arranged everything...even a week's stay at the luxury resort where she'd been hiding out since the Christmas tree lighting.

So far the first two meetings had been a bust. She hadn't liked either one of the businessmen who'd tried to schmooze her, but hopefully the last meeting would go well. The third time was the charm, right?

Even if the meeting went south, it wasn't like she could stay in Star Valley Springs after what had happened. Aiden had made the decision for her when he humiliated her in front of the entire town.

Yet she still couldn't quite make peace with selling out.

Her gaze refocused on the street outside the windows. Would this be the same view she'd see in that little town if she came back five years from now? Not that she didn't like Jackson. It was far more beautiful than most of the tourist towns she'd been in—nestled in a valley between the busy ski resorts. Shops and trendy restaurants lined the streets, which were decorated with evergreen boughs and red velvet ribbons. But Star Valley Springs had this rare simplicity, an authenticity she hadn't experienced during her time in Jackson.

A knock sounded on her door. "Miss Fowler? There's a delivery for you."

Oh, right. Podgurski had told her he would forward more information and some brochures on the luxury properties the final developer owned. "Coming." She hurried to the door and pulled it open, finding a bellhop standing in the hallway. Instead of holding an envelope like she'd expected, he was pushing a cart full of flower arrangements.

"It'll take me a few minutes to get all of these unloaded," the man said with an amused twinkle in his eye. "Someone must be doing a bit of groveling."

Aiden? Had all of those flowers come from him? There had to be at least ten huge, beautiful arrangements—roses and daisies and lilies and dahlias and other colorful blooms she couldn't identify.

One by one, the bellhop moved them from the cart to the dresser, with Kyra reading each card as he went.

Please forgive us. Love, Minnie and Louie

We love you, honey. From, Nelly

You'll always have a home here. Love, Doris

Kyra, we miss you and hope we can see you soon! Love, Tess, Morgan, and Willow

Please don't be mad at me. I can't lose my best friend again. Love, Lyric

Aiden screwed up. —Silas

But he's worth a second chance. —Thatch

She read the few remaining cards from people in town she'd come to know with tears prickling her eyes. She hadn't been angry with any of them. Looking back, their interactions with her had all been genuine. They would've treated her the same regardless.

"There's one more," the bellhop said. "And it's a doozy. I'll be right back."

One more. Darn it. Now she was really crying.

"It's pretty heavy." The man walked back into the room, his face hidden by a massive bouquet of beautiful red roses. There had to be a hundred stems in that vase.

"There you go." He carefully set the bouquet on the small round table in the corner of the room.

"Thank you." Kyra grabbed a twenty from her wallet and handed him the tip before closing the door behind him.

She slowly approached the roses, her heart pounding harder than it had in days. Holding her breath, she withdrew the small card from the envelope.

I'm getting help. Love, Aiden

Tears stung her eyes. "Good," she murmured. There was nothing she wanted more for Aiden than for him to heal and become whole again. But PTSD or not, he'd wounded her on purpose, and that wouldn't be easy to forget.

Her phone rang from where she'd left it on the dresser across the room. She hurried to answer but hesitated when she saw Aiden's number. The thought of talking to him brought pain brimming over in her heart. Still, she would have to face him eventually. "Hello?" Her pulse thrummed in her ears.

There was a lengthy pause before he spoke. "Hey. I'm glad I caught you." His voice held a mixture of relief and apprehension. "I dropped by Kenny's house a few times, but you weren't home. Lyric told me you were in Jackson."

And what if she had been home? What would he have said? *I'm sorry for humiliating you in front of everyone*? "Yeah. I've been staying at a hotel." She held the speaker away from her mouth and exhaled slowly.

"Are you coming back?" Aiden asked the question fast, almost desperately.

"I'll likely only be back in town for the party on Christmas Eve." And she didn't plan to stay long. Thankfully, she hadn't canceled her flight on Christmas Day. And she'd finally submitted her employment paperwork to the hospital in London too. But she didn't tell him any of that. She found it hard to say anything to the man without her voice breaking.

"I'd like the chance to talk to you," he said, as though he knew he didn't deserve the opportunity. "Face-to-face. I need to tell you how sorry I am. How much I've realized about myself and my past since that day in the park."

"You hurt me. Deeply." She needed him to hear that. "God... I have never been so humiliated." Her face burned again as she pictured all of those people staring at her after his very public rejection.

"I know." A rough sigh came through the speaker. "I keep seeing the expression on your face after what I said..." He paused and cleared his throat. "It was one of my worst moments, Kyra. I don't even deserve the chance to apologize..."

There was that tenderness in his tone again, gentle and true. Her heart softened. "Maybe you don't. But we can talk anyway."

"Thank you." He paused. "I'd come to Jackson, but Tess and Morgan and Willow are all sick with strep throat and I'm trying to help out."

"Oh, no." That was all Tess needed right before Christmas. "Are they okay? Please tell me the doctor put them on a strong antibiotic." Strep could get bad quickly if it wasn't treated correctly.

"Yeah. I think they're getting a little better." He sounded tired. "Not that either one of the girls wants to take the medicine. When I try to give it to them, they cough and gag and end up spitting half of it out all over the place."

Yes, in her experience, most kids didn't like the liquid antibiotics. "Try mixing it with chocolate milk—just make sure it's cold. They won't have a problem then."

"I'll try that. Thanks." There was noise in the background. "Willow needs me, but I really have to talk to you. Can you save me a few minutes at the party?"

"Sure. I can spare a few minutes." Minnie had left her a message to tell her that the Ladies, Tess, and Lyric were taking care of the party preparations, so all she had to do was show up.

A relieved sigh billowed through the speaker. "Great. That's great. I'm going to bring the girls as long as they're better by then. Tess said she'd be helping set up."

"She really should rest." Although the party was still three days away. As long as she took the antibiotics, she should be feeling much better by then and none of them would be contagious anymore.

"There's no way she'll miss the party," Aiden said. "And I won't either. I need to see you." There was that inflection again—hinting at a slight desperation.

She looked at the roses, her heart softening. "I got the flowers."

"I know they won't make up for what happened." His voice sounded rough. "I know nothing can make up for the way I treated you. All I can say is I'm sorry I hurt you. And you were right. I need to deal with my issues. I contacted a counselor."

"I'm glad you're getting help." Kyra noticed the clock on the nightstand. She had to get to her meeting or she'd be late. "I have to go. But we can talk more at the party." She truly wanted the best for Aiden. Hopefully now he could finally start to heal.

"Yes, we'll talk then," he murmured before saying goodbye.

She hung up the phone but her heart held on to the conversation all the way to the hotel's main restaurant.

The third and final developer—Christof Duncan—had already gotten a table. The man stood when she approached, offering his hand. "It's nice to meet you, Ms. Fowler. My sympathies on the loss of your father."

"Thank you." She sat in the chair across from him, noting his business casual attire. The other two developers had been dressed in expensive tailored suits, but Mr. Duncan had opted for khakis and a white button-down shirt, earning him extra points. Star Valley Springs didn't need fancy suits.

"I have to say, I was surprised to hear from you." Mr. Duncan took his seat. "I tried to get in touch with your father many times after our first meeting, but he wasn't interested in talking to me."

"My father had no desire to sell his holdings." Kyra glanced at a menu, though she wasn't especially hungry. "But my current circumstances won't allow me to stay in Star Valley Springs. I'm moving to London after the first of the year."

"I see." The man signaled a passing waiter and motioned for Kyra to order first. After the young man had walked away, Christof got right to business. "So I'm assuming you've read over my proposal?"

"Yes, I have. But I also wanted to meet with each potential buyer personally as well. I'd like to hear about your vision for the area, what you'd like to see change." Or stay the same. She needed to get a feel for the man to make certain she was choosing the best possible option for the town of Star Valley Springs.

"Well, it's a beautiful area. I've been fortunate to spend some time there fishing on the river." Fishing for a deal was probably more like it, but she kept quiet.

"Every property I develop commits to a high standard of sustainability and environmentalism," he said proudly. "The goal is to create communities that make a small footprint on the natural world around them."

Kyra nodded along politely, listening to the same spiel she'd heard twice already.

"Everything is designed to fit into the natural beauty rather than take away from it," Mr. Duncan went on. "I was born and raised in Wyoming, and I'd like this state to stay pristine."

There were more points for him. The other two developers were from California. "So what kinds of developments do you envision for Star Valley Springs?"

"It's already a charming place." The man paused while servers delivered their food. "We'd want to preserve some of the character the town already has, of course," he said when they were alone again. "I think we'd be looking at a phased approach. Potentially starting with one mountain resort that would include a few restaurants and a small shopping village. And then we would go from there."

She tried to picture a mountain resort next to the adorable Meadowlark Hotel and Café. "What about the businesses that are currently there?"

"New development can be very good for the local businesses. The more visitors we attract to the area, the more money everyone should make. It's really a win-win."

If that was true, why had her father refused to sell? "Why didn't my father want to talk to you? I mean, you must've interacted with him. I never got to. Unfortunately, we were...estranged." She hated that she had to use that word.

"As far as I could tell, Kenny didn't want anything in the valley to change." Mr. Duncan smiled as though he respected that. "I wouldn't be honest if I said new development doesn't impact towns like Star Valley Springs on some level. But I do believe the benefits to the local economy far outweigh any potential challenges." He refilled his water from the pitcher on the table. "As you know, your father didn't need the money. But I'm assuming you feel differently or we wouldn't be sitting here."

"I don't care as much about the money as I care about preserving what is already in Star Valley Springs." She still had a hard time imagining her life anywhere else after making up her mind to stay. "I'm sure you know the people in town are opposed to any development coming in and running them out." She might as well give him fair warning.

"Yes, I'm well aware of how they feel," Mr. Duncan said. "But, if you chose to move forward with us, I would make it my own personal mission to win them over and work with them to collaborate on our plans as much as possible."

The words were genuine enough. And the man certainly didn't seem as phony as the other two had been. "I know this is a bit unconventional. But would you be willing to come to a party on Christmas Eve so I could introduce you to some very important stakeholders in town?" This was the real test.

"I would make that work," he said without hesitation.

Then maybe she had found her buyer. As long as her friends didn't hate him. "Thank you. I'll text you the details."

For the rest of their lunch they chatted about London and her new job there. She answered all of the man's questions as though she were excited, but her heart felt empty. By the time she walked out of the restaurant she was overcome with an aching loneliness.

"Kyra!" Lyric waved at her from across the hotel lobby.

"Hey!" She maneuvered around the crowds of skiers to hug her friend extra tightly. "What're you doing here?" How did Lyric know she desperately needed someone right now?

"I was teaching some classes at another resort and I thought I'd stop by your hotel to see how your meeting went." She linked her arm through Kyra's and pulled her to a quieter corner. "Besides, I missed you. Star Valley Springs isn't the same without you."

"I missed you too." She'd be missing her friend a lot after she moved. "The meeting went okay, I guess. I like this company the best out of any I've met with." Needing to walk away from the echoing voices around them, Kyra led Lyric out the door. "I asked their CEO, Mr. Duncan, to make an appearance at the party. So everyone can meet him. So he can get to know people."

They stepped outside, where fat snowflakes were floating down to the sidewalks.

"I wonder how that'll go over." Lyric pulled on her hat.

"I'm not sure. Minnie and the Ladies will probably ambush him with kindness." Exactly like they'd done to her when she arrived in town.

"The poor man won't have a shot at getting out unscathed," Lyric said, laughing. "Oh, let's go into this store." She pointed to a souvenir boutique. "This is a fun one."

They ducked into the warmth, the polished wood floors creaking underneath their boots. Right inside the door there was a display of the most beautiful stuffed animal horses. "Oh God. Morgan and Willow would love these." She selected two—an appaloosa and a fluffy brown-and-white paint. "And look..." She held up a silver horseshoe necklace. "Wouldn't this look beautiful on Tess?"

"It's perfect for her," Lyric agreed. "But you know you don't have to buy them all presents, right? You're leaving on Christmas."

"I want to buy them gifts." For a brief moment in time Tess and Morgan and Willow had felt like her family. She'd gotten Lyric something too, but she didn't want to ruin the surprise.

"What about that present you bought for Aiden?" her friend asked while she pretended to inspect a sweater. When they'd been on their girls' trip—before he'd publicly rejected her—Kyra had bought him the most amazing hot chocolate gift set for Christmas—complete with designer marshmallows, reindeer mugs, and candy cane spoons. The memory of that hot chocolatey kiss they'd shared in Tess's kitchen assailed her yet again. "I'll still give it to the girls and him." She could leave the package on Tess's doorstep before she left town.

They moved on to browse at a rack of scarves. "Have you talked to him?" Lyric wrapped a gold-and-purple shawl around her shoulders.

"He called before I met with the developer." Which reminded her... "Thank you for the flowers, by the way. They're beautiful." Even better than the flowers was the fact that Lyric had referred to Kyra as her best friend.

"That was Aiden's idea." Her friend put the shawl back on the rack. "He literally went around to everyone in town you'd met and asked them to send you flowers all on the same day. I meant what I said on the card, but Aiden coordinated the whole thing."

The gesture made her smile. That was the Aiden she'd

fallen for. The thoughtful, tender man who had fallen off a roof trying to surprise his nieces. But he had another side. A side that had eventually shut her out. "He said he's getting some counseling."

"Good. I know how much counseling helped me after my divorce." Lyric continued browsing, but Kyra had lost interest in shopping.

"Was there any other advice my father gave you about starting over?" Because she was standing at a crossroads in her life, and she needed to hear from her dad right now.

"Kenny was full of good advice," Lyric said fondly. "After I moved back home it took me a while to figure out what I was going to do with my life. For months I couldn't decide which way to go. I'd start down one path and then change my mind. Mostly I felt lost."

Kyra could relate.

"One time I was getting down on myself for changing courses yet again," Lyric went on. "And your dad told me, 'Figure out what it is that breathes life into your heart and do that. Whatever it is. Even if it defies logic'" Her smile grew. "'Or especially if it defies logic.'"

"I've never been good at defying logic." But her father's words felt like a gift. She'd always relied on her head to make decisions, but in his honor this time she would learn to follow her heart.

CHAPTER TWENTY-THREE

I don't have anything to wear to the party!" Morgan threw herself down on her bed and stubbornly crossed her arms.

Oh, boy. "What d'you mean?" Aiden sat down on the edge of the mattress and checked his watch again. They were supposed to be at Kyra's—*Kenny's*—house in ten minutes. When his sister had left two hours ago, she'd told him to get the girls ready for the party, making it sound as simple as coloring with them. He hadn't been prepared for a wardrobe crisis. "I thought you were going to wear your red sweater."

"Nope." Her sigh blew her bangs up her forehead. "That's boring. I wear my red sweater to school."

So she must've liked her red sweater. "And you can't wear it to the party because... ?"

"It's a party, Uncle Aiden." Her eyeroll condemned his ignorance. "I have to wear something *special*."

"You're beautiful no matter what you wear."

Morgan uttered a dramatic sigh.

All right, new plan. He got up and walked into her closet, looking through her clothes. "Here." He pulled out a velvety green dress. "How about this? Look, it has sparkles on it."

His niece crawled to the edge of the bed, eyeing the dress. "I don't know..."

"I like that one." Willow came skipping into the room. "It's so pretty! I'll wear it."

"No!" Morgan leaped off the bed. "It's mine. You can't wear my clothes!"

Whoa. "Now, girls—"

"I can too wear your clothes!" Willow ripped the dress out of Aiden's hand and darted from the room with Morgan chasing behind her.

Great. Had Tess been punishing him when she left him to supervise the girls' party preparations? He pulled out his phone and fired off a text.

Your daughters are currently fighting over a dress. What should I do?

He didn't have to wait long for a response.

Figure it out. And then get your butt over here. Kyra's here!

Thus the reason he had wanted to leave a half hour

ago. He'd been aching to talk to her. The heartbreak on her face after their last conversation still haunted him. Now he had one last chance to be honest with the woman. And the sooner her settled his nieces' dispute, the faster he could get to Kyra.

Aiden walked out the room and found Morgan chasing Willow around the couch. "I wanna wear the dress!" his older niece screamed at the top of her lungs. "Gimme it now!"

"How about I wear the dress?" Aiden marched to Willow and stole the garment out of her hand. "Yeah, this is about my size." He held it up against his body. "And green *is* my color. I think this dress would look pretty awesome on me, what d'you guys think?" He made sure to look hopeful, even though that dress wouldn't even fit over his shoulders. "I could totally rock this. Right?"

"Oh, Uncle Aiden." Morgan started to giggle, and it wasn't long before long Willow joined in. "It's way too small for you." She snatched the dress out of his hands. "Willow can wear it." She handed the hanger to her sister. "It'll look really pretty on her. I wanted to wear my red sweater anyway."

It took everything in Aiden not to slap his forehead. All of that for nothing? "Glad that's settled." While Morgan and Willow both ran off to get dressed, he straightened up the living room, which was still a mess from their pillow fight earlier.

"Uncle Aiden?" Morgan crept into the living room—wearing the red sweater, thank God, and a black skirt. "Can you put this on for me?" She held up the delicate heart necklace Jace had given her for her birthday not long before their last mission.

"I would love to." He sat on the couch while Morgan turned her back to him. The same feelings of inadequacy that had always plagued him when he tried to stand in for Jace threatened to rise again, but now, after a few phone calls with the therapist Wakefield had referred him to, Aiden could put them in their place. He wasn't Jace. He would never be Jace. But he didn't have to be. He had something to offer his nieces too.

"You miss my daddy too, don't you?" Morgan peeked over her shoulder while he clasped on her necklace.

"I do." He turned her around to make sure the necklace was on straight.

She wedged herself onto the couch next to him. "It makes it easier missing him together, don't you think?"

"For sure." If it hadn't been for Morgan and Willow, and Tess, he might've gone down an even darker path. "Thank goodness we have each other."

"We'll always have each other, right?" His niece peered up at him, her eyes unsure. "You're always going to be here with us? You're never going to leave?"

"I will always be here for you." Aiden hugged her. "No matter where I go or what I do." He couldn't promise he would live just down the street from the ranch forever. Part of his healing process would mean supporting Tess and the girls while he built a life for himself too.

"I'm ready for the party!" Willow paraded into the room, wearing the green dress and a pair of patent leather shoes.

"Wow." Aiden got off the couch. "You two ladies both look lovely." He ushered them to the fireplace. "All right, say cheese. I have to send your mom a picture." So she could see he'd handled the dress crisis.

Both girls struck a pose, and he snapped a few pictures on his phone, quickly firing off a text to Tess.

On our way. Be there soon.

"Let's go! Let's go!" Willow led the way to the coat closet, and he helped the girls bundle up before they hurried out the door.

"Buckle up," Aiden reminded them after they were settled in their booster seats.

"You have to go real slow under the tunnel of lights," Morgan instructed him. "We like to look at all the colors."

"Aye aye, captain." He drove as slowly as he could, given his sense of urgency to get to the party. They were now officially a half hour late. Thankfully, they didn't have too far to go.

"I can't wait to see Kyra." Willow hummed a few bars of "Jingle Bells" along with the radio.

"Me neither." Aiden turned out onto the two-lane highway that led to Kenny's ranch. He didn't know what he would say to her. But he didn't want to feed her a bunch of rehearsed lines anyway. He only wanted to tell her the truth... that he was sorry he'd hurt her, that he'd acted out of fear, that she'd changed his life, that he was doing his best to move forward, that he wanted to become the kind of man she deserved. He glanced down to turn up the heat.

"Uncle Aiden, watch out!" Morgan's scream rang in his ears.

His gaze lifted to the road ahead. A deer stood in front of them, staring into the headlights.

"Hold on, girls." He pumped the brake and started to swerve. He could get around it. He could—

The wheels skidded on a patch of black ice, sending the truck into a spin. Lights illuminated the trees, the snowbanks. And then Aiden couldn't see. A violent jolt shook the truck as they went off the road.

The girls screamed, and Aiden held his breath, bracing for impact. *Keep them safe, Jace. Protect them…*

The truck slammed into a tree head on, whipping him forward into the steering wheel. The sound of crunching metal and shattering glass deafened him.

Pain gripped his left leg, while the shards of glass seemed to rain down everywhere. Then everything fell silent. Too silent. "Girls!" Adrenaline raced through him. "Morgan! Willow!" Aiden tried to move, but his whole lower body was pinned under the crumpled remains of what used to be the front end of his truck.

"Uncle Aiden." Morgan whimpered behind him and Willow started to wail.

"Are you okay?" He fought to turn his head so he could see them. "Please tell me you're okay."

"I'm okay," Willow said between sobs.

"Me too." Morgan still whimpered.

"Nothing hurts? You're not bleeding?" He could only catch a glimpse of their fearful faces before the pain in his head forced him to turn back around.

There was a pause before Morgan answered. "I'm not bleeding and neither is Willow. We're not hurt."

"Okay." He exhaled relief. "Okay. Everything's gonna be okay." He tried to squirm out of the death grip the dashboard had on his lower body, but a searing pain blinded him. Damn it! His left leg must've taken the brunt of the impact. He couldn't move with the agony grinding into his bones. He reached his arm around to the back of his waist but couldn't get his phone out of his back pocket.

"Are you okay, Uncle Aiden?" Morgan undid her seatbelt and crawled over the seat next to him. "You're bleeding!" Terror laced her voice. "Your head is bleeding!"

"I'm okay." He smiled at her, at his beautiful niece, one of the greatest gifts in his life. "But I need you to go to the back seat, honey." He tried to smooth the rough edges out of his voice. "I need you to crawl into the back seat and find the blanket I keep under the seat. And then I want you and Willow to cuddle up and put it around you. Okay?"

"But you're hurt," his niece cried. "You're hurt bad. I can tell. Your legs—"

"Will be fine." He tried to shift again, to reach for his phone, but the pain in his leg nearly made him vomit. "Go on now." She needed to stop looking at him so she could stay calm. "I need you to listen, Morgan. Get in the back seat and keep Willow warm for me."

Without the truck's engine on, the cold had already started to seep in through the windows. Aiden tensed his shoulders to stop the shuddering.

"Shouldn't I go get help?" Morgan still hadn't moved. "I could go outside and try to find someone..."

"No." He smoothed her hair away from her face. "Someone will come to help us. I promise. It's too cold and dark out there, sweetie. You need to stay here with Willow and me. And I need you to be really strong, okay? We all need to be really strong."

Morgan nodded, her eyes still wide and fearful, but she crawled to the back seat and helped Willow get out of her booster. "I found the blanket, Uncle Aiden."

"That's good." He used his shirt to wipe up the blood trickling down his face. "You two stay warm. Bundle up good."

"We are," Willow said, still sniffling.

"And how about you sing me some Christmas carols?" His teeth had started to chatter, but he couldn't tell if it was from the shock or the cold. "You know how much I love it when you sing 'O Christmas Tree.' "

The girls started to sing, their voices small and weepy, and Aiden tried to hum along to show them he was okay.

He wasn't okay. Forget his leg, the accident had shaken every part of him. Morgan and Willow could've been hurt. They could've been killed. He'd been too distracted. He should've been watching farther ahead. How could he have let this happen?

"O Christmas tree, O Christmas tree..." their little voices harmonized together, fearful but also finding a melody. "How lovely are your branches..."

Aiden closed his eyes, listening to them sing. They had always been able to sing no matter what had happened to them. They were strong girls, and someday they would be a force to be reckoned with. He might not always be able to protect them or stop bad things from happening to them, but he could teach them to come through every storm stronger.

The tremors in his body slowed. He hadn't let this accident happen, just like he hadn't let Jace's death happen. He hadn't put the deer in the road. He hadn't put that sniper in that hovel. Those things hadn't been up to him. He couldn't do anything about what had already happened. He couldn't change the last five minutes or the last few years.

But he could control what happened next. He had to get his nieces through the scary moments until someone on the road stopped to help them. Someone would come. This wasn't it for him. For the first time in a long time he had faith.

Like Jace's letter said, he had to believe the best was yet to come.

CHAPTER TWENTY-FOUR

Maybe she shouldn't have come back here.

Kyra stood on the outskirts of the party in her father's living room, surrounded by the merry murmur of voices, the festive music playing over the Bluetooth, and Christmas décor that could've rivaled any photograph in a Martha Stewart magazine. And yet she'd never been more alone.

It wasn't that everyone had made her feel unwelcome when she'd walked in the door. Quite the opposite, actually. The Ladies and Lyric and Tess had welcomed her into the house with confetti and a cake to celebrate her new life in London. The problem was she didn't want to go. She wanted to stay here. She wanted to chat with these people. She wanted to laugh with them. She wanted to go dance with Lyric and Thatch, who were goofing around to a big band version of "Deck the Halls" in front of the fireplace. Even Mr. Duncan appeared to be genuinely enjoying himself—currently discussing the best fishing spots on the river with Louie near the Christmas tree.

Kyra let out a sigh to ease the pressure in her chest and leaned against the wall. Yes, she'd wanted to take her father's advice and rely on her heart to make this big life decision, but now her heart had started to shy away from the risks. What if she stayed? Would she be able to protect her heart with Aiden living so close by?

She didn't know how she would feel when she saw him again. Maybe her answer would come easily.

"How about some cranberry punch?" Minnie snuck up behind her and offered her a plastic flute. "This is the adult version. Doris spiked it with vodka, the sneak."

"Thanks, but I think I'll pass for now." She glanced out the window into the darkness. Still no sign of Aiden and the girls. Where was he?

"Suit yourself." Minnie drank from the cup. "I have to say, Mr. Duncan isn't at all what I expected."

"He surprised me too." It turned out that Christof Duncan had a wonderful sense of humor. It was no easy task to get Louie laughing like that.

"I think he'll do good things for Star Valley Springs." Minnie set her drink on the nearby bookshelf. "Thank you for being so thoughtful in choosing someone who might actually listen to us."

"I do think he'll listen." But that didn't mean this town wasn't about to go through some big changes. "I don't know, though. Maybe I should wait to sell. Maybe I should spend more time finding a buyer." There was no way Mr. Duncan would love this town the way she had come to. He would always be business first.

Figure out what it is that breathes life into your heart and do that…

Even though he'd passed away, her father had still found a way to speak to her. Now she had to be brave enough to listen.

"You *want* to stay?" Minnie hugged her and then quickly backed off. "You know we would all love for you to be here, of course, but we can't hold you back either. If London is what your heart truly desires, you need to go."

London wasn't what her heart desired.

"Hey, what're you two so hush-hush about over here?" Lyric joined them, still out of breath from dancing with Thatch.

"Kyra's having second thoughts about leaving." Minnie slapped a hand over her mouth. "Darn punch."

"It's okay." Lyric already knew. "I may have been a little hasty in asking Mr. Duncan to come here."

Figure out what it is that breathes life into your heart and do that…

People. These people had breathed new life into her heart. She needed Lyric and Minnie and Doris and Nelly and Tess and Morgan and Willow. She didn't know what would happen with Aiden…if he would be able to let her in fully someday. But she couldn't walk away from these friendships she'd built. She didn't want to go back to isolating herself now that she'd experienced what it felt like to have a family. "I have to talk to Mr. Duncan."

"Don't worry. I've got this." Minnie paraded across the room to her husband. "Louie, I need you in the kitchen, pronto." She had to all but drag him away from his new best friend.

"Go," Lyric said gently, giving her a nudge. "Follow your heart."

Kyra made her way to Mr. Duncan with a sense of purpose that carried her across the room. "Hi there. You seem to be enjoying the party."

"I am." The man scanned the faces around him with a smile. "The people of Star Valley Springs are very hospitable. I'm looking forward to hearing more about their hopes for the future. I know we can work on a development plan that will make everyone happy."

She opened her mouth to speak but didn't know what to say.

"I won't be working on any development plans, will I?" He must've read the look on her face.

"I'm not going to sell. I can't." Saying those words lifted a weight off her. "These people—this place—means too much to me. I can't leave." She didn't even know exactly what her life would look like here, if she could maybe open a clinic since they didn't have one in town or if she could find a job in a nearby city. But her job didn't matter nearly as much as the people she'd come to care about. "I'm sorry you came all this way for nothing."

"You should never apologize for following your heart." The man was nothing but gracious. "Your father did the same thing, and I always respected him for it."

"Thank you." She loved hearing that she was like her father. "I hope you'll stay for the rest of the party and enjoy the desserts."

"I never miss dessert." Mr. Duncan squeezed her hand. "Besides, Louie and I have more fishing spots to discuss. If you'll excuse me."

"Of course." Kyra watched him go in the direction of the kitchen and then slipped into the entryway for some space. Whoa. She was staying. She was really staying.

"Hey." Tess came rushing down the hallway. "You haven't heard from Aiden, have you?"

"No." She checked her phone to be sure. "Nothing."

His sister frowned, worry lines appearing in her forehead. "I'm a little concerned about them. He texted me forty minutes ago and said they were on their way." She studied her phone screen. "I've tried calling him and texting, but he's not getting back to me."

Unease spread through Kyra's stomach. "That doesn't seem like him at all." Aiden always answered the phone when Tess called.

"I know." His sister brought the phone to her ear, shaking her head as it rang. "I'm sure they got delayed leaving. Maybe the girls are fighting again." She pocketed the phone. "But I feel like I should go check on them. Just to make sure nothing's wrong."

"I'm in." Her heart suddenly felt as frantic as Tess looked. "We should get Silas and Thatch too. In case." Maybe his truck had gotten stuck in the snow somewhere along the way.

"Good idea." Tess rushed into the living room with Kyra right behind.

"Hey." She signaled to Silas. "We need you."

He strode to them wearing his signature party-boy grin. "I'm glad you've finally come to your senses, Tess."

Aiden's sister rolled her eyes. "Funny."

"Have you heard from Aiden?" Kyra demanded. They didn't have time to mess around. She waved Thatch over before Silas could answer the question. "Have either of you heard from Aiden? He and the girls were supposed to be here a half hour ago and they haven't showed."

They both checked their phones.

"He hasn't called or texted me." Silas was no longer smiling. "I'm sure he's fine, but we'll head to your place to check things out."

He and Thatch started out the door.

"We're coming with you." Kyra pulled her coat out of the closet while Tess wrapped a scarf around her neck.

"I'll drive." Silas unlocked his truck and appeared to be moving with the same urgency Kyra felt. Something wasn't right.

No one said anything as Silas drove down the driveway. He turned out onto the two-lane highway and blasted the heat. "It's pretty dark. No moon tonight. Everyone keep your eyes peeled. It might be hard to see anything."

Kyra's heart went from pounding to convulsing as she scanned the dark snowbanks along the road. Maybe he and the girls were still at Tess's; maybe—

"Oh, my God." Her chest locked up. Taillights lit up the snow down an embankment ahead.

"That's Aiden's truck." Silas slowed and started to guide the vehicle off the road, hitting some bumps.

Before the truck had even come to a complete stop, Kyra was out the door. "Call nine-one-one!" she yelled to Thatch.

"Morgan!" Tess screamed, tearing out of the passenger's side behind her. "Willow!"

"We're here!" One of the doors opened and Morgan jumped out before helping Willow down.

"Mommy!" the littlest girl screamed and ran into Tess's arms.

Morgan stood still halfway between them and the wrecked truck as if she were shell-shocked.

Silas lifted her into his arms. "You girls okay? What about Aiden? Where's Aiden?"

"We're okay but Uncle Aiden's hurt real bad." Morgan clung to Silas. "He's in the truck. I really wanted to find someone to help us but he didn't want me to get out. He told me to stay."

"You did the right thing, honey." Silas hugged her to him. "We're here now. Everything'll be okay. We'll help him."

"Take them to your truck and get them warm," Kyra whispered before sprinting the rest of the way to Aiden's mangled mess of a truck, which had been wedged into a tree trunk.

"Aiden, talk to me." She yanked open the passenger's door and crawled across the bench seat to get to him. The dash had caved in on his lower body, and blood crusted his head and face.

Oh no. No, no, no. Her throat tightened, but she closed her eyes, forced herself to take deep, even breaths. "Where's the pain?" She did a visual check of his body but couldn't get a read on the injuries.

"Kyra?" His head turned slowly to her, his eyes open halfway. "Are you really here?" His whole body shuddered. He was freezing. "Get him some blankets," she called to Thatch, who was hovering outside, still on the phone with a dispatcher. "Now!"

"I think Silas has some in the truck." The man disappeared.

"Kyra?" Aiden lifted his head.

"I'm here." She pressed her palm to his cold cheek.

"I'm right here. But we need to worry about you right now." Think. She had to think. She had to use her training. "Where do you hurt, Aiden? Is it only your legs? Does your head hurt?" She didn't dare move him, not with the way his leg was positioned under the dash, not with the way blood crusted his face. He could have a spinal cord injury, a head injury. And she had no way to help him out here...

"I'm sorry." His hand reached for hers and held on. "I wanted to tell you. I didn't know if I'd get to tell you..."

"You can tell me," she said firmly, fighting back tears. "You'll have plenty of time to tell me anything you want. But right now you need to save your strength. Okay? The ambulance will be here soon." Helplessness washed over her. She had no tools, no way to bring him relief. God, they'd have to cut him out of the truck...

"I messed everything up." Aiden held her hand tighter. "Everything. I was afraid I could never deserve you, so I wanted you to leave..."

"Shhh." A sob snuck out, and Kyra swallowed hard. She had to be the strong one here. She had to keep it together for him.

Thatch reappeared and shoved a sleeping bag into the truck. "Here. Silas is looking for more blankets. How is he?"

"It's not good." She tried to steady her voice. "There are definitely injuries to his lower body and I'm not sure about his head." Kyra got to work tucking the sleeping bag around Aiden. "We shouldn't move him. We need to wait until he can be stabilized."

"What can I do?" Thatch asked helplessly.

"Wait for the fire trucks." They had to hurry. *Please let them hurry*. "Tell them they'll need tools to cut him out of here."

When she looked at Aiden again, he'd closed his eyes. "Wake up." She climbed under the sleeping bag and sat as close to him as she dared, trying to help warm him. "Aiden, I need you to wake up. Talk to me."

"Sorry." His eyelids fluttered. "I'm really tired."

"I know." Tears slipped down her cheeks. "But you have to keep talking to me. You can't go to sleep right now." Not with his body likely in shock. Not with a potential head injury. Not with the cold seeping in around them. "Tell me everything. Everything you wanted to say."

His gaze found hers, and he stared into her eyes with an intensity that allowed her to see past the dark blood on his face. "I'm falling in love with you, Kyra Fowler. That's everything I wanted to say. I'm falling in love with you and I want to become the kind of man you deserve."

"You alrcady arc." She moved to her knees and kissed his cheek, his forehead. "You are a good man, Aiden." Seeing his eyelids grow heavy again, she moved her lips to his, kissing lightly, gently. "You are a good man. And you know what?"

"What?" he whispered against her lips.

"I got you a Christmas present." Raw fear scorched her throat.

"A present?" His mouth twitched into a grin. "What is it?"

"I'm not going to tell you." She weaved her fingers through his, willing him to fight. "You have to wait and see." He would open the present she'd gotten for him on Christmas, she would make sure of that.

Sirens wailed in the distance. "Listen," she murmured. "Do you hear that? We're going to get you out of here very soon. And then we're going to celebrate Christmas together. You and me and Tess and Morgan and Willow."

Somehow he fired up his grin again. "And what about Christmas night?"

She laughed through the barrage of tears. "I guess what happens on Christmas night will have to be a surprise." The poor man likely wouldn't be in any shape to enjoy a night like they'd had a few weeks ago, but she wasn't going to tell him that now.

"They're here," Thatch called in through the broken window. "You hear that, bro? We're gonna get you out of there, buddy. Just hold on a little longer."

Aiden squeezed her hand. "I'm holding on."

She was too. Kyra was holding on to him with all of her strength.

CHAPTER TWENTY-FIVE

"Can't you drive any faster?"

Kyra checked the map on her phone again. How were they still fifteen minutes away from the hospital? This drive through the mountains had been the longest two hours of her life. After the firefighters had extracted Aiden from the truck, she'd seen the damage to his left leg. He and the girls had all been airlifted to a trauma center in eastern Idaho so they could receive the necessary critical care. As soon as the helicopters had taken off, she had jumped into Silas's truck with him and Thatch, and they'd been driving ever since. "I don't understand why Tess hasn't updated us yet. This is taking forever." There hadn't been one text since she'd gotten into the helicopter with the girls.

"Well, I could go faster, but I'd rather not be the reason anyone else ends up in a hospital tonight," Silas said, giving her an apologetic look in the rearview mirror.

"I know. I'm sorry." She let out a lengthy sigh. Tess

was busy. It was difficult enough for Kyra to be worried about Aiden right now. She couldn't imagine how she would be handing the emotions if she were a mom and her two children had been in an accident. "The girls really seemed okay, though, didn't they?" she asked for at least the fifth time. She'd supervised while the paramedics had evaluated them at the scene, and none of them had identified any obvious injuries. Though without scans it was impossible to know about internal injuries, which was why they'd called in the helicopters.

"They're getting the best care right now," Thatch reminded her. "All three of them. Aiden has been through a hell of a lot worse than a broken leg. Trust me. He's a badass."

"I know." But she hadn't known him when he'd been off at war. Now that she'd found him she didn't want him to suffer at all. Ever. "It's not the leg I'm worried about." Broken bones usually healed well. "He could have a closed head injury. Or internal injuries..." One of the downfalls of being a nurse was that she knew every worst-case scenario.

"He was conscious and talking when they loaded him into the helicopter." Silas was being especially gentle with his tone. "Remember? He told you he couldn't wait to open the present you got him." The man's eyebrows peaked. "What'd you get him anyway?"

"A hot chocolate set." She used her coat sleeve to mop up tears. Hopefully the crying would stop before they actually got to the hospital. "Because he made me hot chocolate the night we sorted through all of the Christmas decorations."

"Ah, yes." Thatch turned around and smirked at her.

"Was that the night he slept on the couch and you slept in the guest room?"

"No, wasn't it Kyra who slept on the couch and Aiden in the guest room?" Silas teased.

"Yes, we slept together, okay?" She shot them her own smirk. "And it was the best night of my life, I'll have you know. There was a really strong connection between us even then." She leaned over the seat, eyeing them. "Have either of you ever had that with anyone?"

The cricket-chirping silence gave her their answer. "I didn't think so." Kyra sat back, satisfied. "So yes, I'm overly emotional, overly worried, and overly obsessive right now. Because I don't want to lose him before we get to have our chance."

"You won't lose him." Silas parked the truck outside of the emergency room doors. "You two will have your chance. You both deserve it." He got out of the truck and opened her door for her, offering her his hand.

"You two aren't so bad," she said as Silas helped her climb out of the truck.

"You're not so bad either." Thatch met them at the doors.

They walked into the quiet waiting room together and marched straight to the desk.

"We're looking for Aiden Steele. And Morgan and Willow Valdez," Kyra announced to the intake nurse. "They were airlifted here after a car accident earlier this evening."

The man moved the computer mouse and clicked a few times while he stared at the screen. "Are you family?"

"Um. Well." Kyra briefly thought about lying, but that would be unethical. "I guess technically we're not, but we're very close—"

"I'm sorry." He taunted her with an overly polite smile. "I'm not able to give out any information right now."

Because of HIPAA. She knew that. She'd said those same words to other people before. "But I need to see him." Considering that the last time she saw Aiden, he was bloodied and broken, she needed to see him right this minute, and she didn't care about any medical privacy laws.

"That's not possible."

"What d'you mean that's not possible?" On some level, she knew she was overreacting, but she couldn't stop herself from saying, "I'll have you know that I'm a *nurse practitioner*, buddy, and—"

"Whoa there, Trigger." Thatch gently tugged on her arm, leading her away from the desk.

"We'll just wait for Aiden's sister over there," Silas said behind her.

"I don't want to wait anymore." Kyra dropped to a chair, hiding her face in her hands. "I need to see him."

"I know you do." Thatch sat next to her. "Silas is calling Tess right now."

Kyra lifted her head. Silas was talking! That meant he'd gotten hold of her. She rose and hurried to the corner to eavesdrop.

"Okay. Good. That's good," Silas said. "So the girls both look fine but are staying overnight for observation?" He nodded at Kyra.

"That's great." The man slowly exhaled. "Thank God. I think Kyra would like to be the one to hear the update on Aiden." He handed her his phone.

"Tess?" The tears started flowing as she brought the phone to her ear. "Morgan and Willow are really okay?"

"They're perfect." Aiden's sister sounded like she might've been crying too. "Neither one of them has a scratch on them."

"I'm so glad." She waited, already knowing the news on Aiden wouldn't be as positive.

"They're taking Aiden into surgery soon," Tess continued, sniffling now. "He's not in great shape right now, Kyra. His leg…it's really bad. It was crushed. They're going to try to save it, but they don't know…"

"What else?" She sank further in her chair to absorb the news. "Any head injuries? Internal injuries?"

"He has a concussion, but they didn't find any other serious injuries besides a few bruised ribs." A sob came through the speaker. "He was hypothermic when they brought him in. I should've gone looking for them earlier. He had to sit in that freezing cold truck badly injured for almost an hour—"

"You couldn't have known." None of them could've known what had happened. "Have you seen him?" She closed her eyes, trying to picture Aiden's face without all the blood.

"Yes." Tess cleared her throat. "I've been going back and forth between his room and the girls'. But they're getting ready to move the girls to the peds floor. I don't know how I'll be able to keep checking on him. I don't want to leave them too long. They're pretty shaken up."

"I'll stay with him." Kyra sprang out of the chair. "If you can come out to the ER waiting room and bring me in, I'll stay with him. Please, I need to see him."

"That would help so much." There was a rustling in the background. "I'll be out there to get you in a few minutes."

"Thank you!" Kyra handed the phone back to Silas and mauled him with a hug.

"Whoa." He stumbled back a step before returning the hug. "Good news, I take it?"

"She's coming out to bring me in there." Kyra finally let go of him and moved on to hug Thatch. "I get to see him." She quickly relayed the information about his surgery and his leg. "But it doesn't sound like the concussion is too serious, and he has no internal injuries." And he was alive and he would heal and she would help him.

"I'm so glad you're all here." Tess came running to them. She hugged Kyra and then Thatch and then moved to Silas, who caught her in his arms.

Kyra didn't miss how Tess seemed to stay enfolded in Silas's arms a little longer than necessary. If she weren't on a mission to see Aiden she would've let Silas and Tess hug all night, but at the moment she couldn't summon any patience. "Ahem." She cleared her throat so loudly that the intake nurse looked over. "We should probably get back there." Before Aiden went into surgery and she lost her chance to see him.

"Right." Tess stepped away from Silas.

"We'll be right out here." The man squeezed Tess's hand and stared at her like no one else was standing there.

Ohhhh. Kyra had to snap her mouth shut before she said anything. She hadn't realized Silas had a thing for Tess. But, wow, now it was pretty obvious.

"Ready?" Aiden's sister started to walk away.

"I've been ready for over two hours." Kyra fell in stride beside her. "I swear that drive felt like three days."

"So did the helicopter ride." Tess paused briefly at the intake station, explaining to the nurse that Kyra was almost family, and then he gave her a visitor pass and they went in through the double doors.

"He's right down this way." Tess guided her through a winding corridor that was much quieter than the ER at her hospital back in Florida. They pushed through a door near the end and walked into Aiden's room.

"Hey, Kyra." He greeted her with a big goofy smile and tried to sit up but winced and held a hand against the right side of his rib cage. "You're so pretty."

She laughed a little. Oh, the wonders of a little pain relief. "Hi there." She walked to the gurney, relieved to see how much better he looked than he had when she'd sat in his truck with him while they'd waited on help. The blood had been cleaned off his face and only one small white bandage patched a spot above his left eyebrow.

"What about me?" Tess moved to the other side of his bed. "I'm not pretty?" She clearly loved to give her brother a hard time.

"Not as pretty as Kyra," he said without pause.

"You're not looking so bad yourself." She eased down onto the mattress carefully to make sure she didn't cause him to move. She'd seen plenty of patients with bruised ribs and knew how painful they could be.

"Morgan and Willow are okay," Aiden informed her. "They're not hurt. They don't have one scratch."

"That's great news." Kyra allowed herself to look at his left leg, which was currently stabilized in an air cast. "How are you doing?"

"Better since you're here." He quickly shifted his gaze to his sister. "We need to be alone. We still have things to talk about."

"I can take a hint." Tess smiled and ruffled her brother's

hair. "I have to get back to the girls anyway. You'll keep me posted on the surgery?" she asked Kyra.

"I'll text you updates as soon as I get them," she promised.

After Tess walked out the door it took every ounce of willpower Kyra possessed to not crawl fully onto the bed so she could wrap her arms around him.

"Did you forgive me?" Aiden rested his head back on the pile of pillows behind him, but his eyes stayed on her. "Or was I hallucinating? I had hypothermia, you know. So I can't be too sure what really happened."

"Hmmm." Kyra rolled her eyes, pretending to search for the answer on the ceiling. "Let me see if I remember what I said..."

"You can't mess with me." Aiden patted the blankets around him until his hand found hers. "I'm in the hospital. I'm about to have surgery. It's not nice."

He had a point. Kyra leaned over him, bringing her lips within inches of his. "How do I know you'll remember what I say now?" she whispered.

"Because I'll never forget this moment." Every trace of levity disappeared as he stared steadily into her eyes. "I'll never forget telling you that you saved me. Before you came, I wasn't living. Not really. I was surviving, existing around the pain, using it to shield myself from more potential pain." He reached to her face, tucking a lock of her hair behind her ear. "I kept thinking it should've been me who died on that last mission. Not Jace. And I couldn't handle the guilt."

"I understand those feelings." She'd worked with enough children who'd survived trauma to see how that survivor's guilt could take hold of a person's thoughts.

"But you made me want more," Aiden went on. "You made me want to deal with the past so I can start living."

Kyra brushed her lips over his, closing her eyes, sealing this moment in a memory too. "And you made me realize I could be part of a family. You brought to life this dream I hadn't even realized I had." She kissed him again, and then sat upright so she wouldn't hurt him. "I'm staying, by the way. I can't sell. I can't walk away from you…from Tess and the girls…from Star Valley Springs. It's my home."

"I was hoping you'd say that." Aiden lifted her hand to his lips and kissed her knuckles. "I want you to know I've started talking to a therapist who specializes in PTSD. In January, I'm going away for a few weeks. To participate in an intensive program for veterans."

"I think that's wonderful." Kyra slowly lay down, resting her head on the pillows next to his. "When you come back, I'll be waiting for you."

She would wait as long as it took for him to fully heal.

CHAPTER TWENTY-SIX

It was a Christmas miracle.

Aiden gazed at the beauty asleep in the hospital chair a few feet away from his bed. Kyra was here with him. And she loved him even though he'd been unlovable. This morning—even though he was in the hospital—happened to be the best Christmas morning in his entire life.

Kyra startled and sat up abruptly, shoving her hair out of her face. "Oh, my God. What time is it?" She scrambled to get to her feet. "Are you okay? Are you in pain? Do you need anything?"

"I'm great. I only need you." He made a "come hither" gesture and patted the sorry excuse for a mattress next to him. "Merry Christmas."

"Merry Christmas." Kyra yawned while she gingerly eased onto the bed next to him like she was afraid he'd break. "How's the leg?"

"I've still got it at least." The doctors had managed to

piece the bones back together, but they'd said he would have a long road to a full recovery. He would walk the road no matter how long it would take, no matter how hard it got. He would do whatever it took to get where he needed to be both mentally and physically. "You should go home and get some sleep." Neither one of them had gotten much with the nurses constantly interrupting to check on his vitals.

"Not a chance." She inched closer to him. "Besides, the doctor said there's only a *slight* possibility you could be discharged later today." As long as his vitals remained stable and they didn't see any swelling that concerned them. "I'm not going anywhere until you do."

"It's not a *slight* possibility." He checked the time on his phone, which sat on his bedside table. "It's only eight o'clock. My goal is to be out of here by three o'clock. I'm not going to make you spend your entire Christmas in a hospital."

"We'll see what the doctor has to say about that," Kyra muttered stubbornly.

Aiden sat up but instantly regretted the sudden movement. Damn his bruised ribs. All he wanted to do right now was pull this woman fully into his arms. "The doctor already said the surgery went much better than he'd expected," he reminded her. "And I'm sure he'll feel very good about releasing me into the care of an incredibly brilliant, compassionate, sexy nurse practitioner."

Kyra shook her head, wearing a smile that tempted him to pull her into a long, pain-defying kiss. "I can't see how my sexiness would have any impact on your recovery."

"Oh, trust me." He slid his hand up her thigh. "I'm gonna be real motivated to make serious progress."

"Glad to hear it." She shifted to her side and faced him, torturing him with an overly gentle kiss. "Because you can't have any vigorous activity until those ribs heal."

"I'm pretty sure they're healed." He patted the sore spots low on his ribs. "Yep. All good now."

"Suuure." Kyra gave him some space. "Let's see you do a sit-up, then."

"Uhhh—" Before he could attempt that feat, the door to his room opened.

"Uncle Aiden!" Morgan dashed to his bed. "You're awake! Merry Christmas!"

"Merry Christmas." He gritted his teeth and opened his arms so he could hug her, catching Kyra in the middle.

"We brought donuts!" Willow traipsed to the bed carrying a box.

"And coffee." Tess came in next, along with Silas and Thatch.

"I could use some coffee." Kyra pushed off the bed, leaving room for both girls to climb up.

"Mama said the doctor fixed your leg." Willow peered warily at the brace holding his new hardware together.

"Yep. With a little time and some exercises my leg'll be as good as new." He checked their faces. "You two girls were very brave last night." A tremor ran through him. "I'm so proud of you both."

"We're proud of you too." Morgan gingerly patted his shoulder. "Mom said you're being very brave too. Even though you had to have surgery."

"Speaking of the surgery." Tess sat in a chair next to the bed, nursing her cup of coffee. "Have you seen the doctor yet this morning?"

"Not yet." He checked the clock again. But they had to get this ball rolling if he was going to break out of here.

"He's under the delusion that he'll be going home for Christmas." Kyra sat at the end of the bed near his bum leg.

"Mama said Santa came to our house last night!" Willow popped up to her knees, shaking the bed.

"Really?" He checked his sister's face. How was that possible when she'd been at the hospital all night?

Tess winked at him. "Yep. Santa and his helpers have the presents all taken care of."

Ah. She must've called the Ladies and told them to put out the presents she'd stashed in the basement. "See?" He looked at Kyra. "We need to get home so we can open presents." Had she really gotten him something?

"We could break you out of here right now." Silas offered Aiden a cup of coffee. "Recon missions always have been our specialty."

"Don't even think about it." Kyra stood up. "You'll have to get past me first."

"Not to worry." Thatch picked up the donut box and held it out like a peace offering. "We'll wait until he has your permission to leave."

"Thank you." She selected a chocolate donut and sat back down on the bed.

"I want a donut." Morgan crawled over Aiden to get to the box on the dresser.

"Me too!" Willow accidentally kneed him in the ribs on her way.

But Aiden refused to wince or groan against the pain. These girls could climb on him all they wanted. They could bruise his ribs again. There'd been a while there in the truck when he wasn't sure he was going to get out of there. He'd never been so cold in his life. But their singing had surrounded him, lifted him up.

"Did you have fun in the helicopter like we did?" Willow crawled back onto the bed with her donut, a dot of chocolate on her nose. "It's the coolest."

"I didn't have too much fun in the helicopter." Not until they'd gotten him warmer and had given him the pain meds, anyway.

"Wait." Morgan wiped her mouth with a napkin. "If we all came here in helicopters, how are we gonna get back home for Christmas today?"

"I'll take you." Silas hovered by the window. "I've got my truck. I can get Tess and the girls home."

But he wouldn't have room for everyone.

"I'll rent a car and drive the rest of the bunch back," Thatch offered. "I'm sure we could return it in Jackson tomorrow."

"Sounds like a plan to me." Aiden winked at Kyra. "As long as the doc says I'm allowed to vacate the premises, that is."

Tess pushed out of the chair. She looked as tired as he felt. "If you're willing to stay here, Thatch and Kyra, maybe we'll head back to Star Valley with Silas so we can get things ready for a big Christmas dinner. Then we can all celebrate later."

"Great idea." Silas finished off his coffee and tossed the cup into the trash can. "We can drop off Thatch at the car rental place first."

"I can't wait to celebrate Christmas!" Morgan was the first one to the door. "We'll get to open presents tonight."

"We can as long as you hug your uncle before we go." Tess nudged her daughter back to the bed.

Morgan and Willow hugged him and smothered his face with kisses. "Get all better so you can come home today," his younger niece said.

"I'll do my best." He could be pretty persuasive when the situation demanded.

"Keep me posted." Tess gave him a hug too. "And be nice to Kyra," she whispered sternly.

"You don't have to worry about that." He'd learned his lesson. He'd never be so careless with her heart again.

Thatch and Silas said their goodbyes too, and then he and Kyra were alone again.

"Is there something between Tess and Silas?" Kyra asked, sitting beside him.

"No. Hell no." Silas knew better than to go after his sister. "Why do you ask?"

"No reason." She shrugged. "I thought maybe—"

The door interrupted once more, and this time the doctor walked in. "How're we feeling this morning?"

"All good." Aiden sat straighter, ignoring the discomfort on his right side. He'd been a gold-star patient all night, but he was itching to get out of here. "I'm ready to head home if you're ready to send me."

"But we don't want to rush." Kyra moved to a chair. "We'll do whatever you think is best, Dr. Blair."

"From everything I've seen, I'd be comfortable releasing you this afternoon." The man went to the computer that sat on a table in the corner of the room. "We need to bring PT in here to get you up and moving with your crutches first, but as long as that goes well, there's no reason you can't be on your way late this afternoon. With a scheduled follow-up visit for next week."

"Perfect." That would give him plenty of time to make Kyra's first Christmas in Star Valley Springs one to remember.

If there was one thing the Steele-Valdez family knew how to do, it was Christmas.

Aiden hobbled into Tess's house with Thatch and Silas flanking his sides and Kyra following behind him reminding him to be careful, to move slowly, to keep his left foot from touching the floor at all since he was supposed to be non–weight bearing for six weeks.

Driving home had been more of a feat than he'd envisioned. Instead of sitting next to Kyra like he'd wanted to, Aiden had to stretch out alone in the back seat of the SUV Thatch had rented, with his leg propped up on pillows Kyra had insisted they stop to buy on their way out of the city. The drive had taken them three hours, and the last section had jostled him around too much, but they'd made it home. Now, though, they were at the ranch on Christmas, where they all belonged.

"I don't know how you pulled this off, sis." Aiden admired the dining room table, which might as well have been set for royalty. She'd put out all of their grandmother's china, complete with the crystal goblets they'd used for every family Christmas celebration he could remember. A Christmas candelabra sat in the center with evergreen boughs circling the base.

"I helped!" Morgan emerged from the hallway carrying a picture. "Look, Uncle Aiden. I made you a get-well card."

He moved to the living room couch and sat down before he took the picture from her. "I love this." It was all of them standing around a Christmas tree together. "Thank you." He kissed the top of her head.

"This is all so beautiful." Kyra wandered to the table on the other side of the great room. "I've never been a part of anything like this. A big family celebration dinner."

"You haven't seen anything until you've been to this family's Christmas celebration." Thatch parked himself on the loveseat near Aiden. "Wait until the gift giving begins. Wrapping paper starts flying and things get wild."

"True statement." Tess refolded a few of the cloth napkins on the table exactly the same way their mother would have if she'd been here. "I'm afraid I got a late start, so the turkey won't be done for about two more hours."

"Turkey?" Kyra looked at her in disbelief. "You made a turkey today?"

"And mashed potatoes with gravy and roasted green beans with brown butter and stuffing from scratch and a few pumpkin pies, unless I miss my guess." Aiden grinned at his sister. He had her pegged.

"After last night, I wanted a normal Christmas." His sister finally left her perfect table and came to sit by him. "So maybe I went a little overboard."

"Well, your work is done for the day." Silas turned on the fireplace switch and then sat on the hearth. "After dinner you're putting up your feet while Thatch and I handle the cleanup duty."

"I can help." Kyra came to sit on Aiden's other side, snuggling in against him. "You should prop your leg up on the coffee table. You have to keep it elevated."

"Right." Aiden did as he was told and slipped an arm around his nurse.

"It's presents time, isn't it, mama?" Morgan ran to the Christmas tree, which had gifts sprawling underneath. Thankfully, Aiden had managed to get hold of Minnie and had asked her to make runs to both his place and Kyra's place to pick up the presents they'd wrapped for the girls and deliver them to the ranch earlier.

"It's present time?" Willow crept into the room from the hallway, her hair sticking out as though she'd just woken up.

"Now that you're awake, we can get started." Tess held her arms open for her younger daughter, and Willow crawled into them. "She was exhausted so she needed a catnap," his sister explained. "You girls can start handing out the gifts if you'd like."

"Yes! Come on, Willow." Morgan pulled on her sister's hand, luring her to the tree.

Aiden never ceased to be amazed that there seemed to be presents for everyone. He always got Silas and Thatch a few gag gifts he couldn't resist. But Tess must've shopped for them this year too. Even Kyra had a few presents under the tree—which he assumed were from his sister and the girls because he couldn't wrap what he'd gotten her.

"Here." Morgan shoved a wrapped package into Aiden's hands. "This one's from Kyra."

"Oh, really?" He shook it lightly a few times before Kyra stole it from his hands. "No guessing until you open it."

When all of the presents were handed out, Tess gave the order for the chaos to begin. "Okay..." She shot the girls her tough mom look. "Remember... you have to thank the person who bought you the present before you move on to the next present."

"We will," they promised in unison.

"On your marks, get set, go!" Before Tess had even finished, the girls were already tearing into their first presents.

"Look at this beautiful horse!" Morgan jumped up and threw herself into Kyra's arms. "I love it! She's so pretty! I'm going to name her Starla!"

"I got one too!" Willow rushed to Kyra and jumped into her lap. "Mine's going to be named Beauty."

"Well, that sure beats the new art supplies and glitter I bought them," Aiden muttered when the girls had gone back to their seats.

Kyra laughed. "Just make sure you don't sniff any of that glitter."

The girls continued opening presents, making the rounds for hugs throughout the room. Eventually Aiden joined in, opening a new cowboy hat from Tess and the girls, a new Battleship game from Thatch, and a potty golf set from Silas, which the girls though was hilarious.

"You can play golf when you're sitting on the toilet?" Morgan giggled. "I wanna try."

"Maybe another time." Right now he had one more gift to open. One he hadn't expected. He picked up the gift Kyra had taken away from him earlier and carefully unwrapped it. "A hot chocolate set." He wasn't sure a gift had ever made him smile so big. "You bought this for me when you were in Jackson?"

"I did," the woman confirmed, her smile sealing a secret between them. "I just couldn't seem to get your amazing hot chocolate out of my head."

"I'm going to make you a cup tonight," he promised, his body already heating. And then one chocolate kiss would lead to another…

"We'll see about that." Kyra gently patted his leg.

But he wouldn't let a little surgery stop him from giving her a memorable Christmas night. She would see.

"Open your presents now, Kyra." Willow came to sit by them.

He focused on watching Kyra open her gifts—a warm sweater and jacket from Tess and the girls, and new gloves and boots from Thatch and Silas.

"I think you all were conspiring to keep me here," she said, trying on the coat right away.

"We were hoping," Tess told her. "For my brother's sake."

"Yeah, we didn't want to live with grumpzilla forever," Silas added.

"Wait." Morgan looked up from organizing the art supplies Aiden had gotten her. "Is that all the presents? Uncle Aiden, didn't you get something for Kyra?"

"Of course I got something for Kyra. But I couldn't put it under the tree." He gave Thatch the signal. "You want to help me out?"

"I'm on it." His friend got up and pulled on his winter gear before jogging out the front door.

"What's going on?" Kyra turned to Aiden.

"I have a surprise for you." He reached for his crutches. "Everyone get on your coats. We're going for a sleigh ride." Once he was balanced, he reached for her hand. "I couldn't bring your gift here. So we have to go see it. All of us together."

"Are you sure you're up for a sleigh ride?" Concern hid behind her smile. "Maybe we shouldn't overdo things."

"I'm sure. Silas and Thatch can do most of the work." He nodded at his friends. It might take a heroic effort for them to get him into the sleigh, but the struggle would be worth it.

"You've got it." Silas slipped outside to help Thatch get the sleigh ready.

"I didn't know you had a surprise for Kyra." Morgan sat down by the door to put on her boots. "Are you two in love or something?"

"Morgan!" Tess shook her head in a silent reprimand. "That's a very personal question."

Was it? Aiden didn't care. "Yes, Morgan." They might as well know. He wanted everyone to know. "I love Kyra." He didn't even know what love was until she walked into his life.

"And I love you." Kyra came up behind him to help him get his coat on, holding the crutches while he pulled his arms through. "Take it easy on the steps." She opened the door for him and moved alongside him.

"Come on." Thatch hopped down from the sleigh, which he'd parked directly in front of Tess's front porch.

"Let's load you in." His friends each took a side and hoisted him up to sit inside the sleigh. Kyra climbed in next, and then Tess and the girls sat on the bench across from them.

"Everyone ready?" Thatch took the reins while Silas rode shotgun.

"We're ready!" Willow climbed into Aiden's lap, and Morgan wedged herself between him and Kyra. "Where're we going?"

"Over the river and through the woods," he joked.

Right on cue, the girls started to sing. "Over the river and through the woods to grandmother's house we go!"

Kyra joined in too. Aiden decided to hum along. No one wanted to hear him actually sing. They moved over the same path they'd traveled on the last day of the cattle drive until they made it to the lower pasture, where the cattle were roaming.

A gasp sat Kyra up taller. "I know where we are." She swiveled her head, looking around. "Where's Brutus?"

"Let's go find him!" Morgan jumped out of the sleigh first, followed by Willow and Tess. Aiden took a lot longer, maneuvering to the ground with the help of Silas and Thatch under Kyra's supervision.

"Brutus!" Willow called, running to the fence. "Come here, boy."

"He's this way." Aiden pointed to the shelter he'd built for the calf and his mom while Kyra had been in Jackson. He painstakingly led her into the pen through the gate and out walked her new pet, wearing a huge red bow.

A delighted laugh slipped out of the woman's mouth. "Look at you." She took the calf's face in her hands. "So handsome." Then she peered back and forth between Aiden and Tess. "You got me a calf for Christmas? Are you sure? I know he's worth a lot."

"He's all yours." Aiden hobbled to her while everyone else hung back. "Tess agreed to let me buy him. And now Brutus will enjoy a long and happy life in the mountains. We can visit him whenever you want."

"Yay!" Morgan and Willow both cheered.

"You hear that, buddy?" Kyra nuzzled the calf's nose.

"You're a pretty big deal now. The mascot for the whole ranch."

Aiden glanced over his shoulder at Tess and grinned. "Told you she'd love this present."

"It's pretty sweet," his sister admitted. "Who knew you were such a romantic?"

"We sure as hell didn't know." Thatch waved everyone in the opposite direction. "But maybe we should give you two a minute."

They all walked to the sleigh, leaving him alone with Kyra.

"Merry Christmas." He wished he could pull her into his arms, but the crutches weren't working in his favor. They were going to be very inconvenient for the next six weeks.

"This is my favorite Christmas ever." She put her arms around him and drew closer. "This whole day might be the best gift I've ever been given." Her lips brushed his, sparking an internal flame. "And I can't wait to see what happens next."

CHAPTER TWENTY-SEVEN

How do I look?" Kyra paraded into the living room wearing the little black dress she'd had to borrow from Lyric. Thankfully, they were roughly the same size, but she still wasn't sure she could pull off the plunging neckline.

Aiden whistled low and, using his crutches to get off the couch, hobbled to her with a devious look in his eyes. "You are smokin'." He took her hand and twirled her around once. "I know you just got dressed, but do you have any interest in getting undressed?"

"Ha." She pulled on the lapels of his jacket to bring him in closer. Luckily, he'd gotten very good at balancing on one foot in a week. "This is pretty much the first time I've been dressed since Christmas." Other than wearing her bathrobe around the house, anyway. There hadn't been much of a reason to get dressed. Since she and Aiden had been staying in the first-floor bedroom at her house—her house!—they'd mostly stayed in bed together. In between cooking meals and watching movies and doing Aiden's exercises, of course.

"I can't believe Star Valley Springs has a swanky New Year's Eve party." Who would've guessed there would be any black-tie events in this tiny little town?

"I'm telling you…everyone looks for excuses to get out of the house around here all winter long." Aiden ditched his right crutch, tossing it onto the couch before setting his hand on her waist. "But this is the biggest event of the year. Minnie and Louie transform the whole lobby at the Meadowlark into a five-star lounge and even hire some of the kids from the high school to walk around with trays of food and drinks."

"Sounds like fun." She stepped away from him before he could distract her with a kiss and they ended up back in bed. That seemed to happen whenever she got up to do the dishes or prepare some food. "We're already late." She handed Aiden his other crutch so he wouldn't get any funny ideas about going without it tonight.

"But I wanted to dance with you." The man had a perfectly kissable pout. "How am I supposed to dance with crutches?"

"We'll figure it out." Kyra turned her back to him and walked into the foyer to get her coat on. "You've figured out how to do pretty much everything else quite well." She shot him a glance of approval over her shoulder. The man had demonstrated that he was surprisingly agile for having a broken leg.

"That's true." Aiden hobbled up behind her and brought an arm around her waist, pulling her against him while he swayed his hips. "Dancing shouldn't be a problem."

"Uh-huh." Kyra rested the back of her head on his shoulder and moved with him. "If we can ever get out the door, that is."

"I'm not sure I want to get out the door." Aiden turned her to face him. "I've really enjoyed being with you this week, alone, just the two of us. Now I have to share you again."

She felt the same way. For six days, they'd shared everything—memories and deep conversation. They'd shared laughter and a few tears too when they talked about what they'd lost in their lives. All day every day, they'd shared their bodies and their hearts, and now walking out of this house almost felt like leaving the protective bubble they'd built around themselves.

"I guess we can't stay hidden away forever." Earlier that morning, Tess had texted them to see if they were coming to the party because the girls were dying to see them—no pressure. "It's probably time to make an appearance."

"If we don't show up, I have no doubt that my sister will be on our doorstep in thirty minutes," he agreed, and then he stole another kiss. "You look incredible. I'm honored to go to the Star Valley Springs annual New Year's Eve party with you." His gaze lowered to her plunging neckline. "But we may have to call it an early night."

"That can be arranged." Kyra slipped into her brand-new winter coat, and they walked outside, navigating the path that Silas and Thatch had shoveled to the driveway after it snowed yesterday.

"I guess we both need to find a car." She'd already sold hers in Fort Myers before coming here.

"I've already been looking." Aiden opened the driver's side door of her rental car for her and then got into the passenger's seat. "I want a truck exactly like my old one. A 1978 Ford F-150."

Kyra laughed, remembering the first time she'd ridden in it. "I did love that truck. But I think I'll opt for something a little smaller." She had so much to figure out here. A car, a job, how to manage all of her father's properties. But somehow none of those things felt overwhelming. For the first time in her life she could pause, she could take time to think through what her heart truly desired. "Do you think I should start a small clinic in Star Valley?" she asked as she drove down the driveway.

"I think that would be the perfect thing for you to do." Aiden put his hand over hers on the gear shift. "If that's what you're passionate about."

They discussed the possibility the whole way to the Meadowlark Hotel. "It would have to be simple," she said, parking the car. "But a clinic would allow me to help people. And maybe I could even find a doctor from a neighboring town to take one or two days a week. That way everyone in town wouldn't have to travel so far for simple issues like ear infections and strep throat."

"I love the idea." Aiden situated his crutches and got out of the car. He met her at the driver's side. "I know firsthand what a skilled nurse you are."

"Well, look who it is." Silas sauntered across the parking lot with Thatch a few steps behind.

When they reached them, Thatch stuck out his hand in Aiden's direction. "Hey. Aiden, isn't it?"

"Very funny." Aiden didn't seem amused, but Kyra laughed. Those three were always giving each other a hard time, but she'd never seen a stronger bond between unrelated brothers.

"So whatcha been up to?" Silas asked while they made their way inside.

"Not a whole lot." Aiden eyed Kyra with the sexy grin she loved so much. "What about you two? Has anyone taken the Battleship trophy home yet?"

"Nope. But I'm up three games." Thatch pointed at Silas. "Your ass is mine, Beck."

"You wish." Silas turned to Aiden. "Louie's got some darts set up over there." He pointed to the opposite end of the hotel lobby. "You wanna try your luck?"

Aiden looked to her, but Kyra shooed him away. "Go have fun with your friends." They'd obviously missed their partner in crime. The three of them likely never went six days without seeing one another.

"Save me a dance." He kissed her before hobbling away with his comrades, already arguing about who was going to kick whose ass.

Kyra wandered past the check-in desk and turned the corner where the lobby opened up into a larger space. Aiden had been right. Louie and Minnie had transformed the place with low mood lighting, black silk material hanging along the walls, and accents of gold decorating tall pub tables that were strewn around the room. On the far wall were the antique slot machines that always stood in the lobby.

"You're here!" Lyric left one of the slot machines and hurried to meet her, grabbing two champagne flutes from a tray on the way.

"It's so good to see you." Kyra hugged her friend tightly. They'd texted a few times, with Lyric mainly checking in on them, but she hadn't seen her since she'd raided her friend's closet.

"That dress looks perfect on you." Lyric stepped back. "It never looked that good on me. You have to keep it."

"Maybe just until I can go back to Florida and get more of my clothes out of storage." Of course, moving here she'd likely need a whole new wardrobe. Another item to add to her list.

"So how are things with you and Aiden?" Lyric nudged her. "I've heard you two have been laying low since the accident."

"We have. And it's been a much-needed break." But she was feeling ready to reconnect with the outside world again. "I've been thinking..." Kyra led her to one of the tables and set down her champagne. "How do you think a wellness clinic would do in Star Valley Springs?"

"A wellness clinic..." Lyric sipped from her glass. "You mean, like a doctor's office?"

"Not necessarily." The more she and Aiden had talked on the ride over, the more she'd realized how nicely her skills and Lyric's skills could fit together. "I mean wellness. I could be there to treat and diagnose simple illnesses and injuries. But you could be there for some preventative care. The gentle movement through yoga and your supplement business to enhance people's overall health."

"It's brilliant." Her friend let out a squeal. "I love the idea so much."

"Let's get together to talk about it next week." Kyra waved at Tess and the girls, who'd just walked in through the door.

"It's a date." Lyric raised her champagne for a toast.

Kyra clinked their glasses together and took a sip before meeting up with Aiden's sister.

"I'm so glad you came." Tess looked around. "Is Aiden here? How's his leg? Any issues with the concussion?"

"He's doing amazing." Kyra pointed. "Right now he's over playing darts with Silas and Thatch."

"Good." Tess sighed. "I didn't want to bug you two, but I wanted to see for myself that he's improving."

"You can bug us whenever you want." Kyra snatched a champagne flute from a passing waiter and handed it to her. "You're family."

Willow tugged on Kyra's dress. "You look like a movie star."

"And you look like a princess," Kyra told her. "You both do. I love those dresses." They were both dressed in what appeared to be Cinderella Halloween costumes.

"Oh, goodness. Look at all this loveliness." Minnie bustled around them snapping pictures.

Kyra admired the woman's sequined gown. "You look so glamorous." How fun for everyone to have an excuse to dress up.

"Why, thank you." Minnie curtseyed. "This was my grandmother's dress, believe it or not. She actually wore it to sing in an old saloon near Casper."

"Wow." Now it was Kyra's turn to take a picture of her.

"I love how it sparkles." Morgan touched the dress in awe.

"If you think it's sparkling now, wait until you see me move on the dance floor." The woman beckoned them away from the tables. "Come on, my dears. It's time to really get this party started."

Even though no one else had ventured onto the dance floor yet, the six of them started to boogie like no one was watching. With Louie behind the DJ's station, they danced to "YMCA" and "Girls Just Want to Have Fun" before Aiden hobbled over on his crutches along with Thatch and Silas to join them on the dance floor.

"Time to slow things down." Louie put on "The Way You Look Tonight" sung by none other than Frank Sinatra.

Silas asked Willow to dance while Thatch took Morgan's hand. The girls stood on the men's feet giggling while they swayed around.

Tess and Lyric both paired up with other gentlemen from town, and Aiden set his crutches against one of the tables before reaching out his hand to her.

Kyra looked back and forth between him and the crutches indecisively.

"I don't need them." Aiden pulled her to him. "I want to hold you. I won't step down on my left foot. I promise."

"Okay." But they were staying next to the table. She wasn't about to let him reinjure his leg for a dance. She wrapped her arms around him and gazed into his eyes, letting her body melt into his. Aiden hummed along to the song low enough that only she could hear. They didn't move much, but it was enough to stand wrapped in his arms with her cheek resting against his chest while they were surrounded by their friends—by her new family. This moment was everything.

CHAPTER TWENTY-EIGHT

Four Months Later

Kyra climbed down off the ladder and stood back, admiring the wall she and Lyric had finished painting in the waiting room of their clinic. "I love the color."

"Me too." Her friend set her paintbrush on the tray. "Oceanfront. That's exactly the right name for it."

Kyra wholeheartedly agreed. The color had a calming tint, not too blue, not too teal. "It sets the perfect tone." Paired with the cream-colored tufted club chairs they'd selected, this room would be one of her favorites in the small house they'd converted into their clinic.

"Aiden is planning to build the check-in counter over here." She walked to the wall opposite the windows. "And we can put some plants in the corners."

"Yes! My herbs will grow great in this light." Lyric retrieved her water bottle and took a long drink.

Kyra was rather thirsty herself. They'd been painting since early that morning, and they still had the yoga studio and the exam room to go. "Do you think we'll really be able to open in a month?" When they'd found the property only a few blocks off Main Street in February, three months had seemed like more than enough time to get the renovations done, but now… "We only have four weeks left."

"That's plenty of time." Lyric sat in the center of the newly refinished wood floors and patted the space next to her. "Maybe we should take some cleansing breaths."

"Yes, we definitely should." Kyra sat next to her, finding length in her spine, and closed her eyes, expanding her rib cage open with a breath and then exhaling all of her stress. "I'm so glad you're a yoga teacher. For the first time in my life, I'm finally learning how to relax." Lyric's laid-back approach to life happened to be the perfect complement to Kyra's intensity.

"You've had a lot going on." Her friend shifted into lotus pose. "That reminds me…how long are you and Aiden going to be in California again?"

"California!" Kyra jumped up. Forget cleansing breaths, she had to get a move on. "Oh, my God, we're leaving for the airport tonight and I haven't even packed." Just like that, stress filtered back in. "What time is it?"

Lyric checked her watch. "It's only eleven." Her friend did an expert's version of a downward dog stretch and worked her way up to a standing position. "Don't worry. I can take care of the cleanup here. And then we'll get back to work when you get home. Everything'll work out perfectly. You'll see."

"That would be great. I really don't want to be late." This long weekend getaway with Aiden and Tess and the girls was a big deal. She hurried into the old galley kitchen down the hall and washed the paint off her hands before getting all of her stuff together.

"Let me know how it goes. Take lots of pictures," Lyric called as Kyra rushed out of the house.

"Thanks again!" Kyra piled her bag into her new cute Jeep and drove across town to her ranch. She plowed through the front door and immediately dropped her bag on the floor. "Hubba hubba."

Aiden stood in the living room wearing a crisp white uniform decorated with medals from his days in the service.

"I forgot how it feels to put this on." He tugged on the coat.

Wearing that uniform had to come with mixed feelings—the honor and sacrifices he'd made, the memories of wearing it with Jace.

Kyra walked toward him slowly, admiring this man who'd devoted his life to others, who'd worked so hard to overcome the scars those sacrifices had left on his heart. "How does it feel?" she asked, straightening his collar.

After a few seconds, a smile reached all the way to his eyes. "It feels like I've come a long way since I took it off for the last time." He looked down at the colored bars over the left breast. "I never wanted to put it back on after I retired. But it feels like it's time now."

"I'm proud of you." Kyra kissed him, letting her lips rest against his while she inhaled. "And I can't wait to see you stand with Thatch and Silas to receive your medals."

For weeks Aiden had struggled with the decision of whether or not he would accept the Navy Cross at the ceremony in California. But as he worked through his feelings about losing Jace, he'd decided to attend. He'd said their team had done everything together, and with Tess accepting on behalf of Jace, they would all stand together once more.

"It means a lot to have you come with me." Aiden's hands reached for hers, squeezing gently. "But there's something I'd like to do before we go. Do you have time for a quick ride?"

"I haven't packed..." But, really, she already knew what she planned to wear, so stuffing a suitcase full of clothes wouldn't take long. "I'll make time." She wanted to be fully present for him as he walked this final chapter on his career in the Navy. She wanted to be part of that closure so they could start the next chapter together. "Do you want to change first?"

"Sure." He smoothed his hands down the sides of his uniform. He stripped down to his boxer briefs right there, and Kyra couldn't resist kissing him.

"I'm not sure I want to go on a horseback ride anymore," she murmured, pressing her body to his.

"You'll love this ride. I promise." He kissed her once more and then disappeared upstairs.

When he came back down dressed in jeans and a flannel he took her hand and led her out the back door. "I've got Pip and Chip saddled up and ready."

"Wow. You've been making plans." She'd wondered why he'd been in such a rush to get out of the house that morning.

"I've been making plans, all right." Aiden boosted her up onto Pip's back. He still walked with a slight limp from the accident, but even that injury had healed well considering how many pieces his leg had been in.

Once he was situated in his saddle, Aiden waited for Kyra to guide her horse in front of him. He'd given her plenty of riding lessons ever since the snow melted, and she'd actually started to enjoy being up so high, seeing the world from a different perspective.

"We're going to head up in the direction of the high meadow." He steered Chip alongside her. "Ready?"

"Ready." She tapped her heels into Pip's girth and brought the horse to a trot. The landscape was still waking up after a long winter sleep, but green hues had started to sneak into the grasses again and buds dotted the trees. Spring had come, and even though the temperatures still warranted a sweater, the sun warmed her face and brought happiness blooming. She couldn't wait to be out here all summer with Aiden and his family—riding and exploring... visiting Brutus. They had a lot to look forward to.

When they reached the higher meadow, Kyra slowed Pip.

"Just a little further." Aiden pointed into the stand of trees down the slope.

Wait a minute...

She recognized this place. He'd brought her up a different way, but they were somewhere near the cattle drive camp. "What're you up to?" she asked, guiding Pip inches away from Chip.

The man grinned at her and then took off at a gallop, signaling for her to follow. Pip pretty much did whatever Chip did, so Kyra didn't have to work hard to get him to follow his friend. "I knew it!" They descended into the trees at a much slower pace, thank God, and stopped at the creek.

"This is where you kissed me." Kyra jumped down into the man's arms. "Right here. This spot." She'd never forget the way the creek had gently babbled over the rocks and the breezes had swayed the grasses, much like they were now.

"I'm pretty sure you kissed me." Aiden held her hand and they started to walk along the creek while the horses grazed. "You turned my entire world upside down that day, Kyra Fowler. And I haven't been the same since."

"I haven't either." She had changed since the day Blondie had taken off with her. "That day was the start of a wild journey."

"I'm glad we're on that journey together." He pulled a small box out of his pocket and lowered to one knee. "I don't know exactly what the future holds. All I know is I want to be with you in the chaos. I want to be by your side, holding you, figuring things out together and then falling asleep with you in my arms every night."

"I want that too." Kyra sank to her knees with him. She couldn't stand anymore.

Aiden slipped the solitaire diamond onto her finger. "Jace said that love is worth whatever it costs." He kissed her. "And I would give up everything else to love you for the rest of my life. I promise to always fight for you, to fight for the love between us no matter what else is going on, no matter how much chaos there is." He gently brushed away her tears. "You don't have to marry me tomorrow. Or next month. Or even next year. But I wanted you to know that my soul is yours. I'll never want anything else."

"Me neither." She touched her lips to his, savoring the warmth of his mouth, the way he knew her so well, the familiarity of their kiss but also the promise of a whole new adventure. "I would marry you tomorrow," she told him. "Or next month. Heck, I would marry you right now if I could."

"Then it's official." Aiden stood and pulled her up into his arms, lifting her feet off the ground. "We're gettin' hitched."

Laughing, she kissed him for all she was worth, wrapping her legs around his waist while he twirled her around.

If only her father could see her now—if only he could see what he'd given her. Maybe he could. Maybe this had been his plan all along. Maybe somehow he'd known that in coming to Star Valley Springs, she would finally become part of the family she'd always longed for.

ABOUT THE AUTHOR

Sara Richardson grew up chasing adventure in Colorado's rugged mountains. She's climbed to the top of a 14,000-foot peak at midnight, swum through Class IV rapids, completed her wilderness first-aid certification, and spent seven days at a time tromping through the wilderness with a thirty-pound backpack strapped to her shoulders.

Eventually Sara did the responsible thing and got an education in writing and journalism. After a brief stint in the corporate writing world, she stopped ignoring the voices in her head and started writing fiction. Now she uses her experience as a mountain adventure guide to write stories that incorporate adventure with romance. Sara lives and plays in Colorado, where she still indulges her adventurous spirit, with her saint of a husband and two young sons.

You can learn more at:
SaraRichardson.net
Twitter @SaraR_Books
Facebook.com/SaraRichardsonBooks
Instagram @SaraRichardsonBooks

Enjoy the best of the West with these handsome, rugged cowboys!

WISHING ON A CHRISTMAS COWBOY
by Sara Richardson

Pediatric nurse Kyra Fowler finally has her dream job at a prestigious hospital in London. But first she must fix up—then sell—the Wyoming house her estranged father just left her. But ex–navy SEAL Aiden Steele isn't letting some outsider sell his sister's home to a ruthless developer. Operation Save Star Valley is foolproof: Show Kyra the sights, work a little Christmas magic, and bam! She won't sell. Except that as Kyra falls for the town, Aiden starts falling for her…

Connect with us at Facebook.com/ReadForeverPub

Discover bonus content and more on read-forever.com

TEXAS HOMECOMING
by Carolyn Brown

Dr. Cody Ryan is back in Honey Grove, Texas, much to the delight of everyone at Sunflower Ranch—everyone except the veterinarian, Dr. Stephanie O'Dell. So he can't believe his fate when a sudden blizzard forces them both to take shelter together in an old barn. Cody's barely seen his childhood crush since he left, so why is she being so cold? As they confront the feelings between them, it's clear the fire keeping them warm isn't the only source of sparks. But once the storm passes, will Stevie and Cody finally give love a chance?

Find more great reads on Instagram with @ReadForeverPub

SECOND CHANCE AT RANCHO LINDO
by Sabrina Sol

After being injured in the military, Gabe Ortega has returned home to Rancho Lindo. But despite his family's wishes, he plans to leave as soon as possible—until he runs into a childhood friend. The beautiful Nora Torres is now a horticulturist in charge of the ranch's greenhouse. She's usually a ray of sunshine, so why has she been giving him the cold shoulder? As they work together and he breaks down her walls, he starts to wonder if everything he'd been looking for had been here all along.

Follow @ReadForeverPub on Twitter and join the conversation using #ReadForever

SECOND CHANCE COWBOY
by A. J. Pine
Ten years ago, Jack Everett left his family's ranch without a backward glance. Now what was supposed to be a quick trip home for his father's funeral has suddenly become more complicated. The ranch Jack can handle—he might be a lawyer, but he still remembers how to work with his hands. But turning around the failing vineyard he's also inherited? That requires working with the one woman he never expected to see again. Includes a bonus story by Sara Richardson!

***Montana Hearts* (2-in-1 Edition)**
by R. C. Ryan
Fall in love with two heart-pounding Western romances in the Malloys of Montana series. In *Matt,* a raging storm traps together a rugged cowboy and a big-city lawyer who can't stop butting heads. When one steamy kiss leads to another, will differences keep them from the love of a lifetime? In *Luke,* a stubborn rancher thrown from his horse is forced to accept the help of a beautiful stranger. But as they begin to feel sparks, will secrets from the past threaten their newfound feelings?